PATH OF PEACE

THE CREMELINO PROPHECY
BOOK III

MIKE SHELTON

The Path Of Peace

ISBN: 0-9971900-5-1
ISBN-13: 978-0-9971900-5-2
Library of Congress Control Number: 2016911269
Greenville, North Carolina

Cover Illustration by Brooke Gillette
http://brookegillette.weebly.com

Map by Robert Altbauer
www.fantasy-map.net

Acknowledgements

I would like to thank my wife Melissa, and our children for always being supportive of me throughout this process. My wife is the sounding board for all my ideas and keeps me in check. As I finish off this trilogy I would also like to thank all of my readers so far. I have received great feedback and appreciate all the reviews.

This book would not have been accomplished without the work and help of Heather Moore and others at Precision Editing Group, as well as my beta readers. I really appreciate all the feedback and support they have given me in developing this story and helping to keep things consistent.

Brooke Gillette has done such an awesome job on all my book covers. Her ability to take my basic ideas and expand it into a rich, colorful, detail oriented cover is truly amazing to me. Robert Altbauer also did an incredible job on the map that is used for the entire trilogy.

-Mike-

Books by Mike Shelton

The Cremelino Prophecy:

The Path of Destiny
The Path of Decisions
The Path of Peace

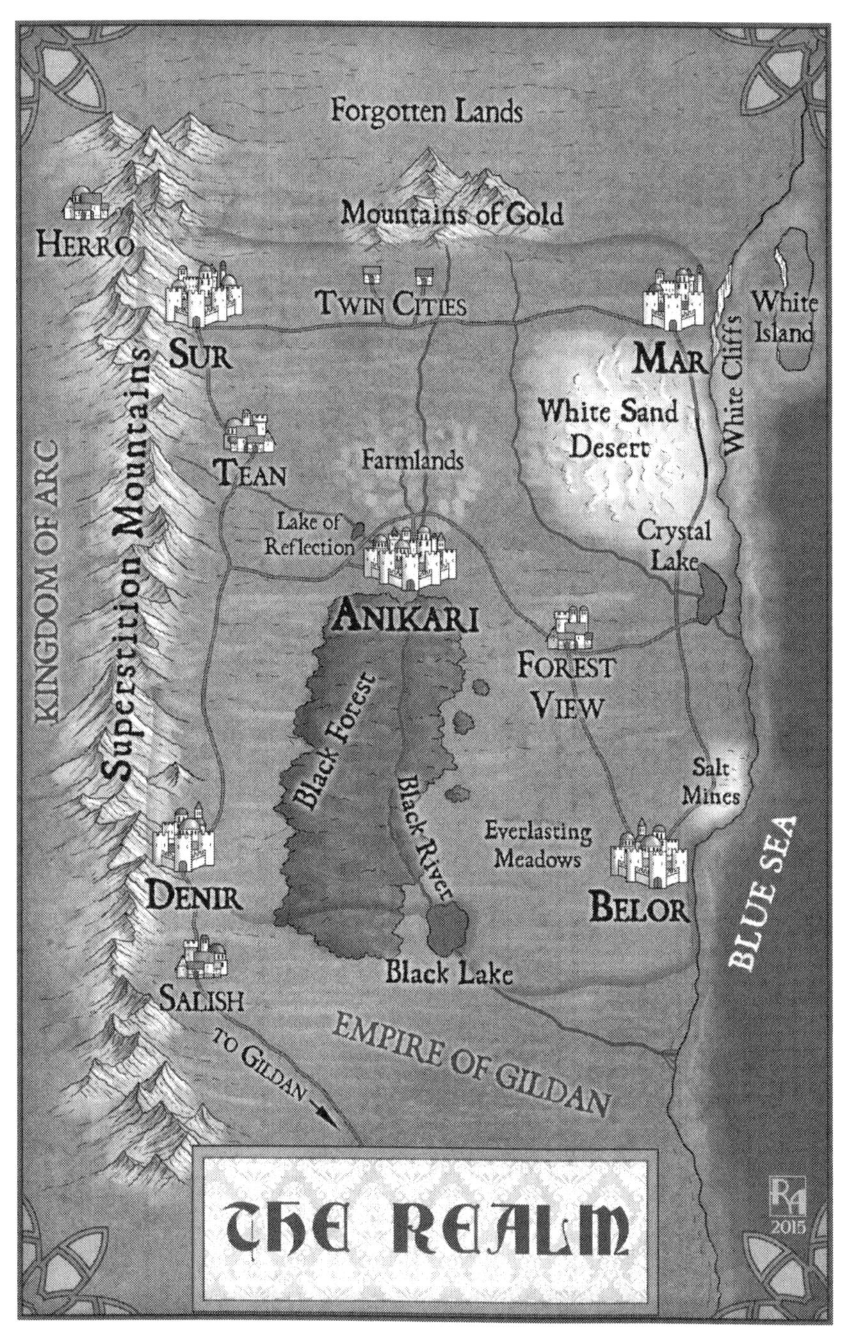

See Color map at www.MichaelSheltonBooks.com

PROLOGUE
(One year earlier in the Kingdom of Arc)

After riding for three days, High Wizard Olan Sallir rode into the Herro on his large black horse. The wizard, dressed in his usual green robes—a color he had discovered brought out the fierceness of his eyes while slimming down his large frame, was hungry and thirsty. The color of his robes was a contrast to the predominate brown drab of most of the Kingdom of Arc.

He strode into the small castle estate to visit the King of Arc. He was glad he had chosen a city at the edge of the mountains at this time of year. The temperature being much more mild helped Olan enjoy the green grass and trees. These were made possible by the storms from the Blue Sea that carried themselves over the countryside of the Realm and spilled over the tops of the Superstition Mountains. Rainfall, while not as plentiful as on the eastern side of the mountain, was much more abundant than further west.

The King of Arc met once a month with the leader of the Wizards' Conclave, always in a different place and always at the choosing of the High Wizard. Today they met in Herro, a medium-sized walled city in the northeastern reaches of the Kingdom of Arc, just west of the Superstition Mountains. It was one of the few places in the Kingdom of Arc that was not desert.

Upon entering the chamber room of the local governor's mansion, High Wizard Sallir saw the King busily passing missives to some attendants. The man was middle-aged and at least forty years younger than the High Wizard himself, but his lighter-colored hair, customary in the kingdom, made him look even younger. Olan moved his hand over his thinning head of hair, not quite as light or full as it once was. He chuckled to himself, though it was loud enough for the King to hear.

"High Wizard Sallir, good to see you again," King Anwar greeted, standing up from his working desk to shake hands. "I think I might make this my summer home. So much cooler than the blasted desert around Arc."

"But it's the desert that made us the strong kingdom we are," the High Wizard responded.

"Or the desert serves to keep others away. It isn't worth their while." The King laughed.

Olan liked King Anwar. He was much more relaxed and humorous than the last two kings Olan had advised. King Anwar didn't take himself too seriously or put himself above others. He was, however, a meticulous administrator. The kingdom's coffers and financial books had never been better. Trade was at an all-time high with the neighboring kingdoms of the Realm and the Gildanian Empire, and the people in Arc seemed happy under his reign.

The Kingdom of Arc, the western neighbor of the Realm, had been organized approximately two hundred years earlier by King Sinwian Arc, a man who unified dozens of warring tribes into one loosely held confederation. Since then, large cities had sprung up in the desert nation, in which local governors were given large amounts of control. A national government still existed under the current King, Samuel Anwar, but it was highly controlled by the Conclave of Wizards, headed by High Wizard Sallir.

"And how is your lovely wife?" Olan asked.

"As beautiful as ever!" Samuel replied. "She is off touring the southern states with my two oldest boys, letting them learn about the kingdom for themselves. They are at the age of manhood now and should see their glorious kingdom. One of them may succeed me some day."

Olan Sallir understood the last statement. Even though most of the time the son followed his father to the throne, in Arc it was not a foregone conclusion, as it was in the Realm and Gildan. Once a King of Arc died or was too sick to carry on his assignments, his sons came forward, and the people voted one of them as King. If they didn't want any, they were free to choose another, and the vote would stand. More often than not, a son had been chosen. In times when it wasn't that way, the vote was usually peaceful for another man of qualification. However, a few times in their two-hundred-year past, small skirmishes would ensue as one faction or tribe tried to promote their candidate over another. In Samuel Anwar's case, he followed his father, and it was most probable his oldest son would follow him as the next King.

"Speaking of kingdoms and successions, our neighbors in the Realm is one item to discuss today, your Majesty." Olan motioned for a servant. "But first I need to replenish myself with some good food and drink." He patted his growing stomach and laughed with a loud boom.

"Get something to eat and refresh yourself from your trip. When you are ready, meet me on the western balcony. We will watch the sun set together as we talk."

The High Wizard turned toward the kitchen and stumbled, trying not to run over the young girl that came running up next to him. After catching his breath, he turned to see who it was. A broad smile filled his flushed face.

"Danijela! How did you grow up so fast?" Olan reached for her hand and kissed it delicately. "My, only six months ago a child stood here, and now a young woman blossoms in her place."

Danijela Anwar smiled, obviously pleased with the praise. She twirled around, sending her dark blue riding cape flying around her slightly plump body. Her hair cut just above her shoulders, while not rare, was at least unique among the higher class in Arc. The nobility lately preferred the longer tresses on their women. The blonde color was very typical of the majority of the girls coming from the northern part of Arc.

"I am fifteen now, Wizard Sallir."

"That is High Wizard Sallir, Danijela," her father said, coming up to join them.

"Oh, no need for such formalities here," Olan said.

"Father, why can't I travel with Momma and the boys?" Danijela pursed her lips in a pout, her ample checks flushed.

"We've been over this. The boys need to understand all of the land they may rule someday."

"Why can't I rule?" she said in the tone of a proud teenager. "The Realm has had queens in the past. I have heard of other lands to the south and west with queens also. Why shouldn't the people vote for me?"

The King reddened. "Danijela! Don't waste the High Wizard's time with your thoughts of fancy. That is not how it is done in our kingdom. It's just the way it is. Why don't you escort our guest to the kitchens and help the cook get him something to eat."

"But—"

"No more!" the King said with firm resolve, but then added "sweetheart" at the end. The King did love his daughter, but she was independent in her thinking. The dangerous part was she had more inclinations and talent to rule than her older brothers did.

No more was said until they came to the kitchen. The seat creaked as Olan lowered himself onto a small wooden bench. The girl went to the cook to ask for meat and ale. He watched her absentmindedly as she talked to the cook and waited to satisfy his hunger. The young girl, though thinner than the last time he saw her, still seemed to hold on to some of her baby fat. However, her exuberance for life, feisty personality, and intelligent eyes were still the same they had always been.

As he waited, he thought about the problems going on in the Realm, their neighbor to the east. King Edward had no heir and apparently was not interested in marrying again or in having any more children. An unstable Realm could bleed over into the Kingdom of Arc. The Emperor in Gildan was also very old, although as a wizard he would live longer than others. However, his son, the general of their armies, was not as patient and peaceful as the current Emperor. Rumors flowed he had designs on expanding his kingdom.

All of a sudden, he heard a small squeak from Danijela. She had dropped a cutting board full of bread from her hands, the sharp knife dropping faster toward her leg. Somehow, however, the knife nor the board nor the bread made it to the floor. The High Wizard watched in fascination as Danijela brought the food and utensils through the air and back to her hands as if nothing had happened. Both of them looked back toward the cook, but she was involved in another conversation with two of her apprentices.

The commotion over with, Danijela walked confidently toward the wizard's table. He looked at her with interest and raised his eyebrows, not saying what was on his mind.

She flashed her bright blue rounded eyes at him and in mock innocence said, "What? You think you're the only one that can do magic?"

The High Wizard had never experienced anyone so informal over magic before. Half-choking on the ale dribbling from his gray beard, he laughed and laughed until he couldn't find any more breath. Finally, Danijela joined in.

"Does your father know?" Olan asked after getting himself settled again.

"I think he might suspect," the King's daughter said with a sparkle in her eye, "but he has never asked me directly. As much as he teases me, with my brothers gone most of the time, I don't think he wants to let me go."

High Wizard Sallir gave a deep sigh. "Bring the rest of the food over here, young one, and join me. I have some questions for you."

Danijela frowned, probably at being called young, but compared to Olan, everyone around him seemed young these days. His powers as a wizard had prolonged his life past the normal lifespan, but he was getting older, and he did need to take on an apprentice.

The girl returned with the rest of the meal and sat down opposite the High Wizard. He could see excitement almost crackling in the air around her.

"So, Danijela, when you do magic, do you think about it first?"

"No, sir, it just happens almost by instinct."

"Do your feelings control it? Does it happen when you are happy or angry?"

The girl thought a moment. Olan took the opportunity to bite into a piece of chicken.

"Very good," he mumbled in praise.

"No, it doesn't work better or worse when I have strong emotions either."

Olan smiled. "Tell me what it feels like."

"Oh, it is so wonderful." Her face lit up, and her eyes opened wide. "It just happens, like it's a part of me. Like the earth around me is coming to help me."

Olan took some bread and smothered butter on it. It was better than what he had eaten on his journey to see the King. He didn't say anything for a moment as he collected his thoughts. He motioned for Danijela to eat something.

Finally, he put his food down and put on his teaching tone. He remembered back to the days in the Wizards' Conclave when he had been a teacher, so long ago. Three Kings ago, in fact.

"There are three disciplines of magic that we know of, Danijela. Magic of the heart, magic of the mind, and magic of the earth. Each draws their strength from different sources. In a general sense, they all can do many of the same things, but each discipline allows the user various abilities or skills that another from a different discipline may not have as powerfully. There are tidbits in some of the ancient writings that allude to a fourth power, but no one in modern history has claimed any but those three."

Danijela smiled at him and, with excitement in her voice, leaped forward in the conversation. "So my power is earth?"

"Yes, child, you are an earth wizard." Olan was surprised that she caught on so quickly. "Most likely a weak one at this point with no formal training, but the power is in you." He continued teaching: "The magic of the mind belongs to a wizard who thinks things through first. He may be slower at committing himself to a cause. He thinks of what he wants to do, visualizes it, and then his mind extends and makes it happen. The majority of wizards have this power. Emperor Alrishitar of Gildan is one of these. I am one of these, though after so many years of study, my powers between heart, mind, and earth have become more balanced."

The High Wizard shoveled in a few more bites of food, and Danijela filled the silence.

"What about a wizard of the heart? Are there a lot of wizards?"

Olan put up his hand. "Hold on, Danijela." He chuckled. "All in good time. A wizard of the heart is much more rare. We don't know why, but there have been relatively few in the last five hundred years from the records we have, at least in these lands west of the Blue Sea. They are ruled by their emotions. They react to what they feel—either anger, love, frustration, or excitement. They don't seem to think about their consequences all the time. Their power is an extension of what they are feeling or experiencing at the moment. A wizard of the heart can be very dangerous and unpredictable if he follows the wrong path; however, one that is ruled by love and fairness and good feelings can make an extraordinary person and a great leader. There hasn't been one in a long time, at least a powerful one. Old King Anikari of the Realm had been one of these. It was also rumored that King Sinwian Arc was one, though by the study of his deeds, I would tend to think of him as an earth wizard."

"Like me?" Danijela asked. "Oh, this is so exciting. I want to show you what I can do." She jumped up and pulled the High Wizard's hand.

Olan shoved the last couple of bites of bread and meat in his mouth. He could tell there was no stopping the young girl. He pushed up on his large frame and followed behind her, still trying to teach.

"Now, Danijela, an earth wizard is not as rare as a wizard of the heart but is rarer than a wizard of the mind. The magic of the earth is more solid, more real. An earth wizard draws power from outside of him, unlike the power of the heart or mind, which comes from within."

"I know that."

The High Wizard shook his head. "How do you know that? You have never learned about wizards before."

"I read books, and I practice my magic." The young girl stopped and turned to look at her older companion. "It's not that hard."

"It's not that hard?" Olan's eyes widened, and he stopped short. "What are you talking about? Wizards take years to perfect their powers. You must be careful, especially as an earth wizard. With so much of nature at your disposal, there is always the danger of taking in too much power and burning your magic out. There are records in the Conclave of this happening before when a wizard either wasn't trained enough or was greedy for power."

At the last words, Danijela was more subdued, and her eyebrows furrowed as she listened to the High Wizard's warning.

"But we shouldn't worry about that just now, since I don't think you have pulled that much power in yet. As untrained as you are. You are most likely in the beginning and weaker stages of your powers."

Danijela's frown turned to a quick smile—a mischievous one. She motioned for the High Wizard to follow her out the back door of the large estate. They walked east down a small sloping meadow, away from the household and prying eyes. Olan didn't know where she was taking him.

Finally, they stopped at the side of a small hill. He could tell pieces of rock had somehow been taken out, he presumed for the building of the estate. He turned to the young girl and was just about to say something when she held her hands up in the air, turned them around, and pointed them at the hillside.

A small rumbling ensued, in which rocks came free of the hold in the earth—large rocks, larger than Olan could imagine. They floated through the air and landed in front of him. The power it took to do that with such finesse amazed him. Once again, he started to speak, but stopped when he could tell Danijela had not finished her performance.

She moved her arms in circular motions, a wide, ecstatic smile stretching from one side of her face to the other. He watched as the rock became fluid and shaped itself into smaller blocks, piled on one another, creating a small, child-sized play structure shaped as a small castle. Extending her hand once again, Danijela drew scraps of dead wood toward her in the air and placed them in neat rows on top of the structure as a roof.

High Wizard Sallir's mouth hung open in surprise. In all his years of teaching, in all his years of traveling, and in all his years of advising kings and rulers across the Kingdom of Arc, he had never witnessed such finesse and precision with the magic of earth powers. He plopped his large frame down on the ground with a grunt, breathing harder than the young girl was. He didn't know what to say.

Danijela sat down next to him. "Oppa? Are you all right?" They had known each other since she was a small child. When she was little, she used to call him her Oppa. He guessed he was old enough to be her grandfather many times over. She hadn't used that term of affection in recent years, a sign she was getting older and growing up. But using it now almost brought tears to his eyes. He had witnessed what might be the beginnings of the most powerful earth wizard to walk the western lands.

Olan let a small smile crease his wrinkled face. "My child. My sweet, sweet child. I am more than all right." He put his arm around her and pulled her in to a close hug. "Do you know how special you are, Danijela?"

"I told my father I could be a queen."

"Oh, no, no, no. You are not meant to be a queen."

Danijela frowned. "Why not?" She began to get up.

Olan carefully brought her back down to the ground with a firm but soft hand on her shoulder. He looked at her sparkling green eyes. "My dear young girl, you are destined to be so much more. Kings and queens will bow to you someday."

"Because I can move rocks?" Danijela squinted up at him, her full cheeks flushed.

The High Wizard smiled at her innocence. "You don't even know your powers yet, and you can do more with those powers than wizards who have studied for decades. I am not sure even then they have the finesse and softness of touch that you do despite your lack of training."

The wizard then stood, pulling the young girl up after him. "We need to talk to your father immediately. You will need to prepare to leave in a week's time. "

"Leave? Where to?" she asked.

"Why, with me, to the Conclave of Wizards, to be my personal apprentice. To learn more of your magic, to become one of the greatest wizards the world has known."

* * * * * * * * * * * * * * *

ONE YEAR LATER
(In the Realm)

Chapter One
THE NEW KING

"Father, stop!" Darius yelled louder than he intended. The lamps in the room flickered from his burst of powerful emotions. Standing up too quickly, he almost knocked over the high-backed, cushioned chair. Papers fluttered off the end of the table they worked at. A scribe, one of three others in the room, reached down to pick up the letters and information. Two other servants waited for any further commands from the King or his father, the first councilor.

"I must leave on my honeymoon. No more papers, no more letters, no more signatures. I trust you can run things without me for a few weeks." He wasn't mad at his father, just frustrated that things were taking so long.

Richard San Williams looked up at his son, Darius, the recently crowned King of the Realm, a questioning look in his eyes. Darius saw a lot of himself in his father. The dark brown hair and gray eyes were similar, but Darius's skin was lighter, taking after his mother. And unlike his father, he was clean-shaven.

Darius offered a pleading smile, trying to take the sting away from his earlier outburst. "Father, you ran the Realm side by side with King Edward for years before he died. I've only been King for three months now. I hardly even understand half of what I am signing. I do trust you." He looked his father in the eyes. His father had ample reason to doubt his son's sincerity. Most of Darius's life, he had hated his father's involvement in politics and his lack of attention and understanding of anything outside of his noble circles. Darius had vowed many times to never be a part of politics. Three months ago, that all changed.

Darius DarSan Williams had been named heir to the throne of the Realm three months before. King Edward, although not an old man, had died a week later from what they now assumed was a slow poison. He had left no children to inherit after him. The strange, though legal, ascension to the throne was brought about by the fact Darius was the great-grandson of King Charles, the previous King before Edward. King Charles had disowned his firstborn son Alric, due to him marrying a girl from the farmlands, outside of nobility. Edward, Charles's second son, had then inherited the throne instead. None of this had been known by Darius, his father, or most of the people in the Realm.

In the last week of Edward's life, he had informed young Darius, who was barely twenty, of the injustice done and the intention to restore the throne back to the line of the firstborn. Richard, who had been alive when the decree from King Charles came down, had also been banned from inheriting the throne, but not Darius.

Richard had been a councilor to King Edward and now remained as a councilor to Darius. It made for a strange relationship with father being advisor to the son, but both of them were trying to work it out among themselves.

"There are some things that do require your attention, Darius." Richard brought Darius back to the present. "You are the King."

Darius sighed. "I know. I know. I am trying to come to grips with that."

"And you are not a bad King either. I have seen you mete out mercy to balance justice. The people like you. You are young, and you and your new wife make a handsome couple for the people of the Realm to be proud of."

Darius had not heard such praise from his father before. Maybe he wasn't doing such a bad job. It did seem overwhelming at times. He could not imagine what ruling would be like without his growing powers. They had awakened in him fifteen months earlier when he had brought a flame forth in his palm when he and his best friend Kelln had been locked in a dark library basement. Since then, he had come to grips that he was in reality a wizard, one with strong powers of the heart. This along with the inherited power of the throne made Darius the first Wizard King in a long time, something the Realm had not had for hundreds of years.

"I will be back in one hour. Have ready only those items absolutely requiring my attention." Darius smiled at Richard. "I cannot keep my Christine waiting forever. A young bride deserves a honeymoon, doesn't she?"

"Yes, she does, though I am afraid it will be a working honeymoon. Traveling the Realm and her neighbors is not all fun and games, my son."

"I understand. But I will do it with her by my side."

The oil lamps blazed brighter as Darius left the study. He walked the hallways of the castle, an attendant guard always following close behind him. Darius realized he could take care of himself, but most of the other men had not grasped the situation yet. Any danger that might arise he could minimize or eliminate with his wizard powers. The servants and guards were still uncomfortable and nervous talking about or even admitting their master was both a wizard and a King. A King they could understand: he was just flesh and blood like them. A wizard, however, carried too many unknowns and still some resentful feelings from the past when wizards hadn't always stayed within the boundaries of the law.

Darius still struggled for total control of his power, though he improved each week. As a wizard of the heart, he was ruled by his emotions, though more often than not now he was able to use love and positive feelings rather than hate and negative ones to do what he desired. This was one of the reasons he was so excited to be leaving on his honeymoon. Part of their itinerary would bring him to the Empire of Gildan, where he would be reunited with his friend Mezar. Mezar, the second heir to the throne in Gildan, was also a wizard—a wizard of the mind—and had mentioned a school and library of learning for wizards in the Gildanian Empire. Darius needed more information about his powers and what to expect from them.

There was no one in the Realm to ask about his powers. One other wizard he had met was known as the Preacher, a man who had tried to take the rule of one of the Realm's major cities, Belor. His powers were part inherited and somewhat learned. The learned portion was a darker side and had been taught to the man while traveling to the eastern kingdoms, across the Blue Sea. The Preacher, through the apparent help of his daughter, Alessandra, had escaped on the day of Darius's coronation. He had taken Sean San Ghant, the son of a minor noble, with him, the same man who had tried to kidnap Darius before he was King to gain power and privilege he thought he deserved. Darius had sent Kelln, his best friend and now his ambassador, to travel to Mar, where they suspected the Preacher and his daughter to be.

The halls of the large rock castle sat empty this time of day. He guessed most of the people were getting ready to gather outside. The royal couple would be leaving on their belated honeymoon, and the streets were sure to be full of on-lookers.

Voices yelling outside a window caught the King's attention right before entering his suite of rooms. He stopped and looked down from four floors up and saw a scuffle outside the city gates.

"Get the outsider out of our castle," one man yelled.

"Put her back in the fields," another said.

Castle guards tried to gather up the rowdy group of five men. By the King's orders, they were not to be punished or jailed, only taken back to their homes with a warning to stay away from the castle.

For the first few weeks as King, those who couldn't accept his impending and announced marriage to someone outside of the walls of Anikari frustrated and angered him. He tried to drive the dissenters away. However, he had over time developed pity and even compassion for them. They had lived in a land so divided by prejudice for so long, it would take some time to be accepting of everyone.

The farmers, referred to as outsiders by much of the city dwellers, had not been looked upon well since the wizard uprising generations before. A group of wizards had tried to take over the rule of the Realm in Anikari. As a result, the most powerful ones were eventually killed while the lesser ones were taken outside the city walls and told to make their living in the farmlands. Since then, the blood of those lesser wizards and the farmers had mixed and diluted, seeming to have eradicated most signs of magic. Ever since, the city dwellers had a tendency to hate wizards, magic, and those that lived in the farmlands.

Darius had met, befriended, and eventually married a girl from the farmlands. That, along with his wizard powers, had shaken things up in the capital city of Anikari. It now saddened him to overhear such harsh words about his wife, their Queen.

The door to their chambers opened, and Darius's heart leaped with joy. The sight of his wife, Christine Anderssn DarSan Williams drove away all feelings but one: love—unabashed, unbiased, all-consuming love. The King gathered the Queen in his arms and kissed her with fervent passion, one hand around her thin waist while the other stroked the back of her long blonde hair. Power engulfed his body and soared into hers. Each could sense the deep feelings of the other.

"Don't worry about them," Christine whispered, nodding her head toward the window. "Give them time."

"I know they need time. It's hard to fully understand how so many people could have so much animosity toward those living in the farmlands. It isn't right."

Christine backed away from Darius but held his hands in front of her. "No, it isn't right, but you have done more to help rectify that situation than anyone. You helped secure the city from the Preacher with both farmers and city guards; you have named a farmer to your council, and have made the rules easier for children in the farmlands to get a better education."

"I just wish they could see you like I do, Christine. I wish they could know you like I do."

"Remember the day we met?" Christine mused. "You had no complaints about helping me back to my home after I fell and hurt my ankle. You are different from them. You accept everyone. It is a gift you have."

"You had me smitten the first time you looked up from the ground with those bewitching green eyes of yours."

Christine laughed and hugged her husband again. He rested his head on top of hers for a moment. "Just be patient."

"I only wish it would change quicker." He walked with Christine into their rooms. The early autumn sunlight streaming in danced along the floor, lightening the mood. Darius smiled.

At the end of the promised hour, he returned to the study with his father. Some documents regarding the leadership in Belor and a new trade agreement with Gildan dominated his time. Mezar had made sure that Emperor Alrishitar of Gildan knew of Darius's desire for peace on all fronts.

The last piece of correspondence would be a letter to Kelln in Mar. Kelln El'Han, a redheaded son of Anikari's once-famous sword maker, was Darius's best friend since childhood. His jovial, happy, not-worried-about-getting-into-trouble attitude had subdued somewhat over the last year. Kelln's travels to Belor and ultimate imprisonment by the Preacher had affected him deeply. He was now in Mar on official business, searching for the escaped Preacher and shoring up the local government that had problems with corruption. Unofficially, he was looking for the beautiful and captivating daughter of the Preacher, Alessandra El'Lan. She had captured and intrigued Kelln's heart multiple times but had betrayed him as many times since. She was thought to be searching for her mother in Mar.

Darius had also asked Kelln to attend to some needs on White Island, the island where the herd masters raised and took care of the Cremelino horses that were used by the King. Through Lightning, one of their own that Darius had given to Christine on her sixteenth birthday, the other Cremelinos had been reaching out to his mind for something. Kelln was tasked with finding out what he could until Darius had a chance to travel to the island.

Finished up with the last minute documents, he shook hands with his father, gave a few more final directions to some of his other councilors, and headed to the front of the castle to begin his honeymoon journey.

An hour later, he still stood in the castle courtyard. As the King, everything took longer. Short speeches to give, dignitaries to placate, entourages to put together, and guards to ride lookout in front of and behind the royal couple. Darius and Christine, changing protocol, had decided to ride on horseback rather than in a carriage.

"Your Majesty," the captain of the castle guard admonished. "This will make it much more difficult to guard and protect you, being out in the open like this."

They still tended to treat him as a vulnerable young man.

"Roland, I have told you many times: I am not defenseless." He would have to teach a lesson now or they would continue to second guess him the entire excursion. "Take your sword and come at me."

Roland's eyes opened wide. "My . . . my Lord. Never. I cannot do that." Roland stood facing his King. The man's leather vest accentuated the muscles bulging from his arms and chest. His stature, square face, and short, dark hair, were the epitome of the royal guard.

"Do it," Darius ordered. His jaw was set firm, and his broadening shoulders held still under his red and black attire.

Roland came at his King, bringing up his sword to strike him. About a foot away from Darius, Roland's sword hit something solid in the clear air. His eyebrows furrowed as he tried again harder. Sweat formed on his brow. The air around Darius held firm. With a flick of his wrist, Darius used his power to grab the sword out of the captain's hand and threw the blade to the ground.

"I can protect myself," he said with maybe too much arrogance, but he had to make a point.

Roland picked the sword up from the ground and bowed low to the new King. "I am chastened, my Lord. Forgive my questioning." The captain's face reddened.

Darius softened, realizing an embarrassed and possibly disgruntled captain could be detrimental and dangerous. "No forgiveness is required. You are encouraged to question me in my safety. However, please don't keep asking once my decision is made." He smiled to try and lighten the moment, his gray eyes holding only friendship toward the man.

The King turned to the rest of the crowd. "As of today, I promote Captain Roland Leeds from captain of the castle guard to captain commander of my own personal guard. He will ride with me today and will be in charge of the safety of our entire entourage as we travel through the Realm and to our neighboring kingdoms."

Roland blushed again, the embarrassment looking out of place on the large, fit soldier. "Thank you, my Lord. You are most kind."

"I trust you can be ready to leave in a few moments?" he asked his new captain commander. "I am anxious to begin."

"Of course. A soldier is always ready." Roland began barking commands at the other guards who would be accompanying the group.

Christine leaned over and put her hand on her husband's arm. "You diffused that in a nice way. Now you will have him close by to keep a watch on him."

"Christine, I trust him. He earned the promotion. He's a good soldier. I may not need protection, but you or others might."

"Darius, you can't trust everyone. Be careful," she admonished.

Christine had previously voiced her worry to Darius that his new power and his ability to love and understand people had made him too trusting and vulnerable. In the first few months of his reign, when someone was brought to him that was in trouble, Darius would blindly trust their assurances they would change their behavior. Three times already a former troublemaker had been brought back in for continuing his law-breaking. It was hard for Darius to understand someone not keeping their promises. His power was growing and his love of the people grew with it; he just had to remember there were still evil hearts and intentions in the world.

Two horses were led to where the King and Queen stood. Lightning, Christine's personal Cremelino horse, was pure white with a long mane. The other horse, although not a Cremelino was just as large but stood black and shiny, waiting for the King to mount. Cremelino horses were a special breed, but neither Christine nor Darius had realized the extent of the horses' magical powers. It was common knowledge that a Cremelino bonded with only one person at a time. No one else was allowed to ride them unless allowed by the Cremelino. If tried, immense pain would jar the insides of the culprit. But the ability to communicate mentally with them took them both by surprise.

Darius looked at Christine and her Cremelino and smiled. He thought back to the time three months earlier when after being gone for almost a year, he had returned to Anikari. He had seen Christine and Lightning on the road outside of the city trying to stop a skirmish between the farmers and city guards. He had used his growing powers to heal Lightning that day.

Remember the prophecy, Lightning spoke to their minds. *It is not yet complete:*

Forgotten lines of ancient magic
and the power of the throne.
One will make them both his own
if his heart sees the true power.
He will bring light to fight darkness
and love to fight hate
if he reaches into the power of his heart.
He will find new allies, turn enemy to friend, and
Find the binding of all power on the path of peace.

Christine responded back, "*He has fought his own darkness and brought light again to the kingdom, and he rules with love. Isn't the prophecy fulfilled then?*"

Not yet, my dear. He has much more to do on his path of peace.

Darius let out a breath of air. He appreciated the fact that they could communicate with Lightning, but their prophecies, hidden meanings, and secrecies were enough to drive him mad.

No one else in the group had noticed the quickly exchanged thoughts between the three of them. The mind-speaking ability of the Cremelinos was only known by a few of them. Lightning had explained to Darius and Christine that she had been prepared to help them fulfill the prophecy. In ancient times, the Cremelinos spoke with wizards, but the practice had been lost since the Realm had kept the Cremelinos for themselves while shunning magic. Lightning's ability to speak with Christine came from ancient bloodlines of lesser wizards that ran in her veins and her special relationship with Darius.

Let's go, wizard! Lightning said.

This time, Darius heeded her words. He smiled and put up his hand in signal to proceed.

"Farewell, my friends," he called out as his own anxious steed galloped across the courtyard and through the castle gates, Christine riding Lightning by his side. "My father and the other councilors are in charge until I return. I will bid your good wishes to the other cities and kingdoms we visit. They will know the Realm is still in control, that her people are proud, and their King will bring them honor."

Among the cheers of its citizens, the group began its descent through the streets of Anikari, the great and ancient capital city of the Realm. Darius spread his hands wide, and flowers bloomed in the windowsills of the businesses and houses lining the streets. The crowds shouted in joy and saluted their new King and his powers. The young people looked up at Christine and Darius in dreamlike stares of hope and longing. They loved their new King and his wife. Bards and storytellers were already singing songs and telling stories of their courtship and wedding.

Darius did notice some of the older residents standing in the back. They did not cheer as loud or join in the celebration as much. They held to the old ways of nobility and separation from others more firmly. Darius tipped his head at those specifically and tried to reach out his magic of love to them. Some responded with amazed looks on their faces; others were too hardened to feel. He had left directions with councilor Martin Halverssn from the farmlands to take things slow and not make any sudden changes. He hoped old prejudices would fade over time.

The autumn day turned warm, but the high heat of summer had left them. They left the western city gates and skirted the outside of the farmlands, turning north and then back east around Anikari. Humble farmers and ranchers stood on the side of the road and let their praises be known. Darius knew many of them and Christine most of them. These were good hardworking people who toiled so those in the city had food and meat. The apple orchards hung heavy with a good upcoming harvest. Berries, watermelon, tomatoes, and other late summer fruit and vegetable gardens could be seen dwindling with their last fruits of the year.

"I've missed riding like this," Christine said to Darius. "We have been in the city too long."

"I agree. By late fall however, the Diamond Palace will be finished enough to spend some time there this winter," Darius said, referring to the large home he was having built out in the farmlands along the edge of the Lake of Reflection. The natural meadow that they had found years before had been named the Field of Diamonds. The palace would give them a chance periodically to be out of the city, while still able to conduct the business of the Realm.

Christine smiled, and Darius felt giddy with excitement of the upcoming trip. They would travel slow, as large royal groups tended to do, stopping at many small towns and villages on their way down to Belor, then up the coast to Mar. He had sent Kelln ahead to make sure Mar was safe for them. He didn't want to put Christine in harm's way. After Mar, they would travel west to Sur. He had sent dignitaries to the Kingdom of Arc to arrange a meeting with King Anwar. Afterwards they would travel down to Denir in the southwest and then onto Gildan.

The trip would last a few weeks at least, maybe a month, but Darius felt it an important part of him being King to be out and meet the people. People seemed to treat others better and gossiped less once they met someone. He knew his quick rise to power, his age, and his wizard magic was already grand fodder for rumors.

As they left the farmlands, he spurred his Andalusian to a quicker pace. They weren't going far that day—only to Forest View—but he needed some fresh air. Lightning and Christine took up the pace beside him.

You didn't want to race, did you, Wizard?

Darius laughed. *"Oh no! It would not be seemly to have the King lose to his lady."*

Christine joined in the laughter, and faint amusement came to their minds.

Someday we will get you your own Cremelino, Wizard King! One that can keep you in your place. You did direct your ambassador to come to White Island, didn't you?

"Yes, I did," Darius answered. *"But you never told me why."*

You will find out soon enough. Just stay alert. There may be trouble on this trip of ours.

Darius considered her warning seriously and looked around. The captain commander seemed to have everything in control. He would tell Roland to keep a special watch for trouble.

* * * * * * * * * * * * * * *

Chapter Two
ADVENTURES IN MAR

Kelln sat outside the assistant governor's office in Mar, the third time in as many weeks. It was infuriating, this sitting around and waiting. He had never liked sitting still and doing nothing. He'd asked to review the trade accounts, which should have been readily available. One excuse after another had him shuffling off to a multitude of people. Now he found himself waiting in the same office as three weeks before. As offices go, this one wasn't a bad place to wait. The chairs were cushioned, stewards came by at regular times to hand out refreshments and sweets, and the ladies in Mar were quite striking with their customary multi-colored skirts hiked up higher than would be proper in Anikari.

Still he was getting tired of not being taken seriously. He had made no headway in finding out anything about the Preacher or Alessandra either. Thinking of the Preacher always made him cringe inside. The man's evil powers had invaded his mind and tortured him while in Belor.

He noticed a man come in through a side door and enter the office. He jumped out of his seat and trotted over to the secretary's desk. The secretary glanced up at Kelln and spoke in a bored monotone.

"May I help you, good sir?"

"Was that Assistant Governor Tamidor coming in?"

"Yes, it was, sir."

"As you know, I have been waiting to talk to him about the trade accounts," Kelln said.

"As you have told me, sir."

Kelln, normally patient and one for some fun, had lost all the patience he had and was not having fun anymore. He smoothed down his official coat and stood taller. "Look here. I am the King's ambassador. I have been ordered to review the books by the King, and I am tired of being ignored."

"I am sure you are, sir. No one likes being ignored," the secretary said.

"That's it, little man." Kelln reached down and grabbed the front of the man's shirt and pulled him up in front of him. Kelln paused for an instant when he grasped that the man stood taller and thicker than him, which wasn't very hard since Kelln was on the short side and had a hard time putting on weight.

The secretary's face grew grim, and his disposition changed. He reached for a dagger at his side. "You don't want to cause trouble here, Ambassador, do you? I don't think you want to cause a scene right now."

Kelln knew when to back down. He put his hands up in front of him and breathed in a deep breath, letting the air out in a slow and patient manner. He tried to relax. The man was right; Kelln didn't want to cause any problems. He was Darius's first ambassador to come to Mar, which had always been a little more independent than the other cities due to its underground Guild of Thieves. Looking up at the big man in front of him, he was sure this man belonged to that guild and had infiltrated the government. Maybe they all had! They were hiding something.

"Fine," Kelln muttered. "I will return in two days. Tell the assistant governor I will review the books at that time." If not, then he would find the governor and deal directly with him.

The large secretary sat back down, resuming his old behavior and form. "I am sure you will, sir." He then continued writing down something in his books.

Kelln groaned under his breath and walked out the door. He wasn't paying attention to where he was going and almost knocked down a lady coming into the building. She glared at him, and he snarled back.

A good walk was what he needed to stretch his legs and clear his head. He wasn't so sure any more about this ambassador position. It took all the fun out of life. He had heard about gardens on the other side of the offices, and so he turned the corner in search of them.

Just as he did so, a man came out of the side door. He glanced around with nervous tics. Kelln slid behind a nearby tree to watch. He was surprised to see Assistant Governor Aron Tamidor sneaking out. The man had on a dark hooded cloak and pulled the hood up over his face. Looking around once again, the man set off at a quick pace.

Kelln smiled. Now maybe there would be something fun to do. He decided to follow the man. Tamidor walked with his head down through the city office building complex and then into the market area. The sun had risen almost to its peak.

The market sounds and smells racked Kelln's senses pleasantly. Fresh sweetbreads tempted him toward the bakery sector, but he needed to stay close to the man he was following so as not to lose him in the crowds. Being a warm day at the edge of the desert, the assistant governor stood out with his hooded head. The man didn't think to turn around and look behind him, which worked to Kelln's favor.

At one point, the man stopped, as if deciding which way to turn. Kelln turned to the nearest market booth and tried to be busy examining their wares. Unfortunately, it was a booth of women's skirts and dresses. Outside of admiring many a girl who wore skirts and dresses, Kelln didn't know much about them. His sisters owned one or two, he supposed.

"Ah, good sir." The female shopkeeper had noticed him. "Looking for a gift for your special lady?"

Kelln tried to follow where Tamidor headed with his eyes. He ignored the lady's question and didn't notice the nicely dressed man who now stood beside him.

"Ambassador, you didn't answer the lady's question."

Kelln turned around, surprised at being addressed in his official capacity. Something didn't seem right. He didn't know the man who had addressed him, and a bad feeling set off alarms in his head. A middle-aged man in white pants and a colorful cloak stood next to him. A small dirk hung ceremoniously at his side. The man smoothed down his long mustache, a style that had become popular lately in Mar, and glared intently at Kelln.

"I'm sorry," Kelln asked. "Do I know you?"

"Probably not," the man said, "but we know who you are."

Kelln tried to turn his head without being obvious. He didn't want to lose Tamidor, but it seemed like he now had.

"Looking for someone?" The man smiled.

Now Kelln realized what had happened. The assistant governor hadn't looked behind him because someone else already followed from behind. He berated himself for such a dumb mistake. He would have to do better than that to be a good ambassador for Darius.

"Just out for a stroll and perusing through your fine market." Kelln put on a happy face. "This is a marvelous place with so much to see."

"You are quite right, good sir. I should get you an escort to show you around. You wouldn't want to accidently find yourself in a bad part of town."

Kelln realized the man had threatened him but tried to remain calm. "I can't believe in this beautiful law-abiding city you have such bad parts of town. I think I am fine by myself. But I do thank you for your offer. Maybe another time."

The man lowered his voice, waved his hands away in a disguised signal, and stepped closer to Kelln. "It's time to leave the market, sir."

Out of the corner of his eyes, Kelln saw other men approaching. He was about to respond when a fair-skinned, dark-haired young woman his age with a younger boy in tow giggled and stepped up next to Kelln.

"There you are, you handsome man. You snuck off without me." She put her hand on Kelln's arm in a seductive manner as her colorful bodice pushed in next to him.

Kelln was confused, and the other man stopped and waved his hand again to hold back the other men.

The young lady drew her eyes around the booth they stood in front of and squealed in delight. "Oh, you were buying me a dress!" She reached over and picked up one of the many items on sale. "You are so sneaky."

Kelln studied the younger boy standing next to her. The scrawny, straw-haired, freckled youth gave him a wink, and Kelln understood what they were doing. He moved in closer to the attractive lady.

"You found me out." He played along. "It was going to be a surprise for your birthday." Kelln put his arm around her and leaned in for a kiss. He might as well enjoy the game.

The teasing girl put her fingers up against Kelln's lips. "Not here in public, sweetie."

Kelln backed up with a pout.

The young boy moved up next to the girl, "Taliana, Mother is expecting us back soon."

"Quite right, brother," Taliana said. She proceeded to loop one arm through his and another arm through Kelln's. "Then we better hurry and find some more dresses." With that, she danced the two boys down the street and away from the man who was giving Kelln trouble. Turning a corner, the boy motioned with one hand for both Taliana and Kelln to follow him down the street. Soon they found themselves in the back of an older plaster-coated building.

Kelln surveyed both of them but didn't say a word. Finally, the two strangers burst out laughing.

"That was fun!" Taliana's blue eyes sparkled.

"You were great, Tali," the young boy added.

"What's going on here?" Kelln felt confused at best. "And who are you two?"

The younger boy stuck out his small hand to Kelln. "My name is Rapp. Nice to meet you, Ambassador."

"Rapp?" Kelln muttered.

"Well it's actually Rappatorian, but you know." The boy seemed embarrassed. "It seems a little too formal for what I do."

"And what is it you do, Rapp?"

"I run errands for people. Help people get out of trouble. You know, that sort of thing," he said vaguely.

"Rapp is being quite modest, sir." Tali spoke to Kelln for the first time since the dress booth. "He is one of the guild's best runners. He works for one of the guildmasters."

"Which one?" Kelln asked with suspicion.

"The Merchants' Guild," Tali answered. The city of Mar had been run by guilds further back than the founding of the Realm. In order to do any kind of business in the city, you had to belong to a guild. Even the thieves had a guild.

"And Tali, if that is your real name, what is it you do?"

Tali laughed and tossed her head in a way that would melt many men. "My name is Taliana Penrose, daughter of Governor Penrose, guildmaster of the Merchants' Guild. I don't work for the guild, but Rapp here asked me for a favor, and I decided to help. Did you like my performance?"

"Yes. Yes, I did." Kelln laughed. "That was quite fantastic. I must admit being a little confused at first."

"Wouldn't it be fun to be an actress and perform with the bards and playwrights all around the Realm?" Tali added.

"Well, you have my vote."

Tali leaned over and kissed him on the cheek. "Thank you, Ambassador."

"And what's the kiss for?" Kelln smiled mischievously.

"Well, you wanted one earlier, didn't you?" Tali teased with a swish of her wide multi-colored skirt, her long brown hair moving around her shoulders.

"Oh, gross." Rapp sighed. "Stop flirting with him, Tali. He's a representative of the King."

Kelln almost said something when they overheard voices outside of the door they hid behind. The man from the market spoke to someone else. They were still on the lookout for him. They stayed quiet for a few minutes, and the voices drifted away.

"Now." Kelln got down to business. "Who was that man?"

"He works for the assistant governor, well, at least unofficially," Rapp said. "We have suspected the assistant governor and his secretary both work for the Thieves' Guild."

Kelln frowned, but had to agree with their suspicions. "I met his secretary. All nice and polite until you do something he doesn't agree with and then . . . he changed very quickly into someone with dangerous undertones."

"My father has been trying to get proof for years on the assistant governor, but they have covered things well," Tali said.

Kelln considered both of them. "So, Rapp, you work for Governor Penrose?"

Rapp beamed. "I sure do. The Merchants' Guild is the biggest guild in the city."

"That is how Daddy got noticed by King Edward. He tried to build up an honest guild. That earned him the governorship four years ago." Tali continued, "But as of late, the Thieves Guild have been trying to cause trouble, skimming money off the top of trade and undermining my father. Now, there are a few new people trying to take over the smaller guilds and form them into one. They have approached my father about siding with him against the Thieves' Guild.

Kelln was amazed at the amount of information he was gathering from these two. It was much more than he had gained by sitting around the city offices for the past month. "How do you two know all of this? You're just kids!"

Tali's eyes flashed. "I'm not a kid, Ambassador. I am not much younger than you, I would guess."

Kelln realized he had said the wrong thing and just nodded his head in apology and said, "please just call me Kelln."

"All right. Kelln, I've been following my father's work for years. When I was little, I brought food into his meetings. Now that I am older, no one pays much attention to me being there since they are used to me, but I hear everything. My father knows there are things Rapp and I can do that he can't."

"Such as what you did today to help me?" Kelln understood. "I do appreciate that."

They stood in silence for a moment.

"I think it's safe to leave here," Rapp said.

The others nodded, and they stepped out of the door and continued walking away from the marketplace into a part of town Kelln didn't recognize. The neighborhood was not the large rich houses up on the hills overlooking the city and the bay, but also it wasn't one of the poorer thief-ridden neighborhoods. He felt quite comfortable walking the streets here. The bright-colored plaster houses stood neatly arranged, far different from the style in Anikari. Many had small courtyards out front with potted flowers, benches, and even some fountains. He imagined families and neighbors visiting outside during the hotter months. The materials used for the houses here came from rocks crushed along the shore that had fallen down from the White Cliffs.

Kelln mulled over all of the information in his head and finally thought of something Tali said. "You mentioned new people coming in and trying to form a new larger guild out of the smaller ones. Why would someone want to do that?"

"Power," Tali said. "If they can form a guild equal in power to the larger guilds, they could have considerable influence in the city."

"But you don't know who it is?"

Tali shook her head. "I have not seen them. Though I have heard descriptions about a large man with short red hair and a woman with long, dark auburn hair."

Warning bells rang through Kelln's skull. He stopped abruptly and grabbed Tali's arm stronger than he intended. When she yelped in pain, he let go.

"What exactly did they look like? What are their names? Where are they from?" Kelln's eyes were intent, jaw set firmly. Had he finally found the Preacher and his daughter?

Tali stepped back from his gaze. A man and his wife glanced up at them from their front garden. Rapp motioned for the three of them to move along. They didn't want to attract attention.

After walking further down the street, Tali answered. "I don't know the answer to your questions, but my father might."

"Does the man have powers? Like a wizard?"

Tali's eyes now opened wide, and she covered her mouth. "How did you know? I have heard someone mention it in passing."

"The Preacher," Kelln could feel apprehension, excitement, and fear hit his gut all at once, "and his daughter, Alessandra."

"You know them?" Rapp swiped his long messy hair out of his green eyes.

"Yes, I do." Kelln's thoughts raced back over the last year. Alessandra had taken him from Anikari to Belor where through misunderstanding and mistrust the Preacher had imprisoned him. Twice Alessandra had betrayed him to her father, the Preacher. The Preacher later had been imprisoned himself in the dungeons in Anikari for trying to rule Belor without authorization from the Realm. His daughter had helped him escape. Kelln hoped she was manipulated or threatened by her father, but he had doubts about her motives and needed to find her and get to the truth once and for all.

The man only known as the Preacher was a wizard who used his powers for evil. Originally, he tried to convince Belor to separate from the Realm. At one point, Darius had contemplated siding with him—two wizards together—to fight the Realm and King Edward. Luckily, Darius had come to his senses and through unforeseen events had actually become the next King. The Preacher hated Darius and Kelln and had promised to destroy them and the Realm in his quest for power and revenge.

Tali, Rapp, and Kelln stopped in front of a larger two story house. The home had a balcony with a view of the street. A trellis in front had vines with white flowers. A man strolled down the walkway toward them. He was a man in his forties, trim and well-dressed, with a comfortable walk. His bright blue hat shaded his face. He approached the three, removed his hat in greeting, and turned to Kelln.

"Ambassador, I am Governor Penrose." He took Kelln's hand and shook it firmly. "I am sorry I haven't been able to meet with you until now. There were important matters that I have been dealing with." Looking up and down the small street and deeming it safe, he motioned for the three of them to join him in the house.

He opened the front door and proceeded to take them down a wooden-floored hallway to a sitting room. A quick hand motion from the governor had Rapp scampering away from the group.

"Taliana, could you please find some refreshments for our visitors?" He smiled at her.

Visitors? Kelln thought suddenly.

Entering the room, Kelln immediately spotted another person standing next to a painting on the far side of the well-furnished room. It depicted a setting sun over the bay, White Island in the distance. Before Kelln could think, the man turned around.

"Ambassador now, are we? My, my, you have risen in rank since we last saw each other." The tall, large man rubbed his short red hair and grinned wolfishly at Kelln.

The Preacher!

****

Chapter Three
THE PREACHER

Rappatorian Hume was small for his thirteen years. In his line of business, it was a benefit. No one stopped to notice a younger child running around. Without any formal education, Rapp had learned the ways of the world through listening and selling tidbits of news. Information was a big business among the guilds in Mar. His father had died years before from an accident while experimenting with glass. He, his mother, and his older sister were becoming destitute when Rapp had decided to sell a secret about the governor. It had been a trap, and he had been caught.

Fortunately for Rapp, the governor felt sorry for the family and agreed to hire on his mother as a cook, and Rapp became, unofficially at first, the governor's newest runner. A runner would run errands for his master. Now he did all sorts of jobs for the man in charge, those things the older men couldn't or wouldn't do. He had a way of discerning people's character and listening without being noticed.

Right now, he judged that his new friend, the ambassador, was in trouble. He hadn't known this other man was going to be at the governor's meeting house. Rapp had been drawn to Kelln instantly and would have warned him if he had known. The governor had informed Rapp, by his hand language, to stay close and alert. The newcomer made everyone nervous to be around.

Through a hole in the wall in a nearby room, Rapp could hear and see the three men talking. All three sat in comfortable high-backed, cushioned chairs. Kelln sat on the edge of his and seemed very guarded and quiet. The other man, who only went by Mr. El'Lan, laughed and charmed his way through the conversation, asking questions about the formalities of forming his own guild. He asked the governor to be his sponsor in return for favors. The governor did not seem interested in the arrangement and excused himself to go and check on the food his daughter was preparing.

That left Kelln and Mr. El'Lan alone in the room.

"I could have you arrested and brought back to Anikari to stand trial," Kelln informed Mr. El'Lan. "I have the authority to do that now."

"Oh, you may have the authority, boy," the man almost growled, his eyes darkening, "but you do not have the ability."

"You cannot threaten me, Preacher," Kelln said. "I have protection from the King."

Rapp was confused as to why Kelln called Mr. El'Lan "Preacher."

"But who will protect him?" the Preacher whispered. Rapp could barely catch the words.

"You will not leave this city alive, you know. You are still guilty of sedition and treason under my command in Belor." The Preacher stood, reaching toward Kelln. "You should still be in prison, or better yet, dead!"

Kelln jumped to his feet and backed away. "Leave me alone. You have no authority here or in Belor anymore."

Blue fire crackled from the Preacher's fingertips, and his eyes blazed almost red. "First you and then that pathetic King of yours. His power is no match for mine or for those I serve."

"You serve someone?" Kelln looked to be trying to distract the man. "I would think you are too powerful a wizard for that."

The Preacher paused. "You know nothing of power. I will rule the western lands for the eastern lords."

"Where is your daughter, Preacher? What have you done to her?" Kelln spat.

Rapp was having a hard time following the conversation, but he surmised that Kelln was stalling, trying to stop the man in front of him from killing him. The man met Kelln's words with murderous gaze. Rapp wondered what he should do. This man, Mr. El'Lan, or the Preacher, seemed to be a wizard from the fire dangling at his fingertips.

Down the wooden hallway, the footsteps of the governor came closer. The Preacher had only moments to recall the wizard's fire back into him before Governor Penrose turned the corner.

"Is everything all right here?" the governor asked.

The Preacher in an instant reverted back to his old self. "Oh, yes. The ambassador and I were catching up on old times."

The governor turned to Kelln, "You know this man?"

"Yes. He is a dangerous man, Governor. I would advise you to have no dealings with him. He is wanted for treason by the King and escaped from prison there."

"Ambassador," Mr. El'Lan jumped in, "I think the governor can decide for himself whom to do business with. The prison thing was just a misunderstanding." Turning to Governor Penrose, he continued, "Sometimes young people jump to conclusions too fast. I am sure that you and I can come to a gentleman's agreement of how things work here in Mar."

Rapp watched his employer think things over. He knew the governor, although trying to abide by the law most of the time, was a shrewd negotiator.

The governor motioned for the other two to sit down. "I am sure we can, Mr. El'Lan." As the leader of Mar sat down, he hand signaled Rapp. Rapp instantly understood the meaning and ran out of the neighboring room to find Tali before she brought in the refreshments. He caught her in the hallway and delivered instructions to her right before she entered the sitting room.

Rapp stood just outside of sight but within earshot. His heart beat faster. Things were always exciting around the governor. He heard Tali serve the governor and the Preacher, then move on to the ambassador.

A small crash erupted from the room.

"Oh, I am so sorry, Ambassador," Tali said in her most sweet voice. "I was merely being clumsy. I am sure we can get the stain out of your clothes if you come with me."

"Sirs," Kelln addressed the other two gentlemen. "It seems I need to excuse myself from the conversation for a few minutes."

"That is all right, young sir," came the governor's voice. "Mr. El'Lan and I will continue discussing his business plans. We can catch up later, Ambassador."

Kelln came around the corner. Rapp grabbed him by the arm and took him into a back room. Rapp and Tali tried to clean him off, Rapp offering him some new clothes. When Kelln motioned his head toward Tali, she got the point and left the room while Kelln changed.

"What's going on?" Kelln asked.

"The governor signaled for me to get you out of here fast. The man inside, Mr. El'Lan, or the Preacher from what you called him, would most likely kill you if he sees you again."

"That's probably right," Kelln mumbled. "He is an escaped prisoner who tried to take over Belor. I need to find his daughter."

Rapp thought for a moment. "We need to get you out of the house first and on your way somewhere. You'll need to leave Mar for a bit. I'll ask around about his daughter."

"What about the governor? He's in danger, too."

"Oh, Mr. Penrose? I think Mr. El'Lan would find quite an opponent in the governor."

"But the Preacher or Mr. El'Lan as he is now referring to himself, is a wizard who learned his craft in the eastern kingdoms," Kelln explained as he finished getting dressed. "He doesn't play by the same rules as others do. The governor is not seriously thinking of working with him?"

"Of course not," Tali said, reentering the room, "but he is wise to politics and the undercurrent of Marian society.

Rapp pulled Kelln out a back door. Tali handed Kelln a pack with food and some other items. Kelln put the pack on. "I need to go to White Island on an errand for the King. I will be back in about a week."

Tali took out a cap and placed it on Kelln's head. "That's to hide those famous red curls." She smiled.

"Just be careful, you two and your father, Tali. Mr. El'Lan is very, very dangerous." Kelln turned to leave.

A dog started to bark in the next yard, and Kelln turned back and gave a nervous glance in Rapp's direction. However, what he saw was Tali making circular motions in the air and then the animal quieting down.

"You?" Kelln stuttered. "You. Are. A. Wizard?"

"Well, I haven't received any formal training to be a wizard, but I do like magic. My father is powerful also. We usually keep magical things a secret around here, so keep your voice down. "She put her fingers up to her lips to emphasize the need for secrecy.

"That's why I said he could take care of himself," Rapp added.

"That's fantastic!" Kelln's eyes lit up.

Tali and Rapp told him he needed to move along. Soon with quiet stealth, he slid between some trees and back to an open property behind the house. Rapp motioned for him to hurry on his way. Afterward, he and Tali went back inside.

****

The King and Queen's visit to Belor and the surrounding villages occurred without any problems or delays. The political structure in Belor was still being worked out, but Darius had sworn in a new governor while he was in the city. He had seen Alessandra's grandfather to ensure that he had a safe place to stay in the city. He didn't have to hide anymore. His wisdom and knowledge of Belor and the Realm would help the new governor stabilize the area.

The citizens of Belor seemed to be doing well coming out from under the rule of their former master, the Preacher. They greeted their new young King with enthusiasm and an almost overwhelming display of trying to make sure they were forgiven for their earlier alliance with the Preacher. Darius and Christine had enjoyed their week in the southern city.

The royal assemblage had spent an afternoon at Crystal Lake, taking some time to relax before heading toward Mar. Darius had sent one of his messengers on up ahead to inform Kelln and the governor of their arrival. The messenger took longer than expected, and Darius was getting worried.

Roland, newly promoted captain of the King's guard convinced the group to stay the night at a small village next to Crystal Lake. The fresh-water lake bordered the Crystal River, which ran from the Mountains of Gold to the lake and on to the Blue Sea. Darius, being closer again to Anikari, had received dispatches from his father. He sat down next to Christine by the river's edge to read them. A few guards stood nearby.

"You look flushed, Christine," Darius noticed after reading the missives from his father.

"I'm fine. Just all the riding in this late autumn heat." Christine smiled. "It's not usually so warm this time of year."

"Mar will be even warmer. The desert holds the heat later into the evening." He brought up his hand in front of her and flourished his fingers back and forth a moment to bring up a cool breeze. "Here you go."

Christine laughed. "Oh, thank you. That's much better."

Even after Darius's hand stopped moving, a magical force continued to blow a cool wind into the queen's face, lifting her curls on the side of her hair.

"What good is being a wizard if I can't use the power to help the ones I love?"

A distant sound alerted Darius, and he stood and gazed around with sharp eyes. His guards noticed his sudden tense behavior and moved in closer, casting a questioning look at him.

"Someone is coming down the road. A lone rider at breakneck speed."

One of the guards went up the small bank to alert the others. The other two guards stood by Christine and Darius. The rider was stopped by Roland, then told him the need to talk to the King. When the rider removed his hooded cloak, the guards gasped. It was a girl. She shook her hair and let it fall back down over her shoulders. Straight, dark hair framed her pale, youthful face. They stood and gawked a moment.

"Haven't you ever seen a girl before, boys?" She mocked them with her sparkling blue eyes but smiled sweetly. Darius walked to where she was.

She bowed to him, "Your Majesty, I presume?"

"Yes, and who are you?" He reached his hand toward her but pulled back before touching her. He didn't know what made him decide to keep his distance from the lady, but he did.

"I am Taliana Penrose. Governor Penrose's daughter. He sent me to warn you. The messenger that you sent to us was ambushed after asking for the ambassador. The ambassador had to leave rather quickly a few days ago after an incident."

Darius raised his brows but said nothing. What had Kelln got himself in the middle of this time?

Taliana continued, "The ambassador ran into some problems. Someone from the Thieves' Guild was following him, and Rapp and I saved him."

"Saved him?" the King asked. He wasn't quite following the girl's words.

"Yes, well, we distracted the man following him and brought him to one of my father's houses. My father, the governor, is a good man, your Majesty, and is trying to clean up Mar and make things better. He and Ambassador El'Han were going to talk about these things, but another visitor showed up, a man named Mr. El'Lan." Taliana paused. "He and Kelln did not get along well. In fact, I think Mr. El'Lan threatened to kill your ambassador."

"Should I know this Mr. El'Lan?" He regarded his wife and the others. They shook their heads in the negative.

"I believe Kelln addressed him as the Preacher."

Darius felt his hand go involuntarily to his sword, his face flushed, and his power flared up inside him. The sword began to glow. The girl standing opposite him appeared surprised at his power surge. She brought her hands up in front of her with obvious intentions of defending herself. Christine put her hand on her husband's arm, and his anger was replaced with the love and concern of her touch.

Darius gave the girl a hard stare. "Where is my ambassador?"

Taliana finished her report. "We sent Kelln away a few days ago. He mentioned having to go to White Island for you. Given the circumstances, my father recommends not coming to Mar at this time. We will let your messenger rest and return to you when he is feeling better. He was roughed up quite a bit."

Darius was about to ask why the governor had sent his teen daughter out on the road by herself, but he sighed as he remembered her defensive posture as his power flared. She had powers also. The others gathered around him, awaiting his decision.

"Your Majesty." Roland came forward. "We can go around Mar, west of the city, and catch the road heading to Sur. Travel will be harder with a group this size since the ground is sandy and not well for traveling, but it is doable."

Lightning nuzzled up next to Darius. His wife's Cremelino was trying to get his attention. *My brothers and sisters would like to meet you, wizard. A side trip to White Island is not too far, and you may find Kelln there.*

"Why do I suspect you keep nudging me to your homeland? I tried to send Kelln there, but now it seems that to find him, I must go also. What are you not telling me?" He sent his concerns to the horse.

An amused feeling came over him from the magical creature. *There are many things we do not share with others; however, we make many exceptions for you, young Wizard King. You are our hope; the prophecy guides all we do.*

"The prophecy again," Darius muttered.

"Excuse me, Sire?" Roland asked.

Darius had been quiet for a few moments while communicating with Lightning. Christine looked at him expectantly.

Darius turned to Roland and said, "Your men will need to care for my wife."

"Darius?" Christine blurted. "What are you talking about? You're not thinking of leaving me, are you?"

I will take care of her, Wizard, as if my life depended on it, Lightning voiced in his mind.

Darius and Christine heard the Cremelino, but the others, who had become somewhat used to this silent exchange between horse and their King and his wife, waited patiently. Darius drew Christine off to one side to speak in hushed tones.

"I don't like this, Darius. Lightning is always so cryptic in her answers. I feel a sense of danger from her."

"As do I." Darius put his arm around his beloved queen. "That's why I think this is the best. You are not feeling well. I need to go to White Island for some reason." He glanced over at Lightning.

"Why don't we stay the night here and think about it some more?" Christine offered. "Maybe send a messenger to Kelln instead."

"No, Christine. More time won't make a difference." Darius knew, as a wizard of the heart, he tended to make quick decisions based on what he felt. Sometimes they were brash and needed to be checked, but he felt a strong compulsion toward White Island.

"I have to go," he continued. "Lightning is right. There is a reason for me to travel to the Cremelino's home. I can feel the importance, though I don't know why. I need to talk to Kelln also and find out what we can do about the Preacher."

Christine hugged him as if she didn't want to let him go. Lightning came over and gave her comfort also.

Darius informed the group that he would travel to White Island while the rest would travel back through Anikari and on to Sur from there. Darius would meet up with them in Sur after taking care of matters on White Island and Mar.

"I will travel to White Island with you also," Taliana declared.

Roland gave a sudden grin. "I will accompany the King also, and I will be happy to be your protector, my lady. My King is used to handling himself." He smiled at Darius.

"Don't patronize me, guard man. I can hold my own," Tali said.

"Guard man?" Roland choked and turned red.

Everyone else laughed at his obvious discomfort.

"I am the captain of the King's guard," he stated formally, "and I will protect you, little girl." He said the last part in mock imitation of how she had addressed him.

Without warning, Roland jumped in the air with a yelp. He reached back and rubbed his behind. "What the . . . ?"

"I am not a little girl. As I said, I can handle myself."

"How did you do that?" Roland muttered. "You didn't even move."

"There are lots of things a woman of power can do." Taliana smiled.

"Oh no, not another wizard," Roland groaned. "Is there anyone else who needs protecting?" He spread his hands wide in mock supplication. The crowd laughed and joined in Roland's mirth.

Darius motioned Roland to the side and addressed the others in the group. "Roland and Taliana will come with me. The rest of you will ride back to Anikari with the queen. After a few days of rest, you will accompany the queen to Sur. Roland and I will meet up with you there to meet with the people of Sur and the Kingdom of Arc's leaders."

Turning, he called Taliana to his side. "Using the power is not a game," he admonished.

Taliana looked down, cheeks red, and curtsied. "Forgive me, Sire."

Darius felt her contrition. "No need to dwell on the past." He smiled at her, and she smiled back.

"My Lord, there are rumors you have powers as I do, though I guess you are much more powerful. Is that true?"

"It is." Darius still had a hard time realizing what he was. "I am a wizard of the heart."

Taliana smiled. "Is that how you convinced your queen to marry you?" she said with a twinkle in her eye.

Darius laughed. "Taliana, you are going to be a handful, aren't you?"

"Call me Tali." She examined the sky and watched a flock of birds flying overhead. They were coming from the west. "Must be a storm coming. We should hurry."

Darius's eyes opened wider at that knowledge.

"My powers are in the earth . . . as are my father's."

"The governor of Mar is a wizard?" Darius found this all too much. At first, he thought he was the only one. Since then he had found Mezar; Alastair, the father of the Preacher; the Preacher himself; and now this girl and her father, the governor of one of his most troubled cities. "And I thought I was all alone." He wondered how many others had powers that they kept hidden for fear of retribution. He would have to remedy that.

Darius walked over to Christine, who was sitting on the ground next to Lightning. She looked pale and sick. "I won't be gone long. In a week or two, we will both be back together in Sur."

"I know." She reached up her hands to him, and he pulled her up and close, her slender body folding into his. "It's just this is the first time we have been separated since you returned to Anikari." Her eyes filled with tears.

Darius held her closer and sent his power of love into her. She relaxed in his arms and breathed out in slow rhythms. Christine turned her head up to his and kissed him.

He whispered, "You need some rest, Christine. You are only a day's ride back to the city. I hate to leave you, too, but I need to go to White Island. It is drawing me more now that we are closer. I will see you in a week or no more than ten days."

Christine stayed in his arms and sighed but didn't say anything.

After a few moments, Lightning nudged them, and they turned around. The entire group was standing and watching

Darius and Christine. They had deep smiles on their faces. Most of them had served under King Edward and were still getting used to the ways of their young King and his wife.

Darius gazed over his subjects and thought of them as his friends. He loved his people. He spread his hands outward and raised his palms up, spreading a trickle of the love he felt outward for them to feel. They received it wide-eyed and dropped to one knee in reverence of their leader.

Roland, always the one to keep things moving, stood back up first. "My Lord, the young girl—" He stumbled on his words. "I mean, the young lady from Mar is correct: it does look like a storm coming. If we all leave now, the queen and her group should reach Forest View before the storm. Those of us going with you might not be so lucky."

Turning to his wife's group, Darius said, "We will meet up with you in Sur." Then he turned and with his group galloped off in a northeasterly direction. He turned around once, waving and smiling at his young wife.

Give greetings and love to my family. Darius listened to Lightning's voice inside his head.

* * * * * * * * * * * * * * *

Chapter Four
THE PRINCE OF ARC

Sean San Ghant sat in the parlor of the mayor's home. The town of Toth sat on the border of Arc and the Realm in a small valley at the mouth of a pass. The road through Toth led between the Superstition Mountains and served as the checkpoint for goods going between the two kingdoms. The road was treacherous but navigable, and through the years, quite a large population of guides and hardened trackers had made Toth their home. Technically it sat on the Arc side of the border, but people from many lands could be found among its citizens. The population held quite a mixed marriage of races and cultures.

The room, much more rustic than Sean's tastes ran, was comfortable, though not large. He had the good pleasure of the mayor's daughter to bring him some morning refreshments. Her skin tone favored a dusty brown mixture of the darker Gildanian and the lighter Arc parentage. Her blue eyes were slightly turned. He rubbed his hand over his close-cropped light hair and winked his thanks at her. She smiled back with flushed cheeks.

Sean had been in the city for over two months now, establishing his front as the son of a successful trader. By his looks, others supposed him of Anikarian heritage, but he never offered the information, and others never pushed it. He was vague on purpose so as not to focus anyone's attention on him. Twice so far, he had to hide from visitors from the Realm that he recognized.

Soon Sean would meet his contact from inside the Kingdom of Arc. He had been planting seeds of discontent against the Realm with the mayor and other local nobles and traders in the important border town. It didn't take much to fire up age-old animosity toward their neighboring kingdom. Historically, the Realm under both Kings Edward and Charles had been monetarily successful, border taxes had been raised, and an air of supremacy had developed. Sean played the part of a disgruntled son looking for opportunity. If that meant betrayal of his country, it didn't matter to him. They had betrayed him by putting Darius on the throne, a man who hadn't cared about his noble heritage.

The door opened, and he felt the cooler mountain breeze blow into the room. In the doorway stood two men dressed in the finery of Arc. They both had on black boots and pants. A white shirt stuck out only slightly from the black jacket and cloaks they wore. Although identical in dress, the two men were opposite in physical stature. One favored the truer Arc heritage of blond hair on top of a tall, slender body. While the other stood shorter, with brown hair, and of a heavier build. Both carried an aura of danger around them.

Sean, deciding these were the men he was to meet, stood up and walked toward them with an air of importance. He smoothed down his own richly made clothes on his way to them.

"Good day, sirs. I've been waiting a long time for you." He looked around to make sure the mayor's daughter was out of the parlor room. "We have a lot of business to discuss."

The thinner man put his hand on his sword hilt and anger flashed in his light eyes. "We don't have any business to discuss with you, Realm spy."

Sean's jaw dropped in surprise. Stammering, he tried to regain control. "Spy? Spy? No, no. You have things all wrong."

"Seems to me *you* might have things all wrong," the thinner man continued. He seemed to be a few years older than Sean. "You say you are a trader, but I see nothing being traded, you reek of Anikarian nobility with your speech and clothes, and you are trying to get in the good graces of our local leaders. What is it you are looking for?"

"Looking for?" Sean repeated, then became angry. "I am looking for you. I was told to meet a contact here, and I've been waiting for weeks trying to keep myself busy. You are wasting my time now."

The larger, older man took a step forward and said his first words. The accent was not one that Sean recognized, but the intent he did. "You will speak respectfully to the prince, or you will be removed from his presence."

The prince? Sean's mind whirled around as he tried to remember who the King of Arc even was. The Preacher had said nothing about getting involved with the Prince. This was more dangerous than he had intended. He had to be careful. He needed to smooth things over.

Bowing low, Sean apologized, "I am sorry, your Highness. I seem to have forgotten my manners while sitting in this mountain pass. I assure you I meant no disrespect. I'm sure you are busy, and I appreciate the time taken to come to me."

The larger man, obviously the younger's body guard, stepped back and seemed to relax, though Sean was sure that could change in a moment's notice.

"You will come with us," the prince instructed. He motioned toward the door. "Now."

Sean was annoyed at having to leave some things behind, but he recognized the opportunity of the moment and followed.

Outside of the mayor's house stood three guards, dressed the same as the two men he'd already met. The prince motioned one of the men forward.

"Tie his wrists and set him on a horse with one of the men. He will be taken and tried," the prince ordered.

Sean couldn't believe what was happening. Maybe these weren't his contacts. "Prince Bronwyn, as I said before, there has been a misunderstanding. I am no spy; just a merchant's son trying to make my way in life. My benefactor told me to meet a contact here to discuss some important business."

The prince ignored Sean's plea. "We ride to Herro. If we hurry, we can be there by nightfall."

Sean tried once again to get the prince's attention, but one of the guards grabbed him in a rough manner, tied a rope around his wrists, set him on a horse in front of another guard, and told him that if he caused any trouble, he would ride unconscious the rest of the way.

Herro was the closest major city to the border, and after riding hard all day, they arrived at the small castle of the local ruler. On the backside of the Superstition Mountains, the ground was not as green and the air drier, but was still comfortable compared to the rest of the desert kingdom.

One of the guards had given Sean some food and allowed him to drink water each time they stopped to rest the horses, but his wrists ached. The skin under the ropes had been rubbed raw. This was the first time the young noble had been outside of the Realm. He thought it would be more exciting. Now he began to fear for his life.

Sean was dragged off the horse and marched into the manor. The prince ordered a guard to get him cleaned up and present him at the dining table to join them in a meal. The Preacher had promised him power, and so he took a deep breath and tried to maintain a show of confidence. Being a noble from the Realm should still get him the respect he deserved.

It was late in the evening when they arrived, but the kitchen staff had obviously been waiting for them. Walking into the dining room, Sean felt his stomach growl and contract. The little food they had given him on the day-long ride was hardly enough to satisfy him. His long legs felt weak, and his mouth watered at the sight. A large formal wooden table sat laid out with platters of meat, vegetables, fruits, and steaming fresh-baked rolls. They all sat down at the table. Sean raised his hands, grabbing the prince's attention.

"My Lord?" he asked, needing the ropes removed.

The prince returned the question with a nod, and a guard untied his wrists. There was quick pain as the blood recirculated, but the smells of the food distracted him enough.

Sean was surprised by the mixture of servants and nobility. A stranger to Sean, the local lord of the manor joined them. All were silent as food was passed around. The men tore with eagerness into the flavorsome pork and venison. Wine was passed around to all, the talk started again, and soon all were laughing with exploits and adventures that grew bigger and bigger.

All except Sean. He didn't know quite what to make of what was going on. The prince sat a few chairs down from him on the opposite side of the table. After Sean tried to get his attention through the meal, the prince finally turned to speak to him.

"I'm sorry about your rough treatment. We had to be careful." His accent was heavy, but Sean understood him nevertheless. "There are eyes everywhere. I am Prince Bronwyn Anwar."

Sean relaxed slightly at the words, relieved that he had indeed found his contacts, and they intended him no further harm.

"I am Sean San Ghant."

Bronwyn continued, "I am hesitant about a man who would sell out his own kingdom."

Sean winced at the slap but answered calmly, "I have been a faithful and strong servant of the Realm, but the Realm has fallen under the influence of a new King. He is young and brash and does not deserve what he has. He has powers that…"

"Powers?" the prince interrupted.

"He is a Wizard King, my Lord, with little training in magic and an even smaller sense of how to run a kingdom. I do not see myself as selling out the land of my birth but as a patriot concerned about its future."

The prince brooded for a moment. "Another wizard sticking his nose where it does not belong. I understand your frustration, Sean San Ghant. The world would be a much better place without wizards meddling in our affairs."

The large wooden door at the end of the dining room crashed open. Sean watched as a large elderly man with graying hair and a full beard walked purposefully into the room. His hefty girth was draped by a large green robe and riding cloak.

"What about wizards, Prince Bronwyn Anwar?"

The room went silent with the presence of the newcomer. Anger flashed in the eyes of the prince.

"Just that there seems to be more of them lately, High Wizard. We were commenting on the new Wizard King in the Realm."

"Ah," the large man said, "I see." He glanced around the room, his eyes settling on Sean for a few moments, but passed by without a word. Sean felt as if the man knew what his motives were.

All of a sudden, a higher female voice broke the uncomfortable silence. "Olan, wait up for me." A young curvy girl came up behind the High Wizard. She stopped suddenly, eyes on the table full of men. Her full cheeks flushed; a broad beautiful smile split her face. "Bronwyn." She rushed up to the prince and, among the chuckles of the men, gave him a big hug.

Hardly reaching his chest, she had to stretch her arms high to grab him around the neck.

"My little sister, Danijela. You have grown. I haven't seen you in over a year. Looks like you are finally losing some of that baby fat," the prince teased, pinching her cheeks.

Danijela smiled but not so warmly now. Her hands moved to her hips, and she stood her ground against her larger and older brother. "Bronwyn, that's not nice to say to a woman."

"A woman now?" Bronwyn said.

"I turned sixteen earlier this year, and you missed my party if I remember right."

Bronwyn did wince at that. "I was out meeting our people. Anyway, what are you doing in the company of the High Wizard?"

"Haven't you heard by now?"

"Heard what? I've been traveling the far reaches of our kingdom, first with Mother and then with my council of men here. We just recently arrived. I had heard you were traveling with Wizard Sallir but hadn't heard why."

Danijela brought her hand up and spun it around. All of the lamps in the room brightened considerably.

Sean watched the prince. His features hardened, and his breathing deepened. He stood up, knocking his chair on the floor.

"What is the meaning of this?" he questioned, striding across the floor toward the High Wizard.

Sean didn't know what a High Wizard was, but from the short conversation moments before, he understood that Bronwyn did not like wizards. He wondered how the prince would react if he knew that the Preacher was the benefactor in this mission of his.

"She is a wizard in training, an apprentice under my care," voiced High Wizard Sallir loudly.

"What did you do to her?" the prince demanded, standing directly in front of the wizard.

Danijela moved between them. "He did nothing, Bronwyn. I knew I had powers for years; I just didn't know what to do about it. He invited me to train with him at the Wizards' Conclave."

Bronwyn looked at Danijela. "You are playing at things you don't understand, little sister. Come back home with me where you belong."

Danijela stood up in front of her brother, not even reaching his chin. Her short blonde hair framed a face that still held a fullness of youth. Her lips tightened as her hands moved to her hips. "I am not little anymore, big brother. I am sixteen. This is what I choose to do."

Bronwyn reached to grab his sister's arm. Instead he was thrown in the air by the stone floor pushing him off his feet. The stone turned to liquid and flowed over the floor. It surrounded the prince and began to make a wall around him, hardening again as it formed. The prince's men rose from the table and drew their swords. Sean sat back and smiled. Oh, yes, these people could be manipulated for sure. Bronwyn's hatred of magic was apparent.

"Enough!" High Wizard Sallir boomed. "Danijela, stop this immediately."

The men still stood with swords out and ready to fight. The High Wizard flicked his wrist and every sword flew to the ground.

Bronwyn stood. His face filled with rage and murderous intent. "You manipulated my sister, Wizard." He spat.

"I am the High Wizard, Prince Bronwyn, and you should not forget that. I have advised three Kings and now do advise your father. He asked me to come and ask you to meet the new Realm King in his place as he is taking care of other matters on the other side of the country. Your lack of control and judgment make me question your ability to do that or to rule in your father's footsteps. I had hoped to raise Danijela to be your advisor."

"We don't need wizards advising us anymore. You take too much power to yourselves and meddle in our affairs. When I succeed my father, there will be no advisor. Neither you or my now-accursed sister."

Danijela started to say something, but the High Wizard stopped her with a touch of his hand on her arm. Tears streamed down her face as she regarded her brother. It was obvious he had upset her.

The High Wizard lowered his voice, almost to a whisper. "Bronwyn, I will excuse this behavior from you because it is late at night. You are young and tired. But make no mistake further. Your succession is not guaranteed. Do not presume too much at this young age."

Bronwyn moved to speak, but the High Wizard put up his hands to stop him. He turned to Danijela. "We are obviously not wanted here tonight. We will go to the inn to rest instead. Come." The two turned back to the doorway they had entered.

Right before leaving the room, Danijela turned back. With a sweep of her hand the stones that had been reshaped, slid back to their original position as tiles in the floor as if nothing had happened. She nodded to the lord of the manor and turned back around.

Complete silence filled the room after the two wizards left. Sean waited for someone to say something. He took a long drink of wine, finishing off his glass. The prince remained standing where he had been left. Sean could take the silence no longer. He stood up out of his chair.

"Now is as good a time as any to get back down to business, my Lord." He was getting tired of doing nothing.

All eyes stared at the foreigner, as if they had forgotten he was in the room.

"I don't think we want to get down to business, as you say, right now. I don't think you would find me a very tolerable person." Bronwyn scowled for a few minutes and everyone fell silent.

"However," the prince started again, "this might be a good night to take care of this situation once and for all."

The guard's faces in the room piqued in interest and slight surprise.

Prince Bronwyn came closer to the group. "Later tonight we will ride to the inn and take care of that overweight meddling wizard once and for all."

"What about your sister?" someone asked.

The prince ignored the comment. The group dispersed to their own rooms to prepare for the attack later that night. The prince came up to Sean and asked to speak with him in private.

They walked outside and stood on a deck with a view of the mountains to the east. The air had cooled, and the stars shined bright in the clear night air.

Sean watched the prince carefully, not knowing where he stood at the moment. Things had not gone according to his expectations.

"Ever been out in the desert?" the prince asked. It was an unexpected question.

"Only the White Sand Desert south of Mar. I went with my father a few years ago. I have never been to your kingdom's great deserts. I am sure they are beautiful."

Prince Bronwyn laughed. "Don't be too sure. Oh, we tout that our strength comes from our desert living, and that may be. And though there are times of beauty and solitude there, for the most part it is a harsh, unforgiving environment. I rather like it here closer to the mountains."

"Have you ever been further? To the Black Forest or to the Blue Sea?

"Sadly, no." The prince motioned for the two of them to sit down on some stone benches. "The wealth of what the Realm contains must be incredible."

Sean could see where this was going, and he decided to be bolder with the young prince. "So having a part of the Realm's resources under your control could be an advantage to you?"

The prince frowned and looked around. "You must be careful of what you say, sir. The Realm has a new young leader."

"Young, yes. He is not experienced in statehood and did not desire his position. People like us—you and me—we want power, we want control. Am I right?"

"Let's just say I would like to take advantage of the weak situation in the Realm right now. An annexation of part of that fruitful land into the Kingdom of Arc would make me very popular here."

"Even more so than your father?" Sean ventured, enjoying the conspiratorial conversation.

The prince leaned back in his chair and looked up at the sky. "Some might call me an ambitious man. But what do you get out of this?"

"I get power and control over Darius," Sean almost spat with vehemence. "He doesn't deserve what he has. If he is weakened or even removed, then opportunities arise for me and my benefactor."

"Speaking of your benefactor." The prince frowned slightly. "I was not informed of who he was or what his plans are."

Sean had to be careful here. He knew that the power of wizards was not popular with Arc's next ruler. "He is a man who prefers to work behind the scenes right now. He has contacts in Belor, Mar, and Sur, and even the eastern kingdoms. Once unrest and discord is spread throughout the Realm, he, too, is looking for power. That is his plan."

The prince stiffened.

Sean continued. "However, he is more than willing to share a piece of the pie with those who help him. He seems to be a reasonable man."

One of the guards came out of the building and motioned toward the prince to get his attention. "We followed the High Wizard and know where he is staying, my Lord. All will be prepared for an attack tonight. He will not expect it here or now. He will not have time to react."

"Good. Good." Prince Bronwyn's smile lit up his pale face, made more so with the contrast of the black clothes he still wore. The kingdom elite, although desert dwellers, prided themselves on their pale skin. Those that were tan were lower caste and worked outside. "Just make sure you do not harm my sister. I am sure she has been brainwashed by that trickster."

The guard went back inside, and Sean turned back to Bronwyn. "Then we have a deal? We can count on you to begin to spread discord down into Sur and the Realm?"

"Oh, yes, my friend. And I know the perfect time to start. As you heard, my father has asked me to meet the new royal couple."

"Remember he is a wizard also."

The prince's face hardened and his teeth clenched. "All the more reason to destroy him."

Sean smiled and laughed softly. Oh, how he longed to see Darius and his little pet girl from the farmlands destroyed.

Bronwyn broke through Sean's revelry. "First, we destroy the High Wizard. Are you ready, my friend?"

Sean nodded and followed.

* * * * * * * * * * * * * * *

Chapter Five
A TRAITOR IN THE MIDST

Prince Mezar Alrishitar, second heir to the throne of the Empire of Gildan, sat in the library of the wizard's school on a hill overlooking the city of Gildan. He kept his black hair long, currently tied in a ponytail behind his neck so as not to bother him as he read. Mezar had been researching the history of King's and Emperor's in the western kingdoms and their connection to the three wizard powers. He had promised his friend Darius that by the time he and his wife arrived later in the fall, Mezar would have some background information to help Darius understand the heredity of the power of the throne along with a history of Wizard Kings.

As a wizard of the mind, Mezar absorbed and remembered all the information he read; however, there were a lot of writings going back over hundreds, if not thousands of years, in multiple kingdoms. He stood for a minute to stretch his legs and paused at a gold-framed mirror hanging in the ornately furnished ancient room. His reflection was a little distorted, but his tilted dark eyes and tanned features looked back at him. His eyes seemed tired, and his face drawn. He marched back to the desk, closed the book, replaced it on a shelf, and headed outside. He needed to breathe some fresh air and move around.

After his excursion into the Realm earlier in the year, he had grown restless and tired of reading.

Before opening the door to the balcony, he caught the sound of whispered voices behind a short wall to his left. Earlier he hadn't noticed anyone else enter the room. The school, closed for a week of holidays, was empty, and he had found himself alone most days. Mezar moved with quiet steps closer to the whispered conversation.

"Everything's all ready, sir. The plans are in place," a man said, his voice low and scratchy.

"All the plans? You know he will not be pleased with any failures. He is a hard man," the second man said.

Mezar didn't know who they referred to, but it was obviously someone they feared to disappoint.

"There won't be failures," the first voice continued. "The first part will be easy. It will appear as if the Kingdom of Arc took the girl. The Realm and the Kingdom of Arc will wage war against each other and forget about us to their south."

Mezar became alarmed and knew he had to do something, but he didn't recognize the voices. What if they were more powerful than he? He started to move closer, stretched out his hand, and felt the power build up in his mind. He thought about what he could do before he acted.

"And here in Gildan?" the second man asked. "That will be more dangerous."

"Yes. It will be slow. No one will notice anything. In a few months, his bad health will have seemed to happen in a most natural manner."

"He is old at that."

Mezar could almost perceive the second man smile.

"The empire will be sad to lose our beloved leader," the second man responded.

Mezar froze. This was an assassination plot. He could jump out and take care of the men, but what he really needed to know was who was behind the plot. He listened further.

"Where will you keep the girl?" the first man asked.

"Her Majesty will be kept safe. The less people that know the location, the better."

Once again, Mezar was surprised. Who were they talking about? The Emperor's wife had passed away years before. Were they talking about Christine? Darius would not let his new wife be anywhere unguarded.

Mezar peered around for a place to hide. If they happened to walk his way and see him, they would know he had been eavesdropping. He hid himself behind a bookshelf. The men continued to talk for another minute, with no new revelations for Mezar, then footsteps receded.

He had to find out what kind of traitor supervised this horrible plot. Once he did that, he would bring the news to the Emperor and his father, the general. He crept behind the men, using his powers to hide his approaching steps. Using magic this way was taxing on his mind but necessary. The two men parted ways.

Mezar decided to follow the one that seemed to be issuing the commands. Maybe he would report back to whoever had sent him. The man glanced back occasionally, but Mezar stayed hidden. He didn't recognize the traitor from behind. For them to be in the wizard compound, the other man must have been a wizard, which made the potential events even more dangerous.

Once outside the gates of the school, they entered a part of town housing wizards and other high-ranking nobles of the city. Evening crept up, but it was still light enough to spot the tops of the domed buildings lighting the darkening sky. Mezar had always loved this time of night. Each domed building had oil lamps that were lit from below and circled the domes underneath their eaves, setting off a soft glow throughout the city. In recent years, some of the more fashionable nobles had begun experimenting with different colors of glass around the lamps, so even though most of the buildings were a soft yellow, a few had dazzling colors of green, blue, and even red.

The man walked down the cobblestone hill and around the stone and cement houses until he entered the merchant district. Eating establishments, a new phenomenon in Gildan, had opened up in this quarter of town. It seemed that more and more of the wealthy, and some not so wealthy citizens, preferred not to cook and eat their meals at home.

Mezar followed the man down the street and into one of the cooking establishments. The man headed to a back room where Mezar couldn't go without being seen. He went back outside and around the side of the building to try and peer through a window or a crack in the wall. He found a small space to view the table where the man sat.

The man he had followed sat facing him, but the other man, his higher up, sat with his back toward Mezar. He cursed silently at his bad luck. There was no other way to see. The man had on a red cloak with black trousers and knee-high boots. Mezar tried to listen to the two speak. Maybe that would give him a clue as to who it was. He caught a few scraps of words from the man he had followed but mumbled sounds in quiet whispers from the other man. The noise in the establishment was too loud. The stranger waved his hands a few times as he talked, and a glint of light reflected off of one of his fingers. A flicker of familiarity passed through Mezar's mind, and his stomach fell.

His father, the general, the heir to the throne of Gildan after the Emperor was sitting with his back to Mezar. The implications were mind-boggling, and Mezar's quick and efficient mind sorted through all he had heard and seen.

Down the back alley, a group of men staggered toward him. He groaned at the distraction. They were drunk and would certainly not leave him alone. He tried to hide behind a crate, but as the men passed, one stopped, leaned over, and puked right in front of Mezar, splashing a few drops on his boots.

"Hey." One of the other men swayed. "That's gross, Dial. Look what you did to the nice man."

The smelled wafted up and met Mezar's nostrils as he stood up and tried to leave. He didn't want to be recognized by the two men or by anyone else. "I'm fine." He started to walk away with his head lowered.

"Hey," one of the other men yelled, "don't I know you?"

People in the eating establishment looked out the screened window to see what the noise was. Mezar thought quickly and, with a trickle of power, knocked a few crates into the wall of the building, taking the attention of the drunken men off of him. He ran fast and turned a corner. He had to get to the Emperor and warn him.

Walking the hills up to the palace, he entered with a nod to the guards, then proceeded to his rooms first to freshen up and then to clean off his boots. It wouldn't be seemly to approach the Emperor in his state. He thought through all he had seen and was ready to present his case when his cousin Lowell came by, flopped onto Mezar's bed, and started chatting about the weather, food, and girls. His clothes, all frills and lace, were the latest rage among many of the young noble class in Gildan.

This particular cousin was two years younger than Mezar and seemed to want to follow everything he did. If Mezar even hinted at going to talk to the Emperor, his cousin would try and tag along. Well known among the extended family was that Mezar was his grandfather's favorite. Rumors floated around in some quiet circles that the Emperor would name Mezar his heir over Mezar's father. The general and the Emperor always seemed to be arguing over something.

After an hour, he convinced Lowell to go and find something for them to eat. As soon as the pesky boy left, Mezar walked with confidence out of his rooms, down the lit granite hallways, and through multiple corridors and floors to the Emperor's wing of the castle. He didn't know if the Emperor had guests this evening or not. Approaching the Emperor's house guards, he slowed. He didn't want to set off any alarms.

"My Prince." The head guard nodded his head in a bow.

"Is the Emperor available this evening?" Mezar tried to sound like it was a normal casual visit. He was sure the guards picked up the sound of his heart pounding. News of a potential assassination was certainly not normal. He still couldn't wrap his mind around the fact that his father was somehow involved.

"The general arrived in the Emperor's study a few minutes ago."

Mezar stiffened. "Have they been talking long?" He had to get the general away from the Emperor.

"Not too long." The guard shrugged. "But you know how it goes with them." The man smiled at Mezar. Much of the time their arguments would last for hours. The general was much more brash than the Emperor. He always wanted to send troops places, take small pieces of land, and flex the Empire's muscles to their neighbors. After returning from the Realm after Darius's surprising coronation, it had taken a lot of pleading and negotiation for Mezar to convince his father to stay out of the Realm and give them time to heal and build. The general seemed even more intent lately to pursuing more power to himself. He had his sights on expanding his nation's borders and was prepared to do so in a time of the Realm's weakness, but Mezar had promised Darius that the Emperor would honor peace.

Since then, a new trade document had been signed. Part of Darius' visit to Gildan in the coming month would be to formally meet the Emperor and sign in each other's presence the trade deal. The general did not agree and was angry at Mezar for representing the Empire of Gildan to the Realm.

"I will let the Emperor know you are here," the guard offered. "That may help to speed things along." The guard smiled knowingly at Mezar.

Mezar nodded back, and in a few minutes, the guard motioned Mezar into the back of the Emperor's study to wait. The study had always been a favorite room of his. Books and valuables from all over the western world jumped out at him. A few maps were mounted in the corner behind a small setting of comfortable leather-stuffed chairs. A stone fireplace stood off to the side. This was where Mezar and his grandfather had had many chats throughout the years.

Voices rose between the two, and Mezar looked at his father. He was hoping that he had been mistaken at the restaurant. But he was not. His father's back was to him. He wore a red cloak with black trousers tucked into black knee-high boots. His stomach lurched. His father's hand flashed with light as a golden ring reflected off of the nearby lamp. He felt his face go pale but starting sweating at the same time.

Mezar looked around the room and for the first time in his life felt out of control. The world tilted, and he breathed in power to settle his dizziness. His mind raced through possibilities and outcomes. None were good. He sucked his breath in too loud, and the two men stopped. His father turned, and they both glanced his way. He willed himself not to faint.

"Mezar," his father said. "Everything all right?" He smiled a predatory grin.

The prince stood still and willed his beating heart to remain calm.

"Father." He kept his voice even. "What were you doing talking to that man in the restaurant in the merchant quarters?" He decided a direct approach might be better.

Giving credit to his father, the man barely twitched, but his eyes grew dark.

"Mezar, what is this about?" the Emperor. "Come here closer to me. You know I have a hard time seeing that far anymore."

"Your Majesty," Mezar responded, "my father—"

And that was as far as Mezar got.

His father slid across the floor in only a moment's thought and stood facing Mezar. "You haven't been invited here, my son."

Mezar tried to peer around his father toward the Emperor. The man looked confused and sicker than he had the day before. Without warning, Mezar felt a shove of air push him backward. He grunted hard and stood his ground, shoving air back toward his father. Mezar ducked low, rolled to the side, and started to move to protect the Emperor. His father spewed fire toward him. It was treason to use power in such a way in the Emperor's rooms, but his father didn't seem to care.

Operating on instincts, Mezar turned around and in defense sent a ball of red fire spiraling toward his father. The general dodged the fire, letting it explode into the strong walls behind him. Small chips of stone flew in to the air. Mezar glanced at the Emperor whose eyes moved from his son to his grandson and back.

"Mezar!" the general shouted. "Stop this instant. I don't know what you are thinking. Let's talk about this."

Two guards came in to the room, then flattened back against the walls, not wanting to get in the way of two wizards throwing fire at each other. The Emperor stood up and had never appeared as frail to Mezar as he did at that moment. The men, the poison, the plan he had heard alluded to, must already be working. But who would believe his accusations?

Mezar drew all the power from his mind that was allowed in a moment's thought. He hoped the suddenness of the magic would surprise his father. Without any more thinking, Mezar sent a hurried thought through the air, a thought that for one moment plugged the ears of the guards and his father but amplified his sound to the Emperor.

"Your Majesty, beware of my father," Mezar shouted. "He is in league with assassins to kill you and to turn his sights northward to take on the Realm."

The Emperor's eyes widened, then saddened. He said nothing out loud and gave no other outside appearance that he understood, but Mezar felt that he did. It was all he could do at the moment.

Leaping sideways against the nearest wall, Mezar launched himself off the wall and over the head of his father and dashed out of the room. He would find help and return. He couldn't let his father get away with this.

His father's shouts from behind told the young prince his father had countered the spell Mezar had used on him. His father began running behind him, using his power to gain speed. Mezar came to a flight of circular stairs and bounded down them five at a time, reaching the bottom in mere seconds. Sliding around a corner, he ran a short distance to an outside door. Shoving the ceremonial guards aside, he jumped down more steps and ran through the garden courtyards. His father still ran behind, but Mezar was younger, and even though he was less trained in the physical aspects of the power, he had more reserves of potential within him.

Visitors in the gardens stood stunned as the two royal wizards raced through the manicured grounds of the palace. A bolt of fire rushed by Mezar's head once, shattering a nearby tree. His father yelled after him, but still Mezar ran. A thin tear slid down his face. He had never imagined his father's lust for power would turn out like this. His behavior was erratic and disturbing.

Entering the noble's district outside the palace grounds, Mezar focused on the task at hand mapping out in his mind the best route to escape through. It became a clear plan in his head.

A man on a horse came around the corner. Mezar grabbed the man and pulled him to the ground, jumping up on the back of the horse. The horse was fresh and, imbued with additional power from the prince, took off at breakneck speed. Dashing around corners, the general fell too far behind to catch his son.

Suddenly bells heralded from the palace, signifying an attack. That meant all gates out of the city would begin to close. Mezar raced for the closest one, arriving just as the gate closed.

"Open the gate!" he demanded, reigning in the horse.

"But the bells?" questioned the guard.

"Don't you know who I am?" Mezar amplified his voice.

The guard flushed, bowed, and stumbled in his speech. "Of course, Prince Alrishitar."

"You don't think those bells are meant to keep me in, do you?"

The guard began pulling back open the gates. "Of course not, my Prince. But what is happening?"

"An attack from inside the castle." Mezar twisted the story. "Someone is trying to kill the Emperor. I am going for help. Can I count on you?"

The guard saluted the second heir to the throne. "Yes, sir. You can count on us to keep watch."

"Get a message to my cousin Lowell. 'Meet me in Salish.' Tell this to no one. You will be rewarded."

"Yes, sir. I will go right now."

Lowell was the one person he knew wasn't involved in the plot. His cousin was foppish – always concerned with the latest fashions - but extremely loyal to him and the crown. Mezar couldn't grasp yet how deep his father's treachery ran. He could only trust his immediate friends.

"Remember, do not tell anyone. In fact, don't take a direct route to the castle at all." Mezar hoped this guard did not mention the message to his father or anyone else. Lowell was not well watched, so he figured the guard could get to him, even with the castle being locked down.

Mezar raced through the gates with the horse, leaving a group of bewildered guards closing the gate behind him. He had to find Darius to warn him, but he didn't know where the King of the Realm was. The visitors from the Realm were still not scheduled for weeks.

Racing northwest on the main road from Gildan, he rode toward Salish. He would make plans there. As a prince in the royal family, in line for the throne, and a wizard, he had resources to call upon if he needed them.

* * * * * * * * * * * * * * * *

Chapter Six
WHITE ISLAND

Darius stood against the railing of a worn out barge hired in a small village south of Mar. The weather turned rough and wet. Taliana, having grown up around the water in Mar, seemed to handle it fine; however, Roland, the horses, and even the old owner of the vessel stood in bad shape. Darius couldn't do anything about the weather more than to slightly speed the wind and send small bursts of power to give feelings of reassurance and safety to the passengers.

Through the sideways rain and thick fog, the slow group started to distinguish the faint outlines of the white-salted cliffs, of which White Island got its name. Some of the tensions began to ease at thoughts that they were not going to drown after all. Darius insisted they get to White Island as soon as possible. Now he almost regretted not staying in the coastal village until the storm had passed.

After some time, the wet group pulled up next to a dock on the island. A few poor drenched deck hands ran from a nearby covering to help them and their animals up and out of the barge. Darius traded money with the owner and invited the drenched men into the nearest inn for a hot meal. Darius handed the horses over to some not very enthusiastic young stable boys, and the rest of the group headed into the nearest inn.

"Make way for the King," Roland announced in a loud voice, drawing unwanted attention to Darius. He sighed, resigned to the fact he could not go anywhere unnoticed anymore. His life was for the people.

The small group in the inn stared at his wet, plastered, youthful body and couldn't quite decide if it was their sovereign leader or not.

"Your Majesty!" a voice shouted from across the room.

Darius smiled. "Ambassador." He greeted his best friend in a formal manner.

Kelln El'Han strode across the room, a slight sway of maybe too much drink in his step. The two embraced, but Kelln pulled away with a face.

"You're all wet!" Kelln stated the obvious. "Aren't your powers good for anything?"

Feeling a little embarrassed, Darius had not thought about drying himself off with his powers. Having lived eighteen years without knowing about them and then up until the last few months either hiding them or using them sparingly, the King frequently forgot about the usefulness of his power. It was easier to remember if someone else needed help, or if there was something grand going on, but for the smaller mundane things in his life, he was content in trying to be a normal person. Using too much of the power also drained him and made him tired.

To make the point to the small audience, Darius did indeed use his powers to dry his party's clothes off with a few waves of his hand. It felt like the right thing to do, and he did it, not really knowing how. The quick drying hardly tired him at all. Steam extended off of them, leaving them as dry as before the storm hit. Somehow Roland produced a small traveling coronet for Darius to wear on his head. Darius gave his captain a perplexed look, but Roland just shrugged as if to say that Darius needed to maintain his image at all times. The crowd smiled and laughed. Indeed it was their King. They stood and gave small bows before Darius motioned for them to continue their meal.

The men's eyes moved from their King to the young dark haired beauty accompanying him. Taliana glared at the men, and they looked away from the fire in her young eyes.

"Hello, young wizard Taliana," said Kelln in a mockingly sweet voice. "Seems like I have only found trouble when I am in your presence.

"Only because trouble seems to follow you." She smiled sweetly.

After requesting a private dining room from the innkeeper, who was more than happy to oblige his King, Darius began asking Kelln about Mar. He was more than worried that the Preacher had found his way there. Kelln hadn't found Alessandra yet but seemed sure she was around if her father was.

"Can we trust her?" Darius asked Kelln.

"Darius, I want to so much."

"But?"

Kelln lowered his eyes. "But I don't."

Darius sucked in his breath. “Kelln, if we find her, we will need to take her to Anikari to be put on trial. There is too much she has done now to be pardoned of her crimes.”

“I know.” Kelln sighed.

“And I can’t let the Preacher run free in Mar. I will send troops there to help you capture him. Belor is barely stabilized after what he did there. I can’t have him infect Mar.”

“My father can help,” Tali offered. “The Preacher has contacted him and wants his support. We could work a trap for him, something he can’t stay away from.”

“Anything that feeds his ego would work.” Darius took a spoonful of soup. The rest took a few minutes to eat some food that the innkeeper provided them. The warm fish soup and fresh bread warmed them inside.

“Roland.” The King turned to his trusted captain. “You will accompany Ambassador El’Lan back to Mar. You will stay in visible places so it will be harder for any harm to come to you. I will send for reinforcements from Anikari that I trust.”

“Sire, my place is with you. A King cannot be alone.”

“Kelln needs you more than I do right now. I can take care of myself.”

Roland seemed embarrassed to continue pushing the King in this. “Sire, please reconsider. It would not be seemly for the King to go riding around by himself without at least one guard with him.”

Darius let out a deep breath. “I surmise you are correct, Captain. It is still difficult getting used to being the King.”

“Miss Penrose here seems more than capable of protecting our ambassador,” Roland added with a toothy grin.

"Hey, why is everyone trying to protect me? I can handle myself." Kelln almost pouted.

Tali rolled her eyes at him but stayed silent and ate her food, though her eyes did sparkle with amusement.

The King rethought his position. "We will visit with the master caretaker tomorrow morning after the storm blows over. Afterward, Tali will accompany Kelln back to Mar, and with the protection of the governor, whom I hope I can trust, Kelln will await for additional troops."

Tali nodded.

Kelln mumbled something about not needing a babysitter to watch over him, but with the flash of Taliana's eyes and a smack of air on the side of his head, he just glared at her.

"Miss Penrose," Darius said in all seriousness, "we talked about not using the power for mundane, silly things. Once this is over, I will need to talk to your father and you about your powers and see what we can do about some training. Seems to be more wizards popping up around the Realm than we knew about. With your impetuous use of the power, you indeed might be a wizard of the heart instead of the earth. Mezar told me about a school in Gildan. Maybe you can study there for a while."

Taliana smiled and agreed to try and be wiser in using her powers.

After that, the discussion moved to small talk about the weather and wondering why they traveled to White Island in the first place. Darius grew tired and excused himself to bed. Roland followed him, leaving Kelln and Taliana in the dining room alone.

The weather did not subside for two more days. Darius was told that the master caretaker was on the far side of the island and wouldn't return until after the rain. They spent their time rehashing their plans and visiting with the few people that came into the inn during the storm.

Darius always found it enlightening to visit with his people and find out their thoughts of the Realm. White Island was unique among cities of the Realm. Most of the physical needs on White Island were funded by the King for the taking care of the herd of Cremelinos. Because of that fact, the people of White Island always stayed very loyal to the crown.

Early on the third day before Darius was even fully dressed, a knock on the door sounded. Roland, who had insisted on sleeping on the King's floor to guard him in the small inn, jumped over to answer it. It was the innkeeper, who informed them that a visitor awaited them in the common room. Darius was excited to meet the caretaker and threw on his traveling clothes. He informed Kelln and Taliana to meet them downstairs.

Sunlight streamed through the windows, brightening up the common room. It was a clean establishment that catered to the locals, with a few traders making periodic visits as goods were exchanged from the mainland. Looking around the room, Darius almost missed the young man standing and looking out one of the rear windows. Darius cleared his throat and the boy, fifteen or sixteen in age, turned around. Darius recognized him from his earlier visit to the island.

The young man took a deep bow toward the King. "Your Majesty, my father Haman bids you to come to our home and visit your herd."

Darius smiled. "Thank you. I have met you before. What is your name again, young man?" The small boy he had seen a year and a half earlier when he had picked up Christine's Cremelino with Kelln seemed a foot taller but still as skinny. His brown mop of hair had a difficult time staying in place, but his firm jaw told of growth to still be had.

"Jakob. Jakob Widing. I will be master caretaker when my father gets older," he said quickly then blushed as if he regretted what he said.

Darius tried to comfort the obviously nervous teen. "I am sure you will make a fine caretaker for our Cremelinos. The one you gave me before was perfect. You were right. It was meant for me. I gave it as a gift to a girl who is now your queen. Christine named the horse Lightning, and her speed has been a help in many circumstances."

Jakob smiled with pride and led the way out. The group followed behind, being careful to not walk in the still existing puddles from the previous storm.

Haman Widing, a large balding man with a happy smile, met them at the gate to his property. His wife had prepared some refreshments of sweets and fruits that she shared with the visitors on the front porch of their modest but sturdy home.

Off in the distance Darius could see a few of the Cremelinos, always a brilliant white. As the horses came closer to the group, Darius began to sense voices in his head.

Wizard of the heart, we greet you and honor you.

A group of ten came to the edge of the fence and knelt down on their knees in respect of their King. Darius walked over to them.

Long has our prophecy foretold of your coming.

"He's talking to those horses again, I'll wager. Just like with the horse of the queen's," Darius heard Roland tell the others.

"He can speak to them without touching them it seems." Haman nodded. "Good. Good."

Are you ready young wizard?

"Ready for what?"

Ready to bring peace and glory in times of darkness?

"Wasn't that already fulfilled?"

Oh no, young King. You have not seen all the darkness yet. You have not seen fear yet. Real fear comes from harm to those you love. Darkness gathers in the south in Gildan, in the west with Arc, and in your own realm.

Darius felt fear tear a hole in his heart. *"What can I do? I am only one person. An untrained wizard at that."*

Remember these three things: Rely on your friends; remember where your power comes from; seek out all the powers at your disposal when the time is right. Only then will you chase evil and darkness away and find peace.

Darius turned and looked at the others. They watched him expectantly, waiting for him to share what he heard. But he did not. He couldn't scare them. He needed to protect them.

Summon the young wizard to us.

Darius asked for Tali to come forward. She did so with glee and delight in her eyes. She approached with caution and began to put her hand out to touch one of the Cremelinos.

"Don't. Stop." Darius grabbed her hand away. "You can't touch them without their permission. Once a person rides a horse, they are bonded together forever."

"But this one spoke to me and asked me to touch his mane."

Darius asked the Cremelino if this was true and received an answer in the affirmative.

Taliana reached out again and touched the smooth white mane of the large powerful horse. Holding her hand there for a moment, Darius knew they were communicating with each other.

"She wants to go with me."

Darius was surprised. These horses traditionally were only held for the King and high-ranking nobles to use to pull their carriages. Lightning had been the first Cremelino he'd known that was given to another. Lightning had explained to him it was because of her proximity to Darius. Lightning had been sent to help guide the prophecy along, and at the time, Darius had not been ready for one.

Times are changing. We have not been used properly for years now. Our original use was to be bonded as a partner to a wizard. You have opened the way for that again, King Darius DarSan Williams. We are meant to work together, wizards and Cremelinos.

Darius informed the group what the Cremelino said.

"What will you name her, Tali?" Darius asked.

Tali thought for a few moments. "Radiance. She brightens my heart."

Haman smiled. "For generations, we have waited for this day, Sire. Histories have been passed down for centuries through each master caretaker. The stories of old are returning. The Cremelinos and the wizards will be united again."

Darius talked to the horse again and was informed that five other Cremelinos would accompany them back to the mainland. When asked who they were for, he was told one was his when the time was right, and the others would be shown in due time.

"How will we travel and take care of them? I'm on my way to Sur after I leave here to meet a delegation from Arc with my wife." Darius looked out at part of the herd.

"I will go with them," Jakob blurted.

His father frowned.

"Father, remember the day that the Cremelinos first spoke to me? They said I would meet the wizard they had felt come into his power. I am meant to be with him. I can take care of the Cremelinos for him."

Haman looked at Darius.

"It would be practical training for him in becoming the next master caretaker," Darius said to Haman. "He will be paid well and protected. If you can do without him here."

Jakob's mother, Nhila, wiped a sleeve across her eyes and laid a gentle hand on her husband's arm. "Haman, I think this is right. This is what Jakob was raised to do. As they said, times are changing. Wizards walk the land again, and these Cremelinos are meant for them. Jakob is well-trained."

Haman agreed. They all made arrangements to meet in town the following day with Jakob and the six Cremelinos, including Tali's. Darius and the group began to walk away when one more message came to him from the lead horse.

Christine says she loves you, my King Wizard.

Darius was taken aback. "*How do you know that?*"

Lightning has told us. We can communicate across distances together through the power of our wizards.

"But Christine isn't a wizard."

No, but Lightning is special, and Christine has enough old wizard blood in her from the farmlands to make the bond work. Lighting was born as part of the prophecy.

"Ah. The prophecy," Darius said out loud. "Why do I sense sometimes I am just a puppet in everything I do?" He didn't say the words in anger, only a feeling of being overwhelmed by what was required of him. Did everything circle around him and this prophecy?

* * * * * * * * * * * * * * *

Deep in Mar's underground, a young, beautiful woman met with the head of Mar's Guild of Thieves. Her mission was the same as her father's when he'd met with the governor two weeks before: They wanted him to help sponsor a new guild for certain favors in return.

Alessandra El'Lan was following her father's commands in order to find her mother. He had told her the Guild of Thieves might know where her mother was, and so she went along with his plan. The outcome of the Preacher's plan was to sow discontent and anarchy in the Realm. Soon he would be meeting with representatives of the eastern kingdoms to finalize their support. Alessandra knew all this, and felt bad for Darius and the Realm, but she needed to take care of herself. The Realm hadn't done anything for her. Except Kelln.

That is what hurt her the most. Her betrayals and dishonesty with him. He was so open, honest, and likeable that Alessandra had found herself falling for him at their first meeting. It had been a year and a half since she had first met him. Even with her shortcomings and ties to Belor, he liked her, and all she did time and time again was betray him. She was a horrible person. She knew that. She didn't deserve him. But that didn't mean she didn't think about him. But once again she was betraying him.

"And what will you do for us?" the guildmaster asked.

"We will remove the ambassador from Mar. We know you almost had him the other day."

The guildmaster frowned at that. "How will you do this? You are new in Mar. You have no ties."

"My father and I share a past . . . let's say a relationship with his royal ambassador. With him out of your way, you can take down the governor and his powerful Trader's Guild, correct?" Alessandra had to be firm.

The guildmaster sat back in his big soft chair. The man had survived now more than seventy years, controlling the guild for thirty of those. Alessandra let him think about it.

She looked around the room, the den of a large mansion. Antiquities from around the world filled cases around the room, almost in a cluttered look. It was as if the guildmaster wanted to show off everything he had ever taken. His glory, his life, was filled with the things he stole. His soul was his mansion.

"There is one more condition," Alessandra added. "We are looking for a woman about twenty years older than me. She used to go by Berlain. Auburn hair, wide eyes, and tall." Alessandra could barely picture her mother in her mind; it had been far too long.

"I have heard of this woman before," the guildmaster remarked, "but I am not sure she wants to be found."

Alessandra's heart dropped.

"But I will ask around and let you know. I wouldn't want to be the cause of that frown on your face," he teased.

Alessandra regained a small amount of hope. "We will proceed with the plans then. I will let you know when things are taken care of."

A servant showed Alessandra out the door and escorted her back into a more crowded part of town. There she met her father.

"Did they accept?" her father asked.

"They did. And they will search for my mother also."

The Preacher waved his hand in dismissal. "Our spies tell me the ambassador is back in town now. He is guarded by the governor's daughter. Although she is gifted with the power, she is no match for me."

"You promised you wouldn't kill him," Alessandra reminded her dangerous father. It was all she could do to ease a portion of her conscience. She wished she could find her mother on her own, just see her one last time, then she would leave. But it seemed she needed her father's connections. When she looked at him, she sometimes had to take a step back to avoid the evil shine from his eyes, but he was still her father and deep inside she still loved and cared for him. It was a twisted life she led, a life of betrayal.

"Yes. I won't kill him. Just remove him far, far away. Maybe the forgotten lands would do him good." The Preacher laughed and laughed, attracting attention from people crossing the small city square. "Unfortunately, the young ambassador won't be around to see my triumphal return to power."

****

Chapter Seven
JUSTICE OR MERCY?

Jakob had a way of finding water in the White Sand Desert. Darius wasn't sure how he did it, but was glad for the boy's talents. Even his own wizarding powers were not adept to that task, though he wondered if an earth wizard would find it easier. The Wizard King was excited to visit with Mezar in Gildan. The thought of a library that might help him understand his power drew him south. It seemed that everything he did came to him naturally when the time was needed, but it was frustrating to not understand how he did it. However, first he must travel to Sur, meet with a representative from the Kingdom of Arc, then travel to Denir, all the while spending time in small villages and towns along the way.

After traveling back to the mainland south of Mar from White Island, Darius bid farewell to Kelln and Taliana with a reiterated promise that he would send soldiers to Mar to help Kelln. Not wanting to get too close to Mar with the Preacher still loose in the city, Darius along with Roland, Jakob, and five Cremelinos cut west through the White Sand Desert. Eventually they would run into the Crystal River and would use that to guide them back north to the road that ran from Mar to Sur.

"Over here." Jakob motioned to the group. Once again, he had found a small spring oasis of water among a few short trees and reeds. The men let the horses get their fill first. Having open access to all the water and food they needed on White Island, the Cremelinos were not used to the dry, barren desert. Their physical abilities were stronger than a normal horse, but the heat of the desert was new to them.

The group sat next to the small pool of fresh water and took some meat and cheese out of their bags. Food was no problem since Haman's wife and the innkeeper had provided them with far more than they would need. Any town they passed through, no matter how small, would declare a feast in honor of their King. The night before they passed through a small sand village. Some nomads that didn't usually have much to do with the Realm as their government still insisted on feeding the group and serenading them with tribal songs.

After resting, they headed west again. Darius was grateful for the cooler autumn nights that kept the desert from getting too hot during the day this time of year. The nomads provided covering for their heads out of a strange white material that seemed to reflect the sun and keep them even cooler. They even retrofitted them to fit on the heads of the Cremelinos.

Two days later, they found the river and a small village next to it. Traveling north for the next few days found them connecting to the main road. Darius, anxious to meet back up with Christine again, wanted to continue riding toward Sur now that they were on the road. However, Jakob recommended they stay for a few days to allow their normal horses to hydrate and regain their strength. The Cremelinos seemed fine.

Knowing the young caretaker was right, he agreed. It gave him time to find a rider and write a message to deliver to his father. He also sent another rider on ahead to Sur to let Christine and the rest of his guards know they were on their way.

It had now been a few weeks since they'd split up, far longer than Darius had been prepared for. He missed sitting beside his wife. His thoughts turned to her, and he smiled. After being reunited again a few months earlier, it had been hard to be away from her. He felt empty without her around.

After taking care of business, Darius went to the stables to make sure the Cremelinos were being taken care of. He grabbed a brush and reached his hand toward one of the white horses, asking permission to touch him as he helped Jakob groom them. Jakob, as one of the caretakers, was given permission to touch the horses without having to be a wizard or bonded.

As Darius brushed the horse, he thought of Christine and Lightning and about the many times that Lightning communicated with him and even let him ride her, but he knew the bond with Christine and the Cremelino was different. He wondered when he would be chosen to have one and how it would feel. Would it be similar to the wizard power he held inside of him?

When the time is right, young wizard, one of the horses spoke to him, *then we will choose.*

"You are all so beautiful and strong," Darius said.

The horse seemed pleased with the comment, and he whinnied his pleasure.

Are there differences between the males and females?

The horse snorted, almost as if laughing at the King. *Are there differences between human men and women?*

Darius smiled, laughed, and spoke out loud. "Yes, there are. I get it."

Loud yelling noises grabbed Darius's attention. He ran out of the stable to see what was happening. A young boy was being dragged behind a horse by a rope. He was screaming for the rider to stop.

Darius jumped out and held up his hand to the rider. The man didn't appear to recognize Darius, but he did stop. The boy picked himself up off the ground and stood in a defiant stance. The urchin was not more than ten years old. The little clothes he wore were dirty and threadbare. His skin was pale, and his light blue eyes sat squinted beneath a mop of brown hair.

Darius confronted the man. "What is the meaning of this?"

"This brat was caught stealing from our garden."

"I was just getting food for my family," the boy explained, holding himself up as tall as he could.

The man spit on the ground in front of the boy. "You're a miner from the Gold Mountains by the look of you. You're a long way from home to be getting food for your family."

Roland stepped between the man and the King. "Sir. Please let the King ask the questions, and refrain from spitting in his presence."

Darius tried not to smile at Roland's way of defending him. His men were indeed protective of him.

"My Lord" The man bowed to the King. "I didn't mean any offense. We don't get royal visitors out this way very often. These urchins from the mines seem to be multiplying lately. They take our food and run off with it."

"Untie the boy," Darius ordered the man.

"Sire. He will run away. He is little but wiry and quick," the man said.

"You heard the King." Roland stepped up to the man with a scowl on his tanned face.

The man sighed and untied the rope off the boy's wrists.

As they had feared, the boy began to run off. The man started after him, but Roland put an arm on his to restrain him.

Darius watched the boy for a moment, feeling sorry for his condition. He thought back to the farmlands outside of Anikari where Christine had grown up. They were hated and treated badly from the city nobles and merchants, sometimes not having much food for themselves. The boy was thin and hungry, but he couldn't let him get away. The King had to serve justice.

With a flick of his wrist and power from his heart, he meant to thicken the air in front of the boy; however, instead he created a wind that came sideways and blew the boy off his feet, landing him hard on the ground. It wouldn't have been so bad, but the wind continued swirling and headed toward some of the other townspeople. With a few screams and scrambling around, they escaped the brunt of it.

The wind dissipated, and Darius's face burned red with embarrassment. He covered it up by walking toward the boy and stopping in front of him. The boy turned, looking up wide-eyed. Darius crooked his finger, asking the boy to stand. The boy shook his head. Darius clapped his hands in front of him, and the ground around the boy shook. The boy's eyes now filled with terror; however, this time Darius's power stayed contained. Again Darius motioned for the young boy to stand up. This time the boy acquiesced and walked slowly next to the King as they returned to the man who had caught him.

A large crowd from the small village had gathered. They watched him with wonder in their eyes and whispered among themselves that now the boy would get what he deserved. The King would not stand for a little brat defying him; however, Darius's heart went out to the young boy.

"Tell me about your village in the mountains," Darius said, ushering the boy to sit down next to him on a large log.

"I live in a small mining town just outside the eastern twin city. My papa and mama work deep in the copper mine. We didn't get much rain early this year in the mountains, not like we usually do, so our crops didn't grow. These people here"—he spread his hands around—"and villages like these don't help us out. My papa said they raise their prices just to hurt us."

The boy stopped talking, but Darius urged him forward in his story. "I'm not old enough to work in the mines, so they send others like me down to these villages to take food that we need to live on."

Darius's heart went out to this young man and his plight. The people in the Twin Cities were as much the King's responsibility as those in Anikari. He could tell their troubles must have been neglected for years under King Edward.

"We work hard for our food, too," the man the boy had stolen from said. "They have no right to steal from us."

Remembering back to the difficulties of the farmers outside Anikari, Darius asked a question of the townspeople. "What would you good people do if you had a harsh spring and didn't have food?"

"We wouldn't steal it," someone said from the back of the crowd. "We would work for it."

"My papa and mama do work, but the mine masters work them too hard to meet their quotas, and they still don't get paid much." With pleading eyes, the young boy turned to the King and begged, "Help us."

"What would you have me do?" Darius stood and addressed the crowd. "What should I do about this small boy only wanting some food?"

"Punish him."

"Send him home."

"Cut off his hand for stealing."

The negative suggestions continued until a small girl, a year or two younger than the boy walked out with half a loaf of bread.

"Here," was all she said. She sat the loaf at the feet of the boy. "I have enough."

The crowd quieted, and Darius's heart almost broke. It was clear to him what he must do.

"I am King of a vast realm of people. It is my job to protect them and care for them, especially those who aren't able to care for themselves. We have suffered this past year in Anikari because of similar problems there." He walked over to the girl who brought the bread. "Is your mother or father here?"

The young girl pointed at a man in the back. The man appeared nervous to be singled out.

"Come forward, sir." Darius gestured to him. "What is your name?"

"Aral Flint," the man said. He wiggled his fingers at his side in nervousness of talking to his King.

"Your daughter has impressed me with her charity. As of this moment, I give you a King's charge. You are in charge of gathering food from this and nearby villages and delivering it to the communities of the Twin Cities. A portion of your bread, vegetables, fruits, and meats will rotate among the villages to provide those in need with food until they can provide for themselves again. My captain will draw up the requisite papers for you to enforce this charge."

There were a few murmurs in the crowd; most were surprised at the King's charge. Darius surveyed the townspeople, then brought his attention back to the young boy. He walked over and ruffled the boy's hair.

"I will travel to the Twin Cities and see for myself what is going on there. This kingdom has enough resources for all men to live in comfort and not in fear or hunger."

Roland moved over to the King and whispered in his ear. "We are on the way to Sur, remember, Sire? There are people there waiting for us."

Darius smiled. "Thank you for the reminder, Captain. You can go on ahead if you would like."

Roland blanched at the idea. "I don't think that is a good idea, Sire. Who would watch after you then?"

Darius smiled. "Then we will first go to the Twin Cities. The dignitaries of Sur and the Kingdom of Arc can wait another week to see their King, whereas I daresay the people of the Twin Cities haven't seen a King in a long time."

Roland's lips sat in a straight line, then he bowed his head.

"Have riders ready to go to Sur, Arc, and the Twin Cities. I will have letters ready in the next hour. And get Mr. Flint all he needs to accomplish his charge." King Darius dispensed his orders to his guard. "And so there are no hard feelings, reimburse the man the young boy has stolen from for his loss."

The man, still standing close by seemed, surprised by the King's justice and mercy. The crowd began talking at once as Darius walked away to write his messages.

He penned a quick note to his wife first, expressing his love for her and his desire to not be separated for so long but stated that what he was doing was the right thing to do. He asked her to placate the officials in Sur and reach out to the delegation from Arc that would be there soon. Darius surely missed having Christine next to him. Her smiles gave him confidence.

Upon exiting the building, one of the Cremelinos came up to Darius. It was the same male he had once spoken with.

"We could communicate to your wife directly through the Cremelino link. Lightning could inform her what you need to tell her."

Darius had not thought of that before. A thought occurred to him: A coordinated placement of Cremelinos around the Realm could be a great advantage in communicating the affairs of the kingdom. Each one would need a wizard with them. He voiced this thought to the horse.

"That is why we are here, young wizard. We foresaw this need."

"Why do I sense that you always know more about things than you let on?"

The horse made a sound like a snicker. "*Maybe we do, but most of the time we need you to make your own decisions. Destiny and prophecy work better that way.*"

Darius decided to send a message along the Cremelinos line as well as send a rider, just to make sure there were not any misunderstandings.

The King, his captain, and Jakob spent the rest of the day preparing for the travels to the Twin Cities. It was decided that Jakob would stay in the village with the Cremelinos and Darius and Roland would travel north with the young boy thief and a few other hired guards from the city. It would be a two-day ride there. Once they left the main road, the path to the Twin Cities was steeper and more difficult. Jakob, the horses, and two other newly hired guards would meet Darius and Roland in six days' time at another village just west of the western road to the Twin Cities. At that point, they would still be a full day's ride away from Sur.

The next morning, after making sure that Aral Flint had his directions and orders clear to gather food and bring it to the mountain towns, the group made final preparations to leave.

Wizard. The Cremelino came up to Darius one final time before they left. *I communicated your message for Christine to Lightning. The answer back was strange. It seems that Lightning has had a more difficult time communicating to the queen of late. They were finally able to get the understanding of the message when they touched, but it almost felt as if there was something blocking it.*

Darius grew concerned for his wife and thought about what he should do. "*It must be the distance, or maybe the queen is just tired. She wasn't feeling well when I left her. That is why I also sent a messenger to Sur, to make sure that the message arrived.*"

Darius relayed the concern to Roland.

"It could also be that you are all new at communicating this way," Roland said pragmatically.

Darius agreed, and though he was still worried and anxious to see Christine again, he decided he had to move forward and be comforted with the thought he would see her soon enough, and they would figure it out together.

* * * * * * * * * * * * * * *

Christine rode through the upper section of Sur with guards on either side of her. The early morning autumn air smelled crisp, the sun already warming the cold ground above freezing. Three days ago she had received the message from Darius that he would be delayed. She had informed the city mayor and sent missives to the Kingdom of Arc dignitaries.

Not feeling well, she decided to get out in the fresh air for an early morning ride on Lightning. She kept the pace steady so as not to upset her stomach further. She and Lightning seemed able to still communicate with each other when they physically touched, but as she moved further away, it became more difficult. Lightning expressed her concern, but Christine wrote it off as being part of whatever was making her sick.

She loved this part of town. It was close to the mountains, and most of the buildings were made from wood. The pine had been smoothed and painted with a host of soft colors. Most of the homes and businesses were three levels, a shop on the first level and living quarters above. Yellows, greens, and blues in light shades made this section of town more cheery. Christine watched as people came in and out of the darker-colored doors.

Christine thought of Darius. Her heart ached to see him again. The first few months of being King had been busy for him. Their wedding was grand, although a little rushed. She smiled at the memory of the grand ballroom decorated in silks and flowers. Dignitaries from all over the Realm had attended. She loved Darius fiercely, but it was a little difficult to get used to being the queen. Their private time together dwindled as matters of state took precedence. This tour of the Realm allowed them more time to be together. Just riding side by side together, Christine relished in Darius's strength of love for her. She knew that part of it was amplified by his power, but she always basked in the feeling.

The buildings thinned around her, and they passed through a narrow gate outside the city. Fields opened up in front of her, and she picked up the pace, her sickness forgotten for a moment. Christine breathed in, letting the cool air fill her lungs. She smiled at the sight of the browning grasses scattered around the farms north of the city. Brief tears came to her eyes as memories of the farmlands where she had grown up flooded through her. Being in a city like Anikari, Belor, or Sur was always astonishing to her since she had been raised in the farmlands. So many people bustling around, so many sounds and smells confronting her senses. Tears slowly slipped from her eyes.

"Are you alright, Your Majesty?" Tad, one of the guards, asked.

"Yes, I am fine. Just remembering the farmlands around my home. I miss them sometimes. Have you ever ridden out into the farms?" she asked.

Tad shook his head. Up until Darius had become King, a huge rift sat between the city and the farmers, unaffectionately called "outsiders" by those in the city. The term had originally been given to some minor wizards who were exiled outside of the city, but over time had been used to refer to anyone that lived in the lands surrounding Anikari. The farmers were looked upon as little more than slaves and definitely inferior to those in the city. Darius befriending Christine years earlier and his announcement of intent to marry her had caused quite a ruckus around the nobles. However, the new King's compassion for all and his fairness already had an impact on the relations of all people in the Realm.

"I guess you wouldn't have ventured outside the city much, given the circumstances," Christine responded to the guard's nod. "I love the smell of the fields and trees."

"Danger!" The warning from her Cremelino horse came in a sudden blast that almost threw Christine from the horse.

Behind them rode a hasty and quick-moving group of men, kicking up a spray of dirt on the small road. The two guards with Christine turned their horses around and stood their ground in front of their queen.

"They look to be from Arc," Tad said.

"Dressing in black is their signature color. I wonder what the trouble is?" the other guard said.

Something felt wrong. Christine looked around for help, but only her guards were visible between the approaching men.

The strangers moved on their horses with a steady yet fast rhythm and soon were within earshot of Christine and her guards. Tad held up his hands to halt them. One of the men on horseback drew a bow and shot an arrow into Tad's chest. He died in an instant, falling off the horse and onto the ground.

Christine screamed and turned Lightning around, not seeing what would become of her other guard. One of the men yelled at her to stop. What was happening?

She leaned lower on Lightning and, with spurts of thought, sent the horse faster than it had ever gone before. Trees blurred around her, their fall leaves forming a stream of color as she picked up speed. A few arrows narrowly missed her at first. Now they came less as she heard the pursuers fade back. No normal horse could keep up with the speed of her Cremelino.

Where to? Lightning asked.

"I don't know this area. Just keep riding until we outdistance them, then we can find a place to hide and circle back into the city later." Christine looked around frantically for a way out of the dangerous situation.

I will reach out to my brothers and sisters. Darius needs to know what is happening.

Without any warning, three other riders appeared in front of them, all dressed in black. She now saw the gold insignia on their left breast. It was the sign of the Kingdom of Arc. She yelled, and Lightning swerved around the men. With the abrupt movement, Christine lost her balance and fell from the horse. Lightning turned, but not before the three riders surrounded the queen. She noticed now that they wore a thin black mesh material across their face so she could not see their features. The lead marauder jumped from his horse.

Lightning once again tried to reach Christine. She rammed herself into one of the other horses. A man lifted a sword and swung it toward the Cremelino. Being faster was the only thing that helped Lightning. The arc of the sword missed her back by inches.

"Run away!" Christine shouted. The link that was always there with her horse seemed to be fractured again. It was so frustrating. She concentrated harder. Lightning was frantic to reach her. With one last lunge, she jumped past the men and came up to Christine, who was now on the ground guarded by one of the men in black. Christine reached her hand and for a brief instant touched her Cremelino's leg. The connection was established again, bright and warm. The familiar feeling flooded through her mind. *"Run for help. Tell the guards. Tell Darius it is Arc. Tell him I love him. Go now!"*

A guard swung his sword again at Lightning, slicing a line down her left side. Pain erupted through the link as the horse pulled away from Christine. With a speed unmatched, the Cremelino jumped between two horses, catching another sword strike by her tail, then faded into the distant fields.

The guard forced Christine to sit up. Dizziness set in, and her stomach cramped. Crying out, she heaved and gave up her breakfast onto the feet of her kidnapper.

The man grunted in disgust, and brought a hand up to slap her, but one of the other man shouted a word to stop the action. His hand froze in mid-air.

Christine, not having much history in languages, did recognize that word, and it was not from the Kingdom of Arc. It was from Gildan. She tried to reach out to find Lightning's bond once again to warn her it was the Gildanians disguised as Arcs, but the link was gone. Why would the Gildanians kidnap her?

The link that had been in the back of her mind since Darius had given her the Cremelino was gone. It was silent. Her constant companion was gone; her mind was empty of Lightning's thoughts. Christine had been frustrated, angry, and even afraid before in her life, but never had she felt terror and dread like this. A part of her was missing.

Another bout of nausea brought her back down to the ground. She heaved, but nothing came out. Dizziness overwhelmed her. Blackness crept in from the corner of her vision.

"Oh, Darius. Help me," she cried out, and then the darkness took her, and she fell in a slump on the ground.

* * * * * * * * * * * * * * *

Chapter Eight
TIME FOR SPEED

Mezar Alrishitar hated feeling this way. Despite his royalty and power, he found himself hiding in a second rate inn in Salish, a small merchant town. Being at the southern door to the Realm and to the Kingdom of Arc, the mid-size town was a rough city consisting of merchants, guards, and those looking to find a deal. Fights often erupted in the poorer quarters, in which Mezar now found himself living. He took a deep breath to steady his nerves again.

It had been over a week since leaving Gildan. He knew his father was still looking for him. Unlike his normal fashion, Mezar let his hair hang down to blend in with the locals. With his change of clothes, he looked more like a hired guard. He stayed at the inn, feigning a few days of vacation after guarding a merchant train around the Realm. The innkeeper didn't care for his story as long as he paid his bill.

Lowell had arrived the day before. He'd received the message in Gildan as Mezar had planned but could not get away unnoticed until the immediate urgency of the search had died down.

He used Lowell as his eyes and ears to catch any talk in Salish regarding the renegade prince of Gildan. Nothing was heard. Through his cousin, he began gathering in a few other trusted friends and acquaintances. These men now settled into the private dining room they had hired for the evening. The innkeeper thought them a group of old guard friends living things up for the evening. A few serving girls brought some steaming bread and broiled meat into the warm room. Mezar had to be careful he didn't flash around too much money or people would get suspicious.

"It is true, Mezar," Gregor, a wizard friend of the prince, started, "that your grandfather seems to be getting more sick. Healers and wizards attend him, but they are only those chosen by the general himself."

"Why is he doing this?" Mezar's frustration rose. His father had ambitions to rule, and he and the Emperor did not agree on many things, but Mezar would have never guessed he would go to this extent to become Emperor. The current Emperor was very old and did not have many years as it was.

"I also saw something, my Prince," Allon, a guard on the palace grounds and one who knew Lowell more than Mezar, said. "I was returning from, uh . . ." He stumbled a bit and blushed. "A meeting with a friend." Smiles grew around the room. Allon was known for the multiple ladies he juggled so well.

"And as I was saying," he began again. "I was returning to my room in the castle a few days ago when I heard the sound of horses and men in the stables. I thought it strange at that time of night, so I went to investigate. A group of men stood close together. Your father stood in the midst of them. He carried a large bag, and he pulled out black cloaks and clothes to give to each man. He told them to keep them hidden until they were ready."

Allon took a drink. "After the general left, the men climbed on their horses and went out the back gates. As they left, I overheard one man remark that he learned from someone else that the new King of the Realm was a wizard and how were they supposed to take the queen with him around. There was an answer, but I couldn't understand it."

At this, Mezar stood. "And when was this?"

"Almost a week ago."

"That means they are probably already in the Realm, probably too far ahead to catch up to."

"We can't just ride into the Realm. They are looking for you, Mezar," Lowell added.

"You are right. We are going to all join a merchant train as hired guards."

Of the five men around the table, some looked excited, and some looked surprised.

"A hired guard?" one of the men of noble birth asked.

"Think of it as going undercover, William. Just like when we used to sneak around the castle at night when we were little boys. Now we will be sneaking around another kingdom, trying to protect its queen."

William smiled. "Ah. Now you're talking some fun. Why didn't you say so in the first place?"

Mezar sent Lowell and Allon out to get them hired on a wagon train leaving in the morning. Darius was touring the Realm and expected to come to Gildan in a few weeks, but Mezar didn't know where he or his wife were at the moment.

The merchant wagons would be slower but would keep the Gildanian men hidden. He needed to find Christine and Darius and warn them, if it wasn't already too late.

Once again, he would be traveling the Realm in disguise. That had been the plan the previous year, for his division of men to form a diversion so that Mezar could sneak around the Realm for a while and return information back to his father and grandfather. His plans were thwarted when Darius had captured him in Denir. For the following months, he saw the Realm in a very different light. He had made friends and had even sworn to support Darius for the rest of his life.

Thoughts of Leandra came unbidden to his mind as he thought about the Realm. She had been caught up in Sean San Ghant's kidnapping of Darius, but she and Mezar had found a friendship along the way. He fingered a ring on his right hand that glowed with a soft power. Linking to it was a similar stone on a necklace he had given Leandra before he left the Realm earlier in the summer. His features softened thinking of her. He would like to visit her again while he was in their neighboring kingdom.

First things first, however. Duty always seemed to call. The balance of power between the Realm and the Empire of Gildan hung on a fragile thread at the moment. Mezar had to find Darius without any more delays.

* * * * * * * * * * * * * * *

Darius sat at a small banquet table in the easternmost twin city. The Twin Cities were more like large villages bordering the edge of civilization up against the Mountains of Gold. The two appointed mayors insisted on honoring the King. Local mine leaders and other high-ranking townspeople attended the event. Roland, embarrassed at the attention, sat next to Darius as an honored guest also. They had taken a tour of the mines and visited people in both cities over the last two days. Tomorrow they would depart back down the mountain to meet up with Jakob and continue on to Sur.

The cool air pressed down the mountain slopes, but the room sat filled to capacity with people and food, all vying for the King's attention. Darius was tired of sitting and took a sip of wine to settle himself down. A walk in the night air would have done him good, but he realized he should never be alone in this faraway city that hadn't had a King visit them for a long time. A few tall dark-skinned men with long braided hair stood mingling in the crowd.

Darius leaned over to one of his hosts. "Who are they?"

One of the mayors smiled. "Bet you don't see them in the capital, do you?" He laughed, and food ran down into his beard. "Those are men from down south—further than Gildan and the southern kingdoms. They say their people live in the mountain divide there – the small kingdom of Mahli."

Darius opened his eyes wide and sat up to inspect the men once again. "I had no idea people lived there." The young King didn't hide his ignorance.

"Not a lot of people from what they say," the mayor continued, "but enough. They are a superstitious lot, talking about the power of dragons and waiting for their prophesied leader to return."

"Their leader?"

"It is taught in legend that a mighty Dragon King will one day arise, bring their people back into civilization and glory, and unite all of the southern Kingdoms. In the meantime, they send out scouts into each kingdom to look for signs of his coming. They are a very strong people and offered to help us move our mine machinery around. They don't seem to mind the darkness in the mines either. They are a happy lot, work well, and treat us politely. We pay them well for what they do, and in the end they tend to stay mostly to themselves."

"Strange. I will have to ask more about them when I am in Gildan," Darius said, realizing he wasn't going to get any more answers about them tonight. "All I know from history books is the last dragon was seen over 150 years ago."

The evening continued until everyone had eaten their fill. Darius stood up to speak. He recognized the parents of the young boy they had brought back with them, standing in the back. He had met them the day before. The boy's father would not be able to work the mines much longer. The mines, the King found out, were hard work on people, the pay and treatment of them not very compassionate. He could change that. He felt their difficulties in his heart, and an idea suddenly came to him.

"I am honored to be here," Darius began, projecting his voice with his power so all could hear. Others stood outside the room, curious as to what a King would say. "Your cities have been hospitable and welcoming."

The townspeople smiled and glanced around at each other.

"I know you have your struggles here, especially after a dry spring and summer this year; food has been hard to get. I have given a King's charge to the villages along the main road to provide you with food until you can grow your own again."

The crowd cheered, and tears came to the eyes of some of the women.

"There is a condition, however, that no more stealing occurs. If you have a problem, you can send a message to me or my councilors in Anikari."

The people nodded.

Darius continued, "I have noticed some sickness here since some of the men and women work too long in the mines without proper pay." He noticed some of the local merchants who ran the mines paying close attention. "I know this is hard work and profits need to be made, but I now make a decree. *No work in the mines will occur on the seventh day of the week.* This will give time for the workers to rest and regain their strength. There will also be proper clothing provided to them."

"My Lord" a man shouted from the back. "We do have to make a profit for the owners of the mines. These actions will make things difficult."

"Sir. Who do you think owns these mines?" Darius asked.

"Well. Uh . . . I am not sure I know," the man stumbled. He was a manager in the mines, given a task to keep the workers working, but he didn't know who he worked for.

"The mines belong to me," Darius stated pointedly. He was now glad his father had made him go to some of the trade meetings with him over the last few years. At the time, he hated his father's assumption that he would follow in his footsteps. Darius had not cared for having the life of a noble. However, once he learned that fate made him the next King he accepted the responsibility. His duty was heavy at times, but he was determined to make a difference and change some things around the Realm.

"By belonging to me—I mean, the King of the Realm is the owner of these mines. So, as owner of this mine and as of this day, I declare ten percent of the value of what is mined will be returned to your communities to upgrade your housing, get needed medical attention, and purchase food and other materials when needed."

The crowd responded with a resounding cheer.

Roland leaned in close to Darius. "Someone will find a way to take advantage of this situation."

"I know. There will always be someone to try and take advantage, but I need to help these people. They are my people. They are desperate and poor. The ten percent coming back to them will hopefully motivate them to work harder and smarter. Even with one day a week off, I expect production to increase."

Roland's eyes widened. "But how do you figure out these things so rapidly, Sire?"

Darius turned quiet for a moment before he whispered back to Roland. "It's the blessing of having the power, Roland. As a wizard of the heart, the power rules my emotions and feelings. When I care for my people, thoughts and feelings come quickly to my mind of what I must do to help them. My power provides answers of what I should do."

"That's a lot of pressure, my King."

"Yes, it is." Darius smiled. "Yes, it is." Being a new King was a lot of pressure. He never quite knew as he jumped to conclusions and answers if they were the right thing to do or not. He supposed he would make mistakes, but if the power would guide him most of the time, he thought he would be fine.

A crowd of dignitaries gathered around the King, thanking him for his attention to their small communities. They bowed in renewed allegiance to him and to the might and glory of the Realm. The festivities lasted well into the night.

In the cool mountain air early the next morning, Darius and Roland, along with the other guards whom accompanied them, prepared to return down to the main road. The two mayors stood by to greet them as they left, once again signifying their appreciation. Darius hoped he had done some good here. He was anxious to get back to Christine, to bathe in her warm smile, and to hold her in his arms once again. They had been separated far too long.

The beginning of the small road had been well-maintained, and they made good time starting down the mountain. A low cloud hung over the Mountains of Gold, signifying that winter would shortly come to the mountains.

At a curve in the road, Darius yelled in pain, grabbed his head, and slid sideways off his horse. Roland and the other guards jumped off of theirs and ran over to their King.

"My Lord!" Roland shouted.

"Christine," the King moaned. "Lightning!"

"What is wrong, Sire?" Roland looked terrified.

"Something is terribly wrong." Darius, still pale, sat back up. "I heard a faraway scream in my mind from Lightning. It penetrated my mind so deep and hard I almost blacked out. It was pure terror. Christine is in trouble!"

The guards helped Darius to his feet and back to his horse, where he slowly remounted. "We need to hurry faster to meet Jakob. Maybe the other Cremelinos know something."

Darius spurred his horse forward at breakneck speed, oblivious to the rocks and twists in the road, relying on the horse to find a way through them.

"You must be careful, my Lord," Roland cautioned.

Darius gave him a firm look that brooked no more argument from his guard. Darius was the King and his captain swore to obey him. Everyone understood that Darius would do anything for his wife.

Even at their quick pace, they had to stop a few times to let the horses drink and eat. At each stop, Darius paced in restless worry and continued trying to reach out to Lightning. But nothing came. At one stop later that evening, he reached one of the other Cremelinos in his mind.

Wizard, did you hear the cry? The Cremelino sounded shaken.

"Yes. What happened?"

Lightning is hurt. The Kingdom of Arc sent men to capture the queen. She was taken by them and Lightning barely escaped, but she is hiding in an abandoned farm north of Sur.

"Is she sure it was Arc?" Darius couldn't understand why they would do this. *"This doesn't make sense. We are on the way to visit them."*

Lightning said they dressed in all black with dark veils over their faces. Christine told her to go for help.

Darius's heart lurched at the mention of his beloved wife. *"Was Christine hurt?"*

The last Lightning saw, her guards had been killed, but the captors didn't hurt her. The Cremelino's voice became louder in his head. Without warning, Jakob and the Cremelinos burst through the clearing where Darius stood.

Lightning is fading. She has lost all contact with Christine, the male Cremelino shouted to Darius's mind.

"What does that mean, to lose contact? What happened? Where is she?" Darius was beside himself. Was his wife unconscious, too far away, or something else? He couldn't dwell on anything worse. He couldn't. It would tear him apart.

Anger built up in the King, anger he hadn't borne in a while. Christine meant more to him than the kingdom or his throne. The emotions amplified his power, and he screamed, "Arc will pay for this treachery."

Lightning needs you, Wizard. She needs your healing power, the Cremelino pleaded. *We must go to her first, then she can help us find Christine.*

The pleading brought Darius back from his cliff of anger. He could still have compassion. The Cremelino was right; he needed to find Lightning and heal her. She was his only way of finding Christine. He had to get there fast. Darius eyed the Cremelino that had been communicating with him.

It is time. The Cremelino trotted up to Darius. *I have chosen you for my bonding, Wizard.*

Darius nodded in agreement, putting his hand out to touch the approaching Cremelino.

"I name you Thunder. Thunder to show forth my power, Thunder to roll across the Realm, Thunder to find Lightning and Christine." He choked up and wiped tears from the corner of his wet eyes. Darius pulled out his sword and thrust it high in the air. Yellow and red lightning crackled around the weapon, and the sound of deep thunder rolled across the sky in a deafening tone.

"We ride now!" he yelled and jumped on the back of the Cremelino. Straightway, new emotions flooded through his mind and heart. A presence filled a new awareness in his mind that he had never felt before. He had communicated with the Cremelinos before, but he hadn't realized what the bond felt like. He envied Christine for what she had been experiencing. It was pure thought with a magical creature. It brought clarity of mind and strength of body. His wizarding powers alongside the Cremelino presented him with increased power and vision.

"Roland, you and Jakob bring the rest of the horses as fast as you can to Sur. I need to go on ahead. I can't wait any longer."

"I understand, my Lord. Good luck."

"If need be, we can communicate with the Cremelinos through Jakob," Darius yelled as he dashed around a curve in the path and out of sight. It would be dark soon, but that would not impact the pair. They would lend their strength and abilities to each other, as it was always meant to be. Wizard and Cremelino, bonded together once again!

* * * * * * * * * * * * * * *

Chapter Nine
THE GUILDS

Richard San Williams, senior councilor and father to the King, left the council meeting frustrated. Too many of the councilors seemed more worried about how they would appear or about how much money they had in their strongboxes than in the affairs of the Realm itself. Richard grudgingly agreed Martin Halverssn, a farmer, was one of the few with a good head on his shoulders. Richard felt he, Martin, and Cray Dreydon, the military advisor, were sometimes the few men of reason in the room. Even Jarad and Michael, the other two senior councilors, seemed to slide back to old ways when Darius was not around. He knew that he was not perfect, and by no means did he agree with everything that Darius did, but he was fiercely loyal to the Realm itself.

He guessed he shouldn't expect everything to change at once. Richard himself should know about changes. It had been a shock finding out only recently he had not grown up as only the son of a poor brick maker, but a son that should have been King after his father. The subsequent information that he and his father had been banned from being King but his son Darius had not been had changed him further. Upon finding out the reason his family had been banned from the throne was because his father Alric, as heir to the throne, had married a commoner from the farmlands, his life had completely tumbled.

The one thing that kept him going through those days was that his friend King Edward needed him. His son's ascension to the throne came much earlier than Edward or Richard had anticipated. He now stayed on in the unique position as councilor to his own son when in fact if his father had never been banished, he himself would have been the King for a time. Oh, there were times he held his tongue and wanted to strangle his son; however he had to admit his son had not done too bad as King. Compassionate to a fault and impetuous, Darius cared little for meetings, but he was young, enthusiastic, and had a genuine concern for all the people of the Realm, from all walks of life. That was something Richard was still learning, and apparently many of the other councilors were also. He had to admit that previously when he thought about the Realm, he had thought about those in the city and their interaction with one another and neighboring kingdoms. Including the farmers and others as part of the Realm had been a difficult transition for him.

"Richard." Cray strode toward him. His age had done nothing to limit his influence and stature.

Richard looked at his old sword master and mentor and smiled, thinking this man had tutored his son also. That was before Darius knew his place and had come to grips with being a King. He chuckled to himself.

Cray cocked his gray head to the side, as if asking what was so funny. A dark-skinned stocky man in his sixties, he had been the most able commander of the King's forces longer than most could remember.

"I was just thinking of you having to teach my son up in the Superstition Mountains. Must have been quite interesting," Richard said.

Cray nodded. "Quite interesting!" He changed the subject. "I need to go to Sur. These other councilors care only about what is happening in their own backyard. Can't they see a buildup of Arc forces, even a small one, is no mere trifle?"

"I agree, Commander." Reports of at least five hundred men from Arc setting up a camp on the border had come before the council. "The King of Arc's son, Prince Bronwyn, is leading those men and used the excuse that they were there to honor the new King of the Realm, but that many armed men close to the border is a worry nonetheless. Take a small battalion of horsemen with you and go now."

Cray raised his eyebrows. The council had decided otherwise.

"With Darius gone, it is my right as first councilor to make decisions in regards to the safety of the Realm. We can say it's an honor guard for our King in meeting with their leader."

"Two can play at their game, huh?" Cray said.

"I don't know what they are up to. It doesn't take troops to meet with the King. Their black-clad riders can be intimidating," Richard added.

"My sources tell me the King's son Bronwyn is more greedy than his father and that he has no love for the Realm or wizards, either."

"Wizards have advised the Kingdom of Arc for centuries." Richard frowned and looked around the long hallway. Lowering his voice, he said, "Though I must admit, I am still not so comfortable around wizard power yet either."

Cray gave the councilor a direct look, as if testing Richard's reactions. "Your son and King is one of them."

Richard jaw drew tense. "Don't try and test my loyalties, Cray. I serve my son as you do, faithfully and fully."

"Of course you do." Cray turned to go. "By your leave, I will go to Sur now."

After a couple of steps, Richard breathed out a puff of air. "Cray?"

Richard watched as his old mentor turned around. Unbidden memories of his father ran through his mind. Cray had known his father as Prince Alric many years ago. From what Cray told him, they had been best friends, and Cray was even aware of Alric's growing powers. When Alric was disinherited for marrying an outsider, King Charles spread the rumor that his son had died in battle. Until Cray had met Darius up in the training camp, he'd thought his friend's line had vanished with him. Darius looked a lot like Alric at the same age. But Alric had changed his identity and assumed the occupation of bricklayer to provide for his wife and son.

"Take care of my son," Richard said with emotion.

"I will, councilor." Cray paused. "He is definitely the best of us all."

Richard nodded. That he was.

"And take young Jain with you as your body servant. It's about time the queen's brother got some training in the real world."

* * * * * * * * * * * * * * *

Kelln had a challenging time telling the difference between rumor and truth in the streets of Mar. And no one seemed to be able to think for themselves before checking with their guild. The Guild of Merchants and unfortunately the Guild of Thieves were the largest, but by no means were they the only ones of significant influence. Kelln had heard of the Guild of Fishermen, the Guild of Dressmakers, the Guild of Bricklayers, the Guild of Weapon Makers, and even the Guild of Wives. Kelln vowed never to get entangled with that one. It had a long reach throughout the city.

Talk of a new guild had surfaced in the last week—a Guild of Protection. The talk around Mar had the ring of the Preacher behind it. No one seemed to know how to contact him, though. The streets said if they chose you, a dark-haired beauty would be in contact. Alessandra!

Kelln sat in the ambassador's office in the city office building. Two guards stood outside his door with two more at each entrance to the building. Dozens more were stationed around the city. Darius had been true to his word and had delivered a battalion of guards to protect his interests in the city.

Kelln sat thinking about Darius. Through Tali's Cremelino, they received the dire news that something had happened to Christine and Lightning. The Kingdom of Arc was on the move. Kelln had wanted to come and help, but Darius needed him to stay in Mar and try to find the Preacher and his daughter. He couldn't afford fighting on one front with another enemy at his back.

Lost in thought, he almost jumped out of his seat when a closet door opened and Rapp came strolling out. The small young man certainly had a way of surprising people. Freckles covered his youthful cheeks. His impish grin and smiling eyes told Kelln the boy enjoyed the surprise.

"Rapp. What are you doing in my closet?"

Rapp tried to pat down his unruly hair, but to no avail. "There's a secret door. All the rooms have them."

"That's fantastic!" Kelln stood up the rest of the way. "I love Mar. Secrets wrapped in secrets."

"Well, I do have a secret for you, Ambassador." Rapp sat on the edge of Kelln's mahogany desk.

The ambassador tried to give a scolding look to the scoundrel, but he didn't have the heart to tell him to get off of the desk. Rapp, although sneaky and squirrely, was an amiable boy, and for some reason he had taken a liking to Kelln. "Out with it then. The secret?"

"Some of the minor guilds are having a meeting tonight. It is rumored a new Guild of Protection will be talking to them and trying to form a loose alliance. This could be your chance to find the Preacher."

"Nothing more than rumors again?" It was the third time in a week a supposed meeting was to take place. When they arrived at the appointed place in disguise, nothing had occurred.

"This one is more reliable." Rapp hopped off the desk. "I heard from the baker, who heard from his wife, who talked to a member of the Tree Grower's Guild—"

"The Tree Grower's Guild?" Kelln threw up his hands in exasperation. "They need a guild for trees?"

"How else would they be planted and cared for?" Rapp said, absolutely serious.

Kelln smiled. How else indeed? Only in Mar. "And this is reliable?"

"Well, the member of the Tree Grower's Guild overhead—"

"Forget it, Rapp. I can't keep rushing out on hearsay."

"The mention of a dark-haired girl was heard," Rapp added.

"Why didn't you say so at first?"

"I was getting to that part." Rapp frowned.

Kelln rubbed his forehead. He could feel a headache coming on. "All right. Is Tali coming with us this time again? What's the disguise?"

"Fishermen Guild," he replied.

Kelln scrunched his nose. "Not again." He remembered the last time. He couldn't get the smell off of him for two days.

"They are a large guild, so not all the members know each other. And others stay away from them due to the stink." Rapp laughed. "Be ready tonight." With that, Rapp walked out the door this time to the obvious amazement of the guards who had never seen him enter. They looked at Kelln for explanation.

"Don't ask," Kelln said. "I can't explain what that boy does."

Later that night, Rapp led Kelln and Tali to an abandoned warehouse. Tali's disguise made her appear older. Rapp, due to his small size, was supposed to be their young son. It was a stretch, but should hold up in the darkened room.

Just outside the warehouse, Rapp produced some fish guts from a sealed bag. Kelln almost passed out as they wiped the mess over their dirty fishing attire. Approaching the door, they were given a wide berth, and no questions were asked. Kelln wore a fishermen's cap, covering his red curls. The three intruders hung in the shadows, watching and waiting.

The gathering crowd grew bigger with an obvious division of each guild standing by their own. There was little trust in Mar. Some held onto lanterns in the dark building, but plenty of shadows covered the fringes of the group. As predicted, people stayed away from the members of the Fishermen Guild, even going so far as to tell them to get to the back.

Soon, a woman with her head covered in a colorful scarf entered the room, carrying a bright lantern. Kelln strained up on his toes. He wished for Darius's height for the hundredth time in his life. But it wasn't meant to be. He would always be short.

"It's her," he whispered to his companions. He knew her walk and stance well after the last year.

Alessandra held up her arms to silence the crowd. She took her time pulling back the hood of her cloak. Many of the men murmured their approval at her good looks, while their wives elbowed them in the ribs. With a slow turn of her neck, she looked around the room. Though he suspected she couldn't see him in the dim light, Kelln ducked back down to avoid being detected.

After ensuring complete silence, Alessandra began to speak. "My father and I are here to form a new guild: the Guild of Protection. Too many of the smaller guilds cannot standup to the larger ones, especially the governor's Merchants' Guild. The governor and his companion guilds are too strict to set the terms and prices of goods and services in Mar."

A few shouts and praises of agreement rippled through the crowd.

"We approached the governor, but he did not understand the need for our guild."

The crowd shouted in anger toward their governor.

"That's because he wants to keep you cowed. He wants control. And who does he work for?"

The crowd was quiet, then a voice from the other side of the room yelled, "The King."

"Yes, the King. The governor does everything for the King, but what does the King do for you?"

Kelln was amazed at her boldness. It wasn't fair. Darius had planned on coming to Mar, but the chaos in the guilds and the Preacher being loose had stopped him.

"Nothing," a lady shouted. "The King does nothing for us. Hasn't even come and visited us."

"That's right," Alessandra continued. "Because the King does nothing, we have to do things ourselves. That is why we are here to protect you against the King and his people—the governor and the ambassador."

Kelln wanted to shout out. She was making this personal now, which was quite unfair. But now he understood what this was. This was the Preacher's way of trying to trap Kelln once again. Alessandra would bad-mouth the King and him, forcing Kelln to confront her and her father.

"But how will *you* protect us?" a man up front asked, still wearing his baker's apron. "What about the Guild of Thieves?"

"They will cooperate with us," Alessandra informed them. "We are reaching an agreement with them. Those that join the Guild of Protection will not have to worry about the thieves."

The people seemed impressed at the breadth of the new guild already. People started talking in small conversations among themselves.

"You are just a girl. How can you protect us?" a large man shouted, from the Guild of Bricklayers by the looks of his clothes.

Someone else took up the mantra also. Soon dissent rang through the cavernous room.

With a flourish, Alessandra lifted up her arms, and the lanterns glowed brighter. She twisted her right hand, and a sword flew away from the side of one of the attendees. She flicked again, pushing out her palms in front of her, and two people fell to the floor.

Kelln receded farther into the shadows. Was she a wizard, too? He remembered conversations they had had, wondering if the powers would flow from her grandfather to her father and then to her or not. Kelln thought about her grandfather, the kindly old Alastair, who had been blinded by the powerful rage of his son, the Preacher. Kelln had learned a lot from the old man, holed up with him for a few days in the Black Forest. That is where he had learned to trust in God, a higher power that directed them. Whenever angry or frustrated, he thought of that teaching and felt peace. He tried to do so now.

Tali leaned close to him, interrupting his reminiscing thoughts. "The power is not coming from her."

"What?"

"I can sense people's powers. I feel Mr. El'Lan, your Preacher friend."

"He's no friend of mine. Tries to kill me each time he sees me," Kelln mumbled, realization dawning on him. "The Preacher? He is here then?"

Tali nodded.

All three of them started looking around. They moved around the edges of the room with care. Most of the crowd was enthralled in Alessandra's performance and did not notice the three of them. A few people looked at them as they moved around, but once they got a whiff of the fish, they moved away.

"There he is." Kelln pointed to a man in the shadows about a quarter of the way around the room from them.

Tali nodded. "That is where the power is coming from."

"Now what?" Rapp asked. "Do we kill him?"

Kelln looked at him and shook his head. "No, Rapp. We'll follow them and watch where they go. We need to find out their full plans. Once I know that, I will bring the guards with me to confront him. He is powerful, so we must be careful."

Rapp looked disappointed they weren't going to kill Mr. El'Lan.

The magic stopped, and Alessandra continued. "Now mark your name or guild on this paper, and we will contact each of your privately about what it takes to join our guild." She motioned them to a small table where a parchment and quill stood waiting for the signatures.

Some of the attendees slipped away, but most gathered to sign. They were interested in anything that could protect them from the Guild of Thieves.

As people left and the dim room became less crowded, the small group of three hung back farther in the shadows and hid behind a large broken doorframe. Soon everyone had gone except for them and the Preacher and Alessandra. Tali used a small amount of her power to amplify the voices of the father and daughter, who stood on the other side of the room by a small lantern.

"You did well, daughter," the Preacher said.

"They are easy, Father. They jump at anything to believe in. But do you think it will work? Will he come?"

"Yes, he will come," the Preacher said. "He won't be able to resist the temptation."

Kelln had an uncomfortable thought that he was the "he" they were talking about.

"Once the ambassador is gone, then we can take down the governor, and I will take control of Mar through my new Guild of Protection, " the Preacher said.

"First, I need information on my mother," Alessandra said. "The guildmaster said he would investigate for me."

"Alessandra!" The Preacher threw up his hands, looking exasperated. "What is this obsession you have with your mother? She is either dead or doesn't want to see you. But I am here, my daughter. I want you. I need you."

"I need to find her, Father. You don't have to understand." Her voice stood on the verge of tears. "I just do—she is my mother after all. I have lived most of my life without her. I need to just see her. If it means betraying Kelln again, I will do it, don't you worry. Your little plans of taking over the city are safe with me."

"Little plans? Alessandra, don't you see what we are doing? Chaos here in Mar, a war brewing with Arc, Belor barely restrained. The Kingdom of Darius DarSan Williams is about to topple over, and there is nothing he can do about it." The crazed wizard paced the floor in front of his daughter.

"Once chaos is in place, I will hand these lands over to the eastern lords. They will save the people from destruction and gain their trust. Then they will give me the western lands to rule." The Preacher lowered his voice. "And I want you by my side to rule with me. Someone has to keep my legacy going."

"But I don't have your powers."

"Not yet you don't. But we will continue to work with them. Any time now we will see a breakthrough. You will see." The Preacher stopped and looked around the darkness with alarm on his face.

"What is wrong?"

"Someone is using the power."

Tali stopped the amplification of the sound, and the three of them huddled in silence.

"There is no one here," Alessandra remarked. "It must be your power residue from earlier."

Rapp's leg twitched against the door, echoing in the dark empty room.

"Who's there?" The Preacher's voice boomed, and a light began to spread out over the room.

"He knows we're here," Kelln whispered.

"Hold on, boys. Here we go." Tali stood quickly and, with a sweep of her hand, sent a blinding light and spray of rocks across the room.

"Go now!" she ordered the other two, and they began to run toward the entrance. Light came through the doorway from the starlight outside, but the opening was still halfway around the room.

The Preacher answered with a bolt of lightning, but because of the earlier blinding light, his aim was not true.

"You?" they all heard the Preacher roar.

He had spotted them.

"I will kill you once and for all."

The three ran even faster toward the door. They looked back over their shoulders, and energy built up around the dangerous man.

Alessandra grabbed her father's arm and screamed, "No, Father, you promised you wouldn't kill him."

Kelln, suddenly glad to overhear the sentiment that could save his life, didn't know if her father would heed the reminder. Still running toward the doorway, the three of them spotted Radiance just outside the doorway. A glow became visible around Taliana, and she pushed a blinding white wind into the Preacher and his daughter, then dove through the doorway. On the other side, she collapsed the doorway around the door and buried the opening in rubble.

Taliana hugged her Cremelino. "Such power. Such emotion. Incredible. Radiance amplified my power tenfold."

"Are they dead?" Kelln asked.

As if to answer, a blast hit the wall from inside and bricks began to fall from the outside of the building.

"Run!" Rapp shouted.

The group ran through the streets. They heard blasts and explosions behind them. The sky lit with fire as one building after another exploded.

"I guess you made him mad," Rapp said matter-of-factly.

The other two laughed.

Soon they were in another secret residence the governor kept, safe from the Preacher and his daughter. After cleaning himself, Kelln sat in a study alone while the other two finished up. He couldn't help think about how Alessandra didn't want to kill him. He could take some consolation in that fact. But he was beyond that now. The words she spoke about taking him and the governor down and the Preacher talking about taking down the rest of the Realm frightened him and solidified in his mind that Alessandra and the Preacher both were now enemies of the Realm, and one of his responsibilities as ambassador was to protect the Realm.

"Berlain," he said out loud. The name of Alessandra's mother. He had known earlier in the year of her desire to see if her mother still lived. He didn't blame her for wanting to see her mother again, but things had gone too far—past the point of reason in that search.

Then a thought came to him. He could find Berlain first and get Alessandra away from her father. By separating the two of them, he would have a better chance of stopping the madness and restoring order to the city.

"Oh, Rapp," he called. "I have a perfect job for you."

* * * * * * * * * * * * * * *

Chapter Ten
SUR

Darius rode his Cremelino at a dangerous speed for a day and a half before he had to stop. Both of their energies were depleted, and though he was wild with worry over Christine, he knew Thunder could not take much more, and he needed some sleep to be able to think clearly again.

The path down the mountain communities had been painstakingly slow. Riding in the darkness of night had been hard, and they had to constantly watch out for turns, roots, and rocks on the poorly maintained road. Since meeting up with the main road running from Mar to Sur, he was able to use Thunder's full resources of strength and speed.

Entering a small village about half a day's ride from Sur, Darius found a decent inn, gave Thunder to the stable boy's keeping, and stumbled into the common room. He had decided to keep his identity hidden, not for any more reason than to be able to eat and rest undisturbed. He vowed to himself to come back at a later time and visit with his subjects as King.

The warm platter of meat, potatoes, carrots, and fresh bread filled his body with new strength almost immediately. After eating his fill, he retired to his room. A few hours of sleep should be enough for him, but he didn't know how much time Thunder needed. He sent the question out to the Cremelino, always a background presence in his mind now. The answer back came in a whisper, signifying the horse's tired condition; however, he said he would be ready to go when Darius was.

Three hours later, approaching midnight, a knock sounded on Darius's door. He jolted out of bed, realizing he had slept deeper than intended. It was the young son of the innkeeper, the boy he had paid to take care of his horse.

"Sir," the boy mumbled, embarrassed to have woken a customer at this time of night. "I am sorry to disturb you, but a trader came in from Sur just now. He was stabling his horse when he caught sight of yours. You told me to tell you if anyone paid special attention to your horse."

Darius nodded for the boy to continue. Darius hoped the man didn't recognize the type of horse it was. That would send rumors flying around the area. The Cremelinos were a breed used by the King and those closest to him. Of course, he had given one to Christine as a gift, and now one had gone with Taliana Penrose also. It had availed him the means to communicate with Kelln about the disappearance of Christine.

"He told me he thought it funny he had come across two white horses of the same size and appearance that same day." The boy yawned. The late night traveler had obviously woken the boy up. "We don't see too many horses of that color around these parts."

Sleep left Darius. "Where did the man say he had seen the other horse?"

"I don't know. I was barely awake." The boy still had a hard time keeping his eyes open. "By some barn outside of Sur or something. You can ask him yourself. He's sitting in the common room drinking ale."

Darius grabbed a coin and stuck it in the boy's hand. "Make sure he doesn't go anywhere." He rushed back into the room, put his boots on, and gathered his things up.

The man sat drinking ale by himself. Two other men were still up at the late hour, nursing their drinks in a far corner. Darius approached the lone man. Sitting down opposite him, Darius began drilling him with questions on the horse he had seen. The man was taken aback and didn't seem to trust Darius at first. A few coins and drinks later, however, and Darius had all he needed.

Sending a quick thought to Thunder just moments before arriving in the stables, Darius informed his horse they were on their way again. As soon as Darius was on his back, Thunder galloped off into the dark night. Even at a fast pace, it would still be early morning before they arrived in the area where the man had seen Lightning.

As the sun began to rise over the Superstition Mountains, Darius noticed more and more villages along the highway. Sur was a short distance away now. The man had told Darius he'd been visiting a farmer friend of his who had found the horse lying down and hurt. He had coaxed her up and into his barn.

After turning off the main road and asking a few directions, Darius found himself riding down a small lane.

A weakened thought came to his mind. *Darius?*

"Lightning. I am close."

Who is with you? Lightning asked.

Thunder! came the proud thought from Darius's newly bonded horse.

A sense of pleasure from Lightning intruded upon his thoughts but no other words.

Soon they found a small farmhouse with a large green barn. Dismounting quickly without stopping, Darius ran to the barn. He found Lightning lying on her side. Taking off a makeshift bandage, Darius found a large gash still oozing pus and blood. Another cut stood out across her white leg. She had been given some straw and food.

His heart constricted to see his wife's horse in such bad shape. He wiped the tears from his eyes and knelt down. Without thinking of what to do, he instinctively covered his hand over the Cremelino's wound. He drew strength from his own heart and opened himself up to the horse. He thought of Lightning and what she meant to him and to Christine. He thought of Christine being taken, and a sob escaped from his throat. He tied to concentrate on Lightning and drew strength from Thunder. Soon a soft glow overlaid the wound, and it began to close up. He then proceeded to run his hand over the smaller wound on her leg.

Sighing from the energy drain, Darius finally opened his eyes. Turning toward a sound in the opening of the barn, he saw a man silhouetted against the barn door.

"I've never witnessed anything like that before, young man. What did you do? Who are you?"

Darius smiled, stood up, and placed his hand on a wooden rail to offer himself support. He could hardly stay on his feet. "Thank you for caring for her, sir."

The man moved closer to Darius. "She was hurt something terrible. Looked like a sword wound, though I don't know who would slice up a horse around here, especially such a beautiful creature like she is."

The two watched as Lightning slowly stood up. Silently she sent her thanks to Darius.

The man stood there, still waiting for an answer to his questions.

Darius put out his hand to shake, "I am Darius DarSan Williams, King of the Realm." The man reached out his hand in shock and surprise. Before Darius could shake it, he collapsed to the ground in exhaustion.

A short time later, Darius opened his eyes. He realized he was laying on a floor, staring up into the underside of the roof of a small modest home. Sitting up with care, though no longer dizzy, he glanced around. The man and his wife were sitting on two chairs, gaping at him.

"You feeling better, son?" the man said.

His wife ribbed him and whispered, "Don't call him son. He's the King. You have to call him Your Majesty or Sire or my Lord or something."

Darius shared a weak smile and held up his hand. "It's fine, sir. Thank you for taking care of the horse and for bringing me in here."

"What you did out there with that horse was truly amazing," the farmer responded. "I wouldn't have believed you were King No offense, Sire, but you are kind of young, except I had heard our new King had wizard powers of old. It must be you."

"It *is* me. I know, hard to believe, sometimes even for me."

The wife stood up and went to the kitchen, "I have some food here for you, my Lord."

"I need to leave right away." Darius stood and wobbled for a minute. He had to find Christine, but he didn't want to alarm these people with that news.

The man helped Darius to the table. "You wouldn't want to miss my wife's cooking, now would you?"

"And you do need your strength," his wife piped in.

Darius was moved by the compassion of these people. He sat at the table and found himself suddenly ravished. He ate three platefuls of potatoes, eggs, and hot griddle cakes. "That was one of the best meals I have ever had. The castle chefs could learn from you." He beamed.

The lady blushed, and the man looked down in embarrassment. Darius realized they were just average farmers trying to make their way in life.

"What can I do to repay you?" Darius asked.

"Oh no. Nothing, Your Majesty. It's our pleasure to help you," the man answered humbly. "Just watching you heal that horse was a treasure for me."

"My powers . . . ?" Darius still didn't know what people thought about his powers.

The lady of thc house smiled. "Don't worry about that. We are not as superstitious against magic around here as they are in the capital. It's like any kind of tool, I gather. You can use it for good or bad. Every once in a while, there will be talk of some wizards from Arc coming into Sur. They've never caused any trouble from what we have heard.

Darius, touched at their humility and understanding, felt proud of how many good people were in his realm.

"You have been so helpful in events that you are not even aware of. I will repay you somehow, but now I need to get to Sur." He stood up from the table and hugged each of them, sending traces of his power into them to thank them.

The two backed up from him with amazement on their faces. Then they bowed low to him and bid him farewell.

Darius climbed back on Thunder, and with Lightning by their side, they rode off at half speed. Lightning, still weak, would be fine after the healing completed.

Wizard, I have lost contact with her. Lightning sounded frightened.

"It's probably the injury you suffered," Darius suggested.

There is a spark every once in a while, but it gets farther away each time I try to find her.

"Have they taken her to Arc then?" Darius mused out loud.

They entered Sur a short time thereafter, and Darius found the Governor's home and the rest of the guards that had been with his wife. They were devastated and afraid of punishment. Darius was tired and frustrated but tried not to take it out on the men. They were doing their best. One of the guards recounted to him that she had gone out on an early morning ride and had never returned. After searching, they found the two dead guards north of the city. Neighbors mentioned seeing black-clad riders in the area.

"Why would Arc take her?" Governor Bree Handover asked out loud. The man was a good steward of the city and seemed genuinely concerned for the queen's disappearance.

"A good question that we will soon find out. Can you send some men up in the mountain pass and see what they can find out?"

The mayor nodded. "The Arcs have a small army camped on the border, Sire. We don't grasp their full intentions. They have said it was an honor guard to meet you."

"An army for an honor guard!" Darius grew angrier. "Are they taunting us now?"

"It is said Bronwyn Anwar, the King's son, waits there to meet with you as you invited."

Darius stood, exhausted beyond measure. He had to keep going. The longer he waited, the further Christine could be. "Then I will ride to meet him and force an answer as to where my wife has been taken."

One of the guards stepped over to Darius. Eric was second in command to Roland. "You are tired, Sire. Why don't you rest first?"

"I can't rest," he almost wailed. "My wife has been taken. I will not rest until I find her." Anguish bubbled up inside him, testing his limits. He reached inside himself and pulled on strength he didn't know he had. He pushed away the tiredness and set his mind for the task at hand.

The guard, Darius's elder by twenty years, continued, "Let us at least get you cleaned up and presentable, my Lord. If you are going to meet the prince of the Kingdom of Arc, let's show him the King of the Realm in all his glory and power."

Darius smiled without it reaching his eyes. "Very well. You are right. We must have a show of power." Turning to the mayor, he gave orders, "Mayor Handover, contact the garrison here, and tell whoever is in charge to bring his battalion. We ride at noon."

Two guards accompanied the King to wash and change clothes. Somewhere in the midst of their help, they also fed him. In the back of his mind, he communicated to Thunder and Lightning for them to be ready to ride. The stable hands were feeding and watering them well.

Their ride in the late autumn air began clear but grew cooler close to the mountains. Leaves hung in oranges, reds, and yellows, sending a glorious splash of color throughout Sur and its surrounding lands. The greener evergreens of the mountains were sprinkled in, growing thicker closer to the mountains themselves.

It was the type of day Darius usually gloried in, the type of day to lift his spirits. Today all he saw in his mind was his wife. Only wed hardly five months now, he couldn't bear the thought of losing her. Not after all they had been through. Not after the persecutions she had suffered in the farmlands, not after the year they had spent apart, not after having her by his side at last. The Diamond Palace was still being constructed for her, a palace set in the meadow by the Lake of Reflection, a place they had spent so much time in as teenagers. The place where she had first kissed him, and where he had asked her to marry him. It would be a grand home away from the castle, where she could enjoy the surrounding farmlands and forest.

Gazing up into the pass, he wiped a tear from his eye. He had met an ambassador from Arc once when younger. His father had introduced him to Darius—an advisor to the King, a large man named Olan Sallir. The thing he most remembered was his vivid green cloak. How dare they take his wife.

"They will not have her!" he growled. "Faster," he called out, and the pace of the three-hundred-man cavalry picked up speed, though they were no match for him and the Cremelinos.

****

Sean stood next to Bronwyn. Bronwyn was a man of action. Sean liked that. The prince was someone that actually got things done.

He remembered back to the night that High Wizard Sallir and Bronwyn's sister Danijela had interrupted Bronwyn and his men's meal. Bronwyn ordered his men to ambush the High Wizard as he slept in a nearby inn. However, the wizard and his apprentice girl had outmaneuvered them. When the prince's men arrived and attacked the room, only a straw dummy met their resistance. Bronwyn was furious and tore the room apart, threatening the innkeeper with sudden death if he did not tell Bronwyn where the two had gone.

All the innkeeper knew was the High Wizard had paid for two rooms and then left, traveling west down the road. After pleading for his life, the men let the innkeeper go with the order that if he saw the High Wizard again, he was to inform Bronwyn or one of his men.

Now Sean stood next to the prince in a small valley on the border of the two kingdoms, surveying the armed men in front of them.

"They are all here, sir," a guard informed the prince. "We are five hundred strong."

Bronwyn smiled. "Perfect. An honor guard for the King of the Realm."

"Oh, I look forward to seeing his surprised face," Sean said.

"Will his wife be with him?" Bronwyn asked.

"They are inseparable. He clings to her like a sick puppy to its mother," Sean spat. "He is not worthy of being King, but she is worthy of even less. An ignorant outsider."

Sean had never understood Darius's obsession with the farmlands, his inclination to spend more time there than in the city. He didn't know how Darius had tricked King Edward into allowing him to be the next King. It must be his powers. Sean could not deny that Darius was a wizard of some sort, but he did not believe the story of him being the grandson of King Charles.

"So the plan is to receive him with honor. He will have only a small retinue with him. We will have a dinner to celebrate, and in his wine we will put the poison that will reduce his powers." The prince looked down the pass. "Then once his powers are reduced, he will meet with an unfortunate accident in the mountains, one that we will regretfully inform the Realm of and offer our condolences and sympathy."

"Then we will take Sur," Sean added with a gleam in his eyes. "A nice expansion to the kingdom. Are your other men in place?"

"Yes, I sent men to Sur, Tean, and the other local villages to stir up trouble. This whole region will erupt into chaos overnight."

"Then I will inform my master all is ready for the complete destruction of the Realm."

The prince turned to Sean. "Your benefactor must be very powerful. Who is he again?"

Sean didn't fall for the bait. The prince had continued to try and pry the information from him. Sean walked a tight line since the Preacher was a wizard and Bronwyn hated them. "Let's just say he has your interest in mind."

Bronwyn frowned. "Or is he using me for his interests?"

A fast rider approached, saving Sean from having to lie again to the prince. The rider informed them that King Darius did indeed ride to meet them, but he had over three hundred men at his back. They were riding fast and would be there soon. Bronwyn didn't seem worried. He ordered his men to be ready.

In less than an hour, the King rode up into the pass. He sat splendidly on a large white horse, dressed with a circlet on his brow and silver armor adorning his body. A flowing purple cape hung down over the armor and a red shirt. Four guards rode on each side, obviously men from Anikari, with a battalion of riders behind. A few horses snorted and stomped, but for the most part the entire company stopped as if on cue.

A slight breeze blew across the small valley in the pass. High rocky mountain slopes guarded the north and south. Silence hung in the air.

Darius, Wizard King of the Realm, shattered the silence. "Where is my wife? Where have you taken her?"

The question shocked Sean, the prince, and the other men. What was the King talking about? Prince Bronwyn glared at Sean.

Sean shrugged. "Her horse is empty." Sean motioned toward the other white horse next to Darius.

"What game is he playing at, Sean San Ghant?" the prince asked. "Have you led me into a trap?"

"No, no!" Sean backed up a few steps.

Bronwyn, still standing a fair distance away, lifted his voice. "I know nothing of the queen, Your Majesty. You invited us to meet with you on your tour of the Realm. We are here to honor the Realm's newest King."

"My wife has been taken by your soldiers, men dressed all in black with a gold insignia, just like the one on your left breast," the King roared back, hand on the hilt of his sword.

Sean saw fear flash across the prince's face. The prince looked around his group, as if to ask if anyone knew what the King was talking about. Sean moved up behind him.

"He lies, my Prince." Sean was furious at this apparent setback. "He uses trickery to goad us into action."

"Why? Why would he do this? Unless he has a reason to." Bronwyn looked angrily at Sean. "You are a Realm man. Maybe you set this as a trap for me." He motioned one of his men to take custody of Sean.

"We are here at your request," Bronwyn replied back to the King. "We supposed your wife would be with you."

"But she is not," Darius boomed, his voice shaking the ground they all stood on. He took a few steps closer on his horse. "Approach me with two of your men, and we will discuss this further."

Bronwyn motioned for two of his best fighters to join him, then as he stepped forward, he grabbed a hold of Sean. "You will come with me also. We will see how your King reacts to seeing you, a Realm noble here in Arc."

Sean struggled, but the prince's strength kept him held. "This is not necessary, my Prince. I am sure the King hardly even knows me." He didn't know how Darius would react to him there. It would not look good. He hated Darius personally and had been part of a plan to kidnap him once. Having escaped from prison with the Preacher, Sean was sure Darius would take delight in taking him back into custody.

Bronwyn approached King Darius with his two men and Sean in tow. The small group stopped within twenty feet of the King, who had dismounted and approached alone.

"Sean!" the King bellowed suddenly, his voice bouncing off the walls of the mountains. "What are you doing here?"

Sean tried to back up, but Bronwyn held him tight.

"He is with me for now," Bronwyn answered, "though the outcome of this discussion will show whether he is still useful to me or not."

Sean went pale and wondered how he would get out of the situation. He had to think fast. Either side would kill him in a moment if he didn't do something.

"This is all a misunderstanding, Your Majesty." Bronwyn bowed his head to the King of the Realm. "I am Bronwyn

Anwar, eldest son of King Anwar. I was sent here at your request. We do not understand the questions about the queen. We are here to feast with you in celebration."

"There will be no celebration," Darius stated.

"We are sorry to hear that. My men were looking forward to greeting their neighboring ruler."

"Why so many men, Prince Anwar?" Darius asked. His knuckles turned white on his sword hilt.

"As an honor."

"Or as an army," Darius said. "I will ask once again. Why did your men take my wife, and where is she?"

Sean looked around. The battalion behind Darius firmed up. Swords were drawn and made ready. The men behind Bronwyn moved closer, unaware that even though they had more numbers, the Realm had superior fighters. Sean still didn't understand what Darius was asking, but knowing him as he did, he knew this was no ruse. Darius was compassionate to a fault, Sean knew, though his temper was something to be afraid of, especially with his newfound powers. Something had happened to the queen and for some reason, Darius thought the Kingdom of Arc was behind it.

Darius turned his attention from Bronwyn to Sean. "Sean, are you behind the kidnapping of my wife?"

"No, no, my Lord, never." Sean trembled at the crackle of power in Darius's gray eyes.

Darius fired rapid questions at Sean. "Where is the Preacher? What are his plans? What are you doing here? Where is Alessandra?"

"Not everyone loves you, Darius Williams." Sean left off the honorifics of his name on purpose. "You don't deserve the throne. You don't deserve what you have." Sean's only chance at this point was to start the battle and escape in the midst of it. He knew Darius's temper and was intent on using it fully to his advantage. "You can't even keep track of your little farmer girl." Sean spat the final insult.

Darius drew his sword, and lightning ran across the length of it, escaping into the sky. Thunder rolled through the air as he pushed his left hand out against Bronwyn's army, many of them having a hard time standing in the sudden gust of wind.

"Christine!" Darius yelled a deafening yell that cascaded with power over the entire valley. Trees split down the middle, and rocks fell down the side of the steep mountain walls. Horses stamped their feet as the ground shook. The Realm soldiers began to push forward. Darius swiped his sword at Sean, but in his blind rage somehow missed him.

Sean pulled away from the prince who retreated back to his men, and ran away from the battle. Calvary on both sides surged forward and took up formation.

Darius remounted his horse and motioned his men forward with one thrust of his arm. Bronwyn did the same. Over eight hundred horse-mounted soldiers clashed together, either avenging their King or fighting for their prince.

The battle had begun.

* * * * * * * * * * * * * * *

Chapter Eleven
CHRISTINE

Christine awoke but kept her eyes closed so as not to alert her captors. She sent out her mind to try and find Lightning but sensed nothing. That had happened more often of late, and she was becoming worried that the companion she'd had for the past two years would soon leave her altogether. Maybe it was because she wasn't a wizard.

The queen of the Realm laid on soft blankets and caught the sound of distant voices. She guessed it was afternoon by the strength of the sun through her closed eyelids. Her head throbbed, and her stomach felt nauseous again.

Opening her lids lightly and turning her head, she ascertained she was alone in the room for the moment. The walls held a cream-colored plaster with pleasant art hanging in organized fashion around the room. The bed sat high up off the floor with lavish quilts covering its frame. High class abductors, she surmised.

Her mind cleared, and she started to remember fragments of the last few days. After Lighting had left her at Sur, the men in black gagged her and placed a dark sack over her head. They had ridden fast and far before stopping that night. She'd been allowed to eat and relieve herself on the way but not speak.

That first night they stayed in a barn, and she had not slept well.

The next day, they covered her head again and rode through the day. At one time she'd heard a struggle and found herself being carried off the horse and told to remain silent. Although they dressed like men from Arc when they took her, they were definitely from further south. The few words they used and the food they brought along signaled them as being from Gildan. She was not well-versed in either culture, but she knew they were not heading through the pass to Arc, most likely south to Gildan.

The door opened, and a young man came in. His light brown face, dark hair, and slightly upturned eyes set him as Gildan before he even spoke.

"Would you like some food?" His accent was heavy but understandable.

"Just some water," she said. Thinking of food made her stomach roil.

The young man returned a few minutes later with a cool glass of water.

"Where am I?" she asked, knowing she probably wouldn't get an answer.

As expected, the young man stayed silent and then took back the glass when it was empty.

He left, and she laid back down. They must have arrived here, wherever *here* was, the prior evening. It was dark when they ushered her into the room. Looking down, she noticed she still wore her riding clothes from many days previous.

She stood and took a few minutes for her shaky legs to stabilize. Walking over to a small window, she peered outside. Her captors had brought her to a large complex on a hill. She had the view of a city, a very large one, one that went as far as she could see. The famed white-domed roofs told her where she had been taken.

"Gildan," she said out loud as the door opened.

"Very good, my dear." The man closed the door behind him.

"Why am I here?" She tried to be regal but knew her clothes looked anything other.

"Simply as a tool of negotiation."

"Negotiate for what?" Christine found herself instantly afraid of this man. His calmness belied a hint of madness underneath. His hair was dark, holding light hints of gray. He dressed in battle attire, which gave added dimension to his thin but muscled body. Without Lightning to give her support, she found herself wavering in front of him.

"Negotiation for the Realm."

Christine looked at the man carefully. He resembled Mezar somewhat. The same mouth and eyes, though on this man they were arrogant and angry, while on Mezar they held eagerness and joy.

"Do you know who I am?" he asked.

Christine shook her head, trying to buy time as she formulated a plan.

The man moved closer to where she stood by the window. "I think you do."

Christine stayed silent. She tried to move further away from him, but the room was too small.

He stretched his hand out in front of him and, without any physical effort, lifted her off the floor mere inches. He bound her arms with air to her sides and brought her closer to him. She could smell his foul breath. Fear gripped her heart. This man was a powerful wizard.

"I will be your next King." The man's heavy breath was warm on her face. "I will rule Gildan and the Realm with an iron fist, not like the current Emperor or your pitiful husband. I have heard of his weaknesses: his temper, his tenuous hold on his emotions, his compassion." The last was said with malice, tiny drops of spittle hitting Christine's face.

He lowered her to the ground and unbound her arms. Christine wiped the drops of spit from her face.

"I am General Alrishitar, heir to the throne of the Gildanian Empire. Mezar has told me about you and your pathetic King," the man said.

Christine took a deep breath. She couldn't believe Mezar had anything to do with this man. He had stood by Darius even though Darius had taken him prisoner.

"You want to know how I will rule the Realm?" The general seemed proud to share his plans, his ingenuity. Although terrified, Christine tried to play cool and get as much information out of him as she could. She could tell his ego had no bounds, and so she fed it with a compliment. "You do seem to have everything figured out, general. I can see why Mezar spoke so highly of you."

The general looked surprised but pleased. "He did?'

Christine fed him another lie. "Oh, yes. When he was in Anikari at my husband's coronation, he told me how great your empire was and that someday you would be the next Emperor and lead Gildan to greater heights."

The general nodded his head. "That is right. Gildan will be the mightiest power in the west when I am Emperor."

"My husband is a new King." Christine brought him back to the conversation. "But he is smart and has the Realm army at his back. You must have a complicated plan to take over the Realm." Christine feigned innocence. She knew of Darius's powers and that Mezar would also never let anything happen to the Realm.

The general walked a few steps away from her. "My plan is easy. Your husband thinks you've been stolen by men from Arc. He will start a war with them, and while his attention is elsewhere, I will send an army into the Realm, taking it piece by piece, starting in Denir, annexing each parcel of the Realm to the empire, one city at a time. By the time your dear husband and King find out what has happened, he will be depleted from his war with Arc, and I will be on the verge of taking Anikari."

"What about me?" Christine drew out the mad man's plans as far as she could.

"Ah. In the end, he will hand over control of the Realm to me as a trade for you. I know of his weakness for you. He will do anything for his young wife. He will not be able to resist."

Now that Christine understood part of the man's plan, she became bolder. "He is powerful. He may stop you, General."

"He is an untrained dog with powers he does not understand. I am one of the most powerful wizards in Gildan.

He will bow before me and my power. He will grovel at my feet." The general raised his voice to a fevered pitch, veins popping out from his neck.

Lowering his voice, he continued, "For now, you will be treated well; have no fear. You are a queen my dear and we royals need to be treated well. I will not have you blemished for your King."

"What if he won't surrender to you for me?" she asked. "Darius understands his duty is to the entire realm, not just his wife."

"Then I will destroy him bone by bone in front of you until you beg to take his place."

Christine blanched and stepped back even further. She could not believe the gall of this man. "You are mad. It will never work. Darius will stop you. Your son will stop you."

"Don't speak to me of my son again!" The general used his power to knock a small vase from a shelf, shattering glass all over the floor. "Your husband softened him. He will learn his place in Gildan or be destroyed with your husband."

The general flung open the door. A guard appeared next to him outside the room, and a servant stood close by.

"Bathe her, and give her clothes fitting for her station. Make sure she eats, and keep her happy." The general looked back at Christine one more time. "And make sure she stays alive. I need her."

Christine felt numb inside. Lightning was gone from her mind. Sitting in a foreign land, she knew her husband most likely searched for her hundreds of miles away in the wrong country. She thought of her mother back in Anikari and her father, who had passed away the previous year. She remembered their faith and hope and love. She remembered the God they spoke of who could comfort and help.

The nausea rose inside her stomach once again. She gritted her teeth against the feeling. It had been constant since arriving in her captivity. In fact, it had been constant almost every day for the past few months. Realization dawned on her, and she gasped. Holding her hand to her stomach, she only dared to believe what deep inside she knew to be true. She had been blind not to see it before now, but things had been so busy. She must be pregnant.

Two servants opened the door and led her to the bath chambers. She hardly noticed as they bathed and dressed her. He mind was far, far away. She reached out for Lighting only to be thwarted once again by something blocking her communication. She closed her eyes as they finished dressing her and prayed for peace in her heart and for someone to find her soon. She couldn't let the general find out. He was a madman.

****

Mezar and his friends had a slow yet uneventful trip through Denir and up the northern road. The wagon train they rode with stopped at most villages and sold their wares. Through listening to rumors, Mezar had discovered Darius and Christine were not back in Anikari yet. Tales of their travels had them somewhere between Mar and Sur. They were sketchy details but enough for Mezar to continue north. There was no news about any troubles further south in Gildan, for which Mezar was glad. Maybe his father had given up looking for him.

Tonight they stayed in Tean and then would be in Sur in the next few days if the weather held out. Mezar felt his ring pulsing with light and had to hide it in his pocket. It meant Leandra was close by. He was excited to see her again.

Mezar and Leandra, a young woman from the Realm, had become acquainted through bizarre circumstances. She'd been used as a pawn by Sean San Ghant to spy on Darius and help to lure him into the trap that eventually had him kidnapped. Mezar, initially a prisoner of Darius, helped rescue Leandra from Sean's clutches when he saved Darius and had grown to care for her. The two had spent only a short time together in Anikari surrounding the new King's coronation.

Mezar had given Leandra a necklace with a small light encased in it the previous summer back in the Realm. It was beautiful and unique, but it also served a purpose: Through the magic infused in her necklace and his ring, Mezar would always know where she was. He felt bad at the way she had been mistreated by Sean, even by Darius, as only a pretty prop. Darius and Leandra had made amends with how they had treated each other. She had gone through quite an ordeal and decided to stay with relatives in Tean for a while. He was happy she still lived in the area.

Entering the town of Tean, the large wagon train of goods attracted a great many people from the good-sized town, the largest one they had been through besides Denir.

Mezar snuck away to find Leandra. He surprised her at the shop where she was working. Her back was to him as he entered.

"Excuse me, miss, could you help me find something?"

Leandra turned around and ran to him. "Mezar!"

They hugged and made small talk for a few minutes. She asked what he was doing there, but he motioned they couldn't talk about it in the shop.

Two other customers came into the general store. Mezar faded to the edges behind some shelves. The men looked rough and spoke with a foreign accent. One kept trying to barter on everything until Leandra told him they had to pay the price or leave.

The man looked around the store. "You all alone here, girl?"

She nodded. "My family is in the back."

"I don't believe you." The man moved closer.

"Where are you from, sir?" Leandra tried to distract him. "You have a nice accent."

The man smiled. "I am going to be from here soon."

"I don't understand." Leandra frowned.

"This land will be ours soon, girl. Part of the Kingdom of Arc."

The other man told the first one to shut up and stop talking. "Just take the goods and leave."

Mezar had heard enough and came around the corner of the shelves. He smiled at them, and they looked surprised to see him there. "From Arc, huh? You're a long way from home."

"There is no law about traveling," the first man said.

"But there is a law about taking land or property that is not yours. That could land you in jail." Mezar moved closer.

The hardened men didn't seem to sense any danger from the slender and young Gildanian and held their ground.

"Where are the rest of your men?" Mezar asked.

"Gathering in the pass," the first replied.

The second man chided him again and grabbed him by the arm to leave. The first man grabbed the goods and started to walk out.

"You didn't pay for those," Mezar said.

The one without the goods pulled a knife and lunged at Mezar. In a swift movement, Mezar moved to the side, grabbed the man's arm, and twisted the knife out of his hand. The other man started to run, but Mezar brought out his hand in front of him and, with a pull of air, lifted up a board under the man's feet, causing him to crash to the floor. Leandra brought some rope over, and the two of them tied up the would-be thieves.

"Now, tell me about the men in the pass. What is going on there?"

The men were silent until Mezar used his power to pull the rope tighter. They began to gag, and their eyes bulged.

"Tell me or it goes tighter."

"Mezar?" Leandra gave him a warning look that told him not to be too harsh.

He mouthed a "sorry" to her. He was just anxious to find Darius and warn him of his father's plans.

The first man gave in. "Prince Bronwyn is going to attack and take this area for the kingdom. He sent some of us out to disrupt things."

Leandra stepped up to the men, hands on her hips and a scowl on her face. Her cheeks were red, and she looked angry. "This land is not yours to take. Our King will protect us."

Mezar turned to the other man. "Your turn. When is this attack?"

The other man stayed silent until Mezar pulled tighter. The man started choking and couldn't breathe. He signaled that he would talk.

Between broken sobs, he told Mezar that King Darius and his queen were supposed to visit in Sur and then with the prince of Arc. The two thieves had lost track of time, but they thought the meeting would be soon.

"We can't let anything happen to Darius and Christine," Leandra said to Mezar.

Mezar nodded. "We won't."

Mezar kept them tied up and took them out front. He slid away from the group as he had Leandra call over a city guard to take them to jail.

"How did you get them tied up?" one of the guards asked Leandra.

"Can't a girl protect herself?" was all she said.

The guards shook their heads, seemingly confused, but took the thieves away.

After they were gone, Mezar and Leandra went back into the store. Leandra grabbed Mezar into a fierce hug and let a few tears fall. She was almost as tall as Mezar, the top of her head reaching his eyes.

"I have missed you, Leandra," Mezar whispered into her soft brown hair. It was still short and framed the soft features of her face.

"And I you, prince of Gildan." Leandra pulled away and looked at Mezar. "Your disguise is horrible. I would recognize you anywhere."

Mezar laughed. "But you know me. People see what they want to see. But my speech can give me away; it is not perfect. So I must be careful around others."

"Is it true that Arcs are trying to take part of our land?" Leandra looked worried.

"I didn't know about that until now. There is even a greater threat to Darius and Christine." Mezar paused and puffed out some air. "My father is causing problems and plans to kidnap Christine."

"Mezar, we have to help them," Leandra pleaded. "You know I still feel bad about what I did to him, how I turned him in."

"Darius forgave you, Leandra," Mezar said. "It was Sean's doing. He threatened to hurt your family."

"I know. I know. But I want to do something to show them I am really loyal to the Realm."

Mezar took Leandra with him back to where his other friends remained with the wagon train. They made a plan to escape the city that night. Leandra would go with them so their accents would not give them away. She ran off to gather clothes, food, and horses for them from her uncle's farm and to tell her uncle's family that she would be gone for a while.

Mezar now knew exactly where to go to find Darius. He just hoped he wasn't too late to warn the King about Christine. He also hoped he wasn't too late to stop a war between Arc and the Realm when the biggest worry for the Realm right now should be Gildan and his own father.

* * * * * * * * * * * * * * *

Chapter Twelve
A CHANGE OF HEART

Darius and his men fought hard, but the men of Arc were stronger than Darius had realized. He wished he could use more of his power to move things along, but with the pace he had kept in recent days and lack of sleep, he was barely able to stand and fight. He didn't know if it was his untrained abilities or if it was the same for everyone, but using the power exhausted him terribly. He was always hungry afterward, and it took some time to recover.

Grief over his wife steered him forward through his exhaustion. He took some men with him and raced through the enemy's camp, searching every tent for any sign of her. Nothing had turned up yet. He was getting frantic. His men were getting tired. They were outnumbered, and even though they fought better, it was becoming difficult. He hated watching his men die for him, but he hated more the thought of his wife gone from him.

He pushed on, tent after tent, until he reached the largest tent. About to enter, Darius turned at the sounds of horns and hooves behind him. A large army came up through the pass from Sur. At first, his stomach dropped. He thought the riders to be more of the enemy ambushing them but noticed the standard of the Realm held high above one of the thundering horses.

"Form back to ranks," he yelled from atop Thunder. He turned the large horse around and rode back to the new group, bringing his men with him. There were far fewer returning with him than had started. He stomach churned, and his heart fought, weeping for the fallen who lay dead, scattered across the small valley.

He pulled up by the commander of the troops and smiled in surprise at Cray, his general and old mentor.

"Good day, my Lord." Cray bowed his head. "Seems you need some help."

"Yes, General. Glad to see you. How did you know we were here?" A soldier offered Darius a drink of water.

"We heard of a gathering of soldiers on the border, and your father sent me to investigate. When I arrived in Sur, the governor told me where you had gone."

Darius nodded but didn't have much energy to do anything else.

"You look horrible, pardon me saying, your Majesty. Have you had any sleep?"

Darius swayed on the horse, and two men helped him off. He glanced at the other side and spotted the Arc army retreating toward their camp. They would try and get away, but they couldn't run quick enough to get very far; the valley ended in a tight mountain pass that would only allow a few through at a time. A few minutes of rest would help his men and not give too much advantage to the enemy.

He sat down on the ground next to Cray and informed Cray of his wife's abduction.

"It doesn't make any sense for them to take her," Cray said.

"I know." Darius shook his head. "But her Cremelino, Lightning, and other witnesses in the area saw the men."

Cray shook his head. "I am still not used to the idea of communicating with these horses. I knew they bonded with their owner, but I thought it was only a strong bond of feeling and purpose, not that they could actually communicate.

Darius smiled. "Cray, you have no idea of the power of the bond. They are marvelous creatures." Next to him, Thunder neighed loudly.

"And this?" Cray motioned around him. "Your doing or theirs?"

Darius smiled without humor. "Both. Seems they brought a five-hundred-man army as an honor guard—I am sure with other intentions. Sean San Ghant is here, sowing seeds of trouble again." He glanced around the area, realizing he hadn't seen him in a while. "When they didn't offer up my wife, we attacked."

"Have you found her?"

Darius groaned with exhaustion. He couldn't think straight. He barely sensed his own power. He struggled to hold his grief in check. "No. We haven't. Maybe they took her up the pass."

"You need to rest, my Lord. I have fresh troops." Cray motioned around. "We can finish off this skirmish and find out what they are doing here and where your wife is."

Evening came early in the mountains, and the sky began turning dark. Without warning, down the mountain behind the Arc camp came another group of men.

"Who is that?" Darius asked out loud.

"More troops from Arc, I surmise. It seems they might have been planning a little more than an honor guard." Cray frowned, dark lines showing on his forehead. "Now the battle won't be so easy. I think it's best to plan tonight and attack in the light of day tomorrow."

Darius just wanted to find his beloved. "No. We attack now."

Cray saluted and ordered the ranks to form up. The fresh men rode out in front, getting to the enemy before their troops arrived down the pass.

Men fought from horseback and the ground. Sounds of swords striking and men's yells filled the valley and echoed off the walls of the steep cliffs. Cray had brought with him a company of archers, who began to decimate the Arc troops.

Soon their enemy's reinforcements arrived, and they, too, had archers, who began pushing back the Realm army. They battled deep in the night; however, at some point both sides slowed to a stop. The dead littered the ground, the wounded still groaning. All suffered exhaustion. The battle was not going to be won that evening.

Cray's men, to speed their ride, had little provisions with them. Cray sent a few men back to Sur to procure more food. Some men set up a makeshift tent for the King. Darius stumbled inside hardly able to stand. Men helped him out of his armor and he quickly fell into a deep slumber. He dreamed of

Christine's face. He could see it but never seemed to be able to touch it. The stable presence of Thunder in his mind brought a modicum of peace. Lightning had retreated to the back of the battle without a rider and also lent the King some of her power. Finally, he was able to relax and slipped into a deep sleep.

In the morning, a group of men returned from Sur and handed out food. The enemy began forming ranks. The air, cloudy with fog hanging low over the valley, lent an air of doom to the battle.

* * * * * * * * * * * * * * * *

Off to the side, Sean had stayed hidden from the battle the previous day. He found himself now in a precarious situation involving enemies on both sides. Not for the first time that day did he curse the Preacher and his plans. This was a disaster. Darius didn't trust him, which Sean felt very little remorse about. He didn't care what the upstart King thought about him. Bronwyn, on the other hand, was going to be his ticket to invading the Realm and establishing chaos to hand to the Preacher. Still confused on what had happened, he tried to piece together a new plan, one that kept him alive.

Darius had been ranting about the abduction of his wife, but Bronwyn had been as surprised as Sean about the information. Another player had entered the mix, and Sean planned to find out who it was. His best bet would be to side with Bronwyn.

Sean caught the sounds of battle beginning again. The King's men were on the offensive against the prince. He went to the battlefield to find Bronwyn and assure him of his loyalty. The battled roared around him. Twice he had to duck from being hit by a stray arrow. The two sides fought each other fiercely on horseback, hacking away at each other's army.

In the middle of the foray, Sean spotted Darius on his white horse, flashing with brilliance through the fog. His golden sword glowed with power.

Sean, not dressed in Realm attire, was attacked by a soldier from Anikari. Paring his way around the man, he left him bleeding and clutching his side.

Looking around, he saw Bronwyn. The prince had fallen from his horse and fought off a trio of enemy soldiers. Sean joined in.

"The traitor returns," Prince Bronwyn spat.

"I am not a traitor, my Lord. I had nothing to do with the King's men, the taking of his wife, or this new army." Sean swatted away a sword strike and dove into the battle, eliminating one of the men attacking the prince. "My intentions with you have always been clear."

"I should never trust a man who is willing to sell out his own kingdom." The prince continued to fight off his attackers, taking a slice across his arm. He returned it with a stab to the gut. One more fell. "I still don't even know who you are working for."

Sean and the prince fought the last remaining attacker together. The two of them pushed him toward a drop-off. A small ravine went down thirty feet at the edge of the battlefield. The Realm soldier was quick but no match for two trained swordsmen. Down went the third man.

Sean heard a loud yell and turned toward its source. Darius had seen the two of them and began pushing through the crowd. Everyone else fell away from his advance. Desperation seized Sean's mind. The next moments would determine his fate.

"My benefactor will hold all of the Realm, letting you take the fertile grounds of Sur."

The prince breathed deeply, still holding his sword in his hand. "What if I want more?"

Sean's eyes opened wide. "More? Don't be greedy, Bronwyn. And don't be a fool." Sean didn't want the plan to fall apart. "Take what you are given. The man who gives it to you is more powerful than your entire army."

The fighting moved closer to them with Darius nearing them. Sean smiled at the opportunity. The two of them could take him and end this folly.

The prince laughed. "How is one man more powerful than my army?"

Sean grew angry at the prince's doubts, and Darius was almost there. Seconds away. "He is a wizard more powerful than the King. Don't cross him."

Bronwyn lunged at him just as Darius arrived. "You are in league with those blasted evil sorcerers. I knew you were a traitor." The prince swung his sword at Sean.

Sean jumped back and brought his sword in front of him with both hands. Back and forth they went. Sean pushed the prince back, but then with a desperate move, the prince rolled in front of him under Sean's sword and hit him in the knees, taking him to the ground, the deep ravine mere inches away.

Sean tried to stand, but the prince, bigger than him, rolled on top. Sean's sword fell to his side. Prince Bronwyn brought his sword high in the air, aiming at Sean's head.

"Traitor. Now justice will be done. " Bronwyn began to bring the sword down on Sean.

His life would be ended in a valley in the Superstition Mountains. No glory. No power. No rule. *What a waste,* Sean thought. He closed his eyes, bracing for the killing blow.

It never came.

Sean San Ghant opened his eyes again and saw Darius, now off his horse, blocking the prince's killing stroke. Sean was amazed. Why would he do that for him? Sean had hated Darius his entire life, teased him, kidnapped him, turned traitor against him.

"Why?" Sean yelled. "Why?" Why would a man that he hated and detested save his life?

Darius was busy fighting off the prince's attack. Sweat poured down his face. His purple cape fluttered behind him, hanging over armor and thick clothes. His sword glowed brighter, and the King pushed the prince back.

Bronwyn tripped and fell to the ground, much in the same position as Sean had just been in. Time slowed for Sean. He peered around the battlefield. Hundreds lay dead, but the battled raged on. Wounded horses and men lay across the valley, but strangely it was only the three of them left alone to determine the fate of the battle.

Sean sucked in a quick breath and yelled at Darius again. He needed an answer. "Why did you stop him from killing me?'

Darius, keeping his sword at the neck of his enemy, shifted his attention to Sean. "It's not his right to condemn you, Sean San Ghant. As much as I think you were part of this plot, you are not the power behind it. It's the Preacher. It's him I want. The prince does not have a right to kill you. You are still a noble member of the Realm and my responsibility. I will decide your fate." His face was wolfish, but his eyes held some compassion. "I am not the same person you kidnapped and brought into the cave months ago."

Sean was drained of energy and sunk back to the ground. He didn't know what to think. He had never warranted such attention or compassion. All he had believed about Darius came into question. In one swift act, his nemesis had shifted his whole outlook on life.

"What about him?" he said, arms pointing to the prince.

"I will not kill him. At least not until I get more answers." Darius motioned two soldiers to tie the prince's hands.

The ground began shaking violently. Rocks starting to move around them, coming up out of the ground and forming small barriers around the fighting.

Sean studied Darius, and the young King shook his head, signaling that he didn't know what was happening. It wasn't his power causing the quake. The rolling continued until two people rode down into the valley. They glowed with power. The fighting had ceased with all men from both sides watching the two newcomers ride full speed toward Darius, Bronwyn, and Sean.

Darius kept his sword drawn, power crackling on its tip. Two men held the prince tight between them.

Up rode the two wizards Sean had seen at the lodge weeks before: the old man with his green cape and gray beard and the young girl, barely of age to be out on her own, with her short, blonde hair, flushed cheeks, and determined gaze.

They continued riding, stopping directly in front of Darius. The horses were breathing hard. The girl noticed her brother being held and brought her hand up in front of her. The earth exploded at the guard's feet, knocking them over. The prince tried to move, but Darius intervened. He blasted a powerful wind at the girl. The guards stood up and grabbed the prince again. He fought against them but was held tight.

"Stop this now!" the older man shouted. Flinging his arms in the air he stilled all motion. He sent the girl a grave look, and she subsided.

"King Darius DarSan Williams, I presume." The man spoke in a deep booming voice.

Darius nodded. "And who might you be?"

"I am High Wizard Olan Sallir, personal advisor to King Anwar of the Kingdom of Arc."

"And her?" Darius motioned to the girl.

Olan smiled and held in a laugh. "Oh. She is my headstrong apprentice, Danijela Anwar. A growing earth wizard, daughter of the King, and younger sister to Prince Bronwyn, whom you hold behind you." Olan examined the prince and frowned. Turning back to Darius, he smiled. "I am sure this was not the reception you had planned."

Darius, who still looked angry, let out a deep breath. "It is well to make your acquaintance, High Wizard. I've heard of you." Darius held on to diplomacy by a thread. "Your prince here has abducted my wife, the queen."

"I did not," the prince said, sounding defiant.

"I will speak to you in a minute." Olan dismissed the Prince with a wave of his hand.

Darius continued. "Eyewitnesses saw men in black, garbed in the Kingdom of Arc's battle attire, attack my wife and carry her off. We came to meet the prince as previously arranged for a friendly meeting. Your prince had over five hundred men waiting here with him."

The High Wizard looked at Bronwyn and raised his eyebrows. "Seems like a lot of men for an honor guard to meet the new King of the Realm, my Prince. I remember your father directing a few dozen."

"You still attacked him on our soil." Danijela's first words were directed toward Darius.

"He took my wife." Darius gritted his teeth. The ground quivered slightly at his retort.

Olan glanced around a moment then back to the King. Men had begun to retreat back to their own sides, stepping over the small rock walls that had been erected.

"A lot of bodies fill this valley, King Darius. The young lady does have a point."

"I had reinforcements arrive when they heard of an army building up in the pass. Then shortly afterward, another battalion of Arc soldiers came down the pass just ahead of your arrival." Darius pointed to the soldiers. "They had obviously been directed ahead of time."

Olan glared at Bronwyn. "A fine mess you have gotten us into, my Prince. You will be taken back to your father."

"High Wizard, with full respect, I cannot let you take him back until I find out about my wife. He will be a prisoner of the Realm, though I will let his remaining men leave in peace."

Men from both sides started to tense up and move farther away from the small gathering. The young wizard lifted her hands once again; the rocks once more rose up and flowed together. Dirt and trees began to fall, and a wall erected itself between the two camps.

"Don't do me any favors, sister," Bronwyn shouted. "All of you wizards are an abomination. No one should have that much power." He pulled away from the guards and ran toward the group along the edge of the ravine. His unfocused and wild eyes missed seeing a large root sticking out of the ground. With no warning at all, the prince tripped on the root, his speed carrying his body off the cliff and down the embankment. His wailing echoed off of the walls until he landed with a distant thud on the rocky bottom.

"No, Bronwyn!" Danijela yelled, jumping off her horse and running to the edge of the ravine. Tears filled her eyes and surprise and frustration filled the other men standing close by. She sat staring into the deep opening while everyone else stood still.

Danijela stood, turned around, and faced Darius. Her young eyes, red and blurred with tears, burned at him. She lifted her arms, and fire crackled from the foggy sky. Elements of earth began to gather around her, and her brother's body lifted out of the ravine, settling onto a cleared patch of dirt in front of the group.

Sean wanted nothing more than to be farther away from this dangerous group of wizards. He began to back away. Darius glimpsed him moving and shook his head. Without much thought, Sean found himself obeying and stopped. He watched as Darius walked with slow but deliberate steps toward the young girl. She bristled and stiffened as he entered her personal space. With gentleness, he wrapped his arms around her, closed his eyes, and held her. Rigid at first and crying, she eventually relaxed and fell into his arms.

The small group gasped. Sean was certain they all felt a calmness and tranquility reach into their hearts, just as he did. Swords lowered, deep breaths were taken, and the battle ended. Sean found tears coming to his own eyes as he gasped in admiration and wonder at his King.

Lowering himself to the ground on one knee, Sean, with newfound respect in his eyes, gazed up at his King, still amazed his life had been spared. He had never known such feelings of devotion before. His heart was open and bare. There was only one thing to do.

In a voice raw with emotion, Sean bowed to his King and stated, "Darius DarSan Williams, King of the Realm and wizard of the heart, I pledge my life to your service as your humble servant until the end of my days."

* * * * * * * * * * * * * * *

Chapter Thirteen
FRIENDS REUNITED

The day after the battle in the mountain pass, Darius sat in a room of the mayor of Sur's office. Gathered around a table with him was Roland, who had arrived with Jakob and the rest of the Cremelinos, High Wizard Sallir, Danijela Anwar, and Cray Dreydon. They would have to send word to the King of Arc about his son Bronwyn.

The group had just eaten a light lunch of open-faced roast sandwiches with gravy and slices of melon. So far there was not much talk. Everyone was exhausted, and frustration and anger still hung in the air between the two kingdoms.

"I've sent the rest of Prince Bronwyn's men back to Herro except for a small group of loyal soldiers I have kept with me," the High Wizard informed Darius.

"Herro isn't very far away. What is to stop them from coming back as soon as we leave?" Darius still hadn't found any clues to his wife's disappearance or why the prince had brought so many men to the border.

"You have my word as representative of the King of Arc that they will not return."

"A King whose son may have captured my wife but in the least had other plans of invasion into my realm."

Olan's voice rose, but he maintained control. "Young Bronwyn's views did not reflect the views of his father. He was young and brash. The men were following his orders, and may I remind you that some of those orders came from sources inside your realm."

Darius groaned inside and put his hand out to settle the High Wizard down. "Forgive me. I am exhausted and not thinking clearly. I do take responsibility for Sean San Ghant as a member of the Realm. It appears he was part of the plans of an old nemesis of mine, known as the Preacher. He is a wizard of evil, learning his trade among a sect in the eastern kingdoms. He tried to take Belor, and now he has broadened his plans of chaos. We do seem to be trying to find a path for peace."

"May I make a suggestion, my Lord?" Cray asked Darius.

Darius nodded his head in assent and took a drink from his glass.

"This is not going to be solved today. You need rest."

Darius began to interrupt, but Cray continued. "You need rest to be able to think. I know you want your wife back, but you are King of the entire Realm. Word has come in just an hour ago that another army is forming on the border of Gildan across from Denir."

Darius slammed his fist down. "I thought Mezar had things under control in Gildan."

"It appears our neighbors are testing the new King of the Realm." Cray said. "How will you meet these tests, young wizard?"

Darius laughed out loud. "You give good advice. You are right as always. How will I meet these tests? I am young and untrained, and so they all push against me. The Preacher in Mar, the Arcs in Sur, the Gildanians in Denir." He paused for a moment to think.

Rest, my young wizard. Things will work out for you. Just remember where your power comes from. Thunder interrupted the King's thoughts. *Help is on the way.*

"Help from where? Do you know where my wife is?"

No, we still cannot feel her presence. Lightning intruded in the conversation. Darius could sense the sadness in her heart.

Send the young girl wizard to us before she leaves, Thunder said.

Darius smiled and stood up. "I am going to rest for a bit. You all should also. It has been a long few days, and I am afraid things are going to get worse before they get better. Rooms have been arranged for all of you at the mayor's lodge." He turned to Cray. "General, before you rest, send out some fresh men to once again study the area where the queen was taken and ask around for any more information. If we can believe them, both the prince and Sean say they had no knowledge of the abduction."

They all stood and bowed to the King.

"Danijela." Darius put his hand softly on her arm. "Stay for a minute please."

The young girl glanced at her mentor. He nodded.

After the others left, Danijela looked expectantly at the young King. "My Lord, have I offended you?"

Darius smiled, "No, no. You intrigue me. Your power out in the mountain pass was impressive. Your ability to reshape rock and the earth . . ."

"Pretty amazing huh?" She smiled, seeming almost younger than her sixteen years.

"I must admit, I am still a novice when it comes to my power, but what you did, I cannot even comprehend."

"It comes with the power of the earth I am told. I, too, am just a young apprentice, only taken in with the High Wizard this past year," Danijela said.

"Apprentice or not, you obviously have the makings of one of the most powerful wizards in the west."

Danijela laughed and twirled around, her cape flowing behind her. "That is what I am told. Won't it be fun?" There was a sparkle of amusement in her eyes.

Darius couldn't help laughing also. "It won't all be fun and games. Power is dangerous if not used in the proper way."

The girl grew somber. "I know. My brother was afraid and didn't trust it. Look what happened to him."

"I am sorry about that. I was angry at him, but truly I would not have wished him dead like that."

"In my moment of anger and sadness, you held me. That was amazing. The comfort you sent into my being was beyond my powers. Thank you."

"A wizard of the heart does have some advantages, even if I can't create walls out of rock."

There was an awkward silence for a moment.

"The main reason I wanted to speak to you is this: I want our kingdoms to be allies. I don't want hatred or fear to govern us. We both have the ability to do tremendous damage to one another."

The girl started to say something, but Darius stalled her with his hands. "As a token of my appreciation and by their consent and asking, one of the Cremelinos has chosen you to bond with. "

Danijela's eyes misted over, and she covered her mouth with her hands. She bobbed a short bow. "I don't know what to say. I've read about them in my histories, but I never knew the Cremelinos of the Realm still bonded like old times."

"You have books about them?" Darius was excited. "All I know is from what they tell me themselves, and they aren't forthcoming about things very often."

Darius felt a brief flicker of amusement in his mind.

"In the time of the founding of most of our kingdoms hundreds of years ago, the Cremelinos were companions to the wizards," Danijela said. "Each wizard had one to bond to. They gave their master power and strength in times of need and shared information among each other even over long distances. They are a race predating many of our western civilizations. They are the guardians of our land."

"Once again I find that I have a lot to learn." Darius made himself a note to discuss with his Cremelino the sharing of power.

Thunder and Lightning sent their approval through their bond with him.

"The Cremelinos already think highly of you, earth wizard," Darius said.

"You just talked to them?" Danijela asked excitedly.

"Yes, I did, in my mind. Now I need to rest if I am going to be any good to anyone, but the Cremelinos would like you to go to the stables with them."

Danijela bowed again. "This treasure will not go unrewarded, my Lord. My father will hear of your generosity. Just let us know when you need our help, and we will be there."

Darius and Danijela headed out of the room, she going one way, Darius the other. He almost ran into his captain commander.

"I am sorry to disturb you, my Lord." Roland was almost out of breath. "A group of men and a lady just arrived. They appear, ah, shall I say, like thieves or mercenaries. They say they have an urgent message for you."

"I guess sleep will have to wait, Roland. Did they give names?"

"One with a slight Gildan accent said to tell you that your old prisoner has returned." Roland frowned. "What does that mean?"

"Mezar is what it means." Darius hurried down the hall toward the reception room. "The prince and second in line to the throne of Gildan."

"Oh!" was all Roland said, obviously taken by surprise.

Darius entered the room and saw a group of men dressed as Roland had explained. They did look either like thieves or mercenaries. A pretty girl stood next to them with short dark hair and dark eyes. Her lips turned upward in a warm smile as he walked into the room.

"Darius," she said. Roland's brow furrowed.

"My King" she added.

"Leandra, good to see you again. You look well. And I see you brought some friends with you."

Mezar stepped out from behind the larger men; his muscular but slender body was much smaller. His black hair was down around his shoulders, unlike the ponytail he had worn as Darius's prisoner earlier in the year.

Darius ran to his prisoner-turned-friend and gave him a hug. "What are you doing here? We were planning to be in Gildan next month."

Mezar smiled at seeing his friend, but then returned to his grave look. "There are troubles in Gildan."

"I have heard of troops on the border. What is the meaning of that, Mezar? I thought you were going to take care of things in Gildan."

Mezar cringed. "That is a long story. First, is Christine here with you?"

Darius grew solemn and gathered his emotions before speaking. "No, Mezar, she has been abducted by the Kingdom of Arc, but we don't have any clues and cannot find out any information about her. My guards are combing the area again."

"I thought to get here in time," Mezar groaned.

"What do you mean?"

"Can we meet in private, please?" Mezar asked.

Darius had a dire impression overtake him. What did Mezar know about his wife? Was she still alive? Every time he thought of her, he was almost taken to his knees in grief and pain. Thoughts of her running in the rain with him in the forest around Anikari and finding their Field of Diamonds. Thoughts of seeing her pleasure when he gave her Lightning. Thoughts of her kissing him for the first time and running his fingers through her soft, golden hair. Pain when he remembered their year apart and what it had almost cost both of them.

With an aching heart, putting his grief into a small corner of his mind, he nodded to Roland to clear the room. After everyone had left, the two young men sat on stuffed, high-backed chairs. They were centered around a fireplace glowing with a small fire. The late autumn chill had begun to set in this close to the mountains.

Darius motioned to offer Mezar a drink. Mezar shook his head.

"My Lord, my friend," the prince of Gildan began. "Gildan has taken your wife."

Darius was struck with a blow he had not anticipated. He leaned his head back and closed his eyes, forcing the tears away for the hundredth time in the past week.

"How? Why?" the young King tried to say.

"When I say Gildan, I really mean my father, the general of our armies and heir to the throne of Gildan. He is slowly poisoning his father, the Emperor, and he has abducted your wife as well."

"But why, Mezar? What does he hope to accomplish?" Darius raised his voice louder and in anger. "And why didn't you know about this or warn me earlier?" Darius glared at Mezar. Maybe he wasn't what he pretended to be. Maybe he wasn't a friend. A powerful young wizard in his own right, maybe he had tricked Darius.

Mezar leaned forward to the edge of his chair. "You must believe me, Darius. I had nothing to do with this. My father tried to kill me, and I barely escaped. He is mad with desire for power. He intends to take over the empire and the Realm."

Darius stood in fury. "Why does everyone want the Realm? My realm? Her people are not for sale or to be captured. If Arc, Gildan, the Preacher, or any other group or kingdom try to take her, they will face serious consequences." Bright light erupted from his hand and smashed a table into pieces. A wind wiped around the room, blowing out the fire and darkening the area where they sat. "I may be a young King, but I can be a dangerous one!"

Mezar jumped out of his seat. Darius turned on him. His eyes were unfocused, and he sent forth a bolt of fire. In his mad grief, Darius lashed out at anyone and everything in the room. Mezar pushed the incoming fire away from him with a bout of air.

"Darius. Listen to me!" he yelled.

Darius stood, chest heaving with exertion, fuming at Mezar, and thinking of his next move.

"I can help you find your wife. I know my father's places and his people," Mezar pleaded.

"My wife!" Darius's eyes cleared, and he came out of his rage, realizing what he had done. He groaned and sunk back into the cushioned chair. Tears came unbidden and uncontrolled to his eyes, running in streams down his haggard face.

The door to the room opened with a soft creak, and Roland stuck his head in.

"Your King needs to rest," was all Mezar said.

Roland nodded, went to a corner, and found a rough blanket. He put it tenderly over his weeping King.

Mezar and Roland slowly backed out of the room. They were about to close the door when Darius whispered Mezar's name.

"Mezar. I am sorry. Forgive me."

"Always, my friend." Mezar smiled. "Now get some rest. We'll talk again later." He closed the door softly.

Darius, alone with his grief and pain, tried to think of solutions, but his thoughts drifted aimlessly, and in a matter of moments, he fell asleep.

* * * * * * * * * * * * * * *

Chapter Fourteen
RAPP

Rapp moved deep into the Guild of Thieves' territory. Even though they tried to influence the entire city, there were places that were solely under their control. The governor's Merchants' Guild had been growing in strength, and the Thieves' Guild was having a harder time finding corrupt people to deal with.

Luckily for him, once again most people tended to ignore a small-looking boy wandering around. He had left his hair messy, which wasn't much different from his normal style, and his clothes were ragged and torn. Though educated in the governor's household, he could without much thought revert back to the language of the slums.

Begging for pieces of bread earned him a hard glare from a guild guard, so he moved on. He had been searching for the last week for the mysterious Berlain that Kelln wanted to find for Alessandra, the same woman whose father tried to kill them the prior week. He didn't always understand why nobles or government officials did what they did, but he was up for the challenge.

Bits and snippets of information he had gleaned were starting to come together. There indeed had been a lady named Berlain who'd been born in Mar but had left to Belor as the wife of the man now known as Mr. El'Lan or the Preacher. At one point, she had left him and their young daughter to return to Mar for reasons unexplained. Rapp, having met the Preacher a few times firsthand, could surmise why she left. He did not seem like a very nice person.

"Hey, get out of my way, boy," a man yelled at Rapp as he exited the back door of an old building. Rapp feigned to move away, but as he did so, he stuck a small piece of wood between the door and the frame, stopping it from closing all the way and locking.

Once the man disappeared around a corner, no longer concerned with the apparent street urchin, Rapp opened the door, removed the wood, and let himself in to a large dark room. Lights in the distance down a hallway sent eerie shadows along the walls. He wound his way carefully down the hallway until he heard voices. Trying the knob to a door, he slipped inside another room. It was full of boxes of parchment and scrolls, labeled by year and month. A small dirty window in the room gave enough light for Rapp to read. The find was astounding.

Rapp had found records and proof of the guild's dealings for years. This would be invaluable to the governor to legally shut down the Guild of Thieves for good, but he closed the lid and moved back to listen at the door. The records were not why he was there that day.

The voices receded, and Rapp went out into the hallway again. The halls and doors began to be cleaner and nicer. He rounded a corner and found himself entering the back of the kitchen. His stomach growled just to be around the potential meal. A growing boy, he had a hard time not constantly being hungry. Peeking around the room, he stepped out and reached for an apple sitting in a bowl.

"Hey, what are you doing?" An older lady in an apron came around a corner and caught Rapp red-handed. "How did you get in here anyway?"

A quick solution raced through Rapp's mind, and he put on his childish slum accent. "Just one of the runners, ma'am." The Guild of Thieves had young boys run errands like any other guild.

The woman relaxed. "Well, if you don't have anything else to do but to grab some fruit, why don't you run an errand for me? The guildmaster is meeting with some men, and they are hungry. You can help me bring them the food."

Rapp couldn't believe his luck. Of course, he hoped the guildmaster or any of the men he was meeting with wouldn't recognize him.

"Can I clean up a bit first?" he asked.

The woman smiled. "Want to make a good impression on the old man, huh?"

"Yeah. I want him to notice me. I wanna work for him as a thief someday." Rapp put on his best smile to cover his lies.

The cook laughed. "Well, you better do better than trying to steal some apples from under my nose. Go wash up. There is a room at the side of the kitchen with some decent clothes."

Rapp took a few minutes to clean his face and change clothes. Now he looked more like a young servant. Servants were ignored almost as much as street urchins. He took the platter of food from the cook and headed down the hall. Not knowing where to go, he followed some faint voices until he came to a partially opened doorway.

His contacts had told him that the guildmaster's headquarters were here. It was said that the man used to have a daughter named Berlain. Rapp was hoping it was the same Berlain that the ambassador had asked him to find.

He glimpsed inside and tried to keep from being seen. A lady stood with her back to him, middle-aged and dressed in fashionable attire. She blocked the face of the man who sat in a chair in front of her.

"Father, you wanted to see me?" the lady said.

"A dangerous man is here in town. I think you need to leave and go into hiding again."

"We have been through this before. I am done hiding. I have a right to be your heir and to earn respect in the trade before you die."

"You realize I have protected you all these years. You will take my place, hopefully still a long way off, though." The man chuckled and then started coughing in violent bursts.

"What is the danger?" the lady said.

"Your ex-husband has been asking around about you, Berlain."

Rapp watched the woman move over to the man. His nerves almost made him drop his tray. It was the Guild of Thieves' guildmaster himself, and by their conversation, he spoke to his daughter.

"What is he doing here?"

"From what I have heard, his plans in Belor didn't work out, and now he comes to sow discontent in Mar. He was never one to leave trouble alone." The guildmaster raised his voice. "He is trying to form his own guild by amassing the smaller ones. He is ruthless and has hidden agendas."

"I am not afraid of him anymore, Father."

The man smoothed the wrinkles out of his pants and then looked back up, as if trying to think of what to say. "His daughter is here with him."

"His daughter?" The woman turned to the side, and Rapp recognized someone who had aged well. She still wore her dark hair down, though most likely dyed to keep the gray out, yet her face was marred only by a few wrinkles. She looked familiar. "You mean our daughter?"

"You gave her up when you left him," the guildmaster said cruelly.

Berlain gasped. "I left her with her father. That was the best for her at the time."

"I have spoken to her, but she did not know who I was."

Berlain gasped and fell into a nearby chair. "You did not tell her where I was, did you?"

"No. No. I pretended I had heard your name long ago. It seems she and her father have come to some kind of agreement. She will try and steer the ambassador and governor away from the guilds if she is able to meet you."

"She wants to meet me . . . after all these years?" Berlain spoke to herself then went into silent thought for a moment. . "Did she look well?"

"Berlain, you cannot be thinking of meeting her." The guildmaster's voice boomed. "You must leave as I told you to."

"Maybe just once." Berlain paused. "It would be nice to get the attention of the ambassador and the governor away from us."

The guildmaster sat in silence. Rapp took the opportunity to walk into the room as if he hadn't been standing there listening. The old man motioned for Rapp to put the food on a table in front of his chair. As Rapp had thought, the man didn't pay much attention to him.

He glanced at the woman, memorizing her features, a plan forming in his mind. He needed to get back to Kelln. Voices behind him indicated more people arriving. Berlain stood up as if to go.

"We will talk later, Berlain," the guildmaster said to his daughter.

Rapp looked over his shoulder for a moment, then turned back to his task. One of the men entering the room had been the one trying to talk to the ambassador when Rapp had first intervened with Tali at the dress stall in the market. He didn't know if the man would recognize him or not.

Quickly, he finished setting out the food then backed away toward the door, trying to keep his face hidden. Just as he was to the door, the old man called for him.

"Boy, bring us some wine."

Rapp glanced up at them out of habit. "Yes, sir."

The other men looked at him and continued seating themselves. Then the man he had recognized whipped his head around. "I have seen you before."

Rapp shook his head. His heart pounded. He would have a hard time outrunning these men without a diversion. He was thick in the Guild of Thieves' headquarters. He would be lucky to get out alive.

"Your mop of hair." The man appeared deep in thought, as if trying to remember. All of a sudden, his eyes cleared. "The ambassador."

That was all it took for Rapp to decide it was time to leave. He threw the empty platter of dishes and food, causing a moment of chaos. He turned, slammed the door shut, and ran down the hall, the same way he had come from the kitchen. He only had a few seconds' head start.

He ran through the kitchen, the cook trying to stop him, but he sped past, zig-zagging through the halls to the back door. Multiple sets of feet pursued him close behind.

Opening the door to the outside, he continued running. Just as the men came out of the building, he ran into the back of another one. Not knowing where he was, he almost fell into a pool of water. It was a bathhouse. And not just any bathhouse, but a women's one. His eyes opened wide as women stood and sat around two pools of water. He looked down quickly, cheeks turning red, and ran as quick as he could through the room. He heard loud laughter behind him.

Running out to the front room, he found clothes hanging on a peg. He grabbed a robe and slipped it on, pulling a hood around his head. He sat in a chair and turned it toward the wall. He hoped his crude disguise would work. The men raced into the room. All they found was a young woman sitting in a corner with a hood and robe.

"Did you see a boy run through here?" one of the men asked.

Rapp, in his best girl voice, said, "No."

He could feel the man's eyes on the back of his head and heard him take a few steps toward him.

"You men are not allowed in here," a woman said, coming into the room. "Get out."

The men tried to tell her what they were looking for, but the woman took no excuses. They were shooed out without any further explanation.

Rapp breathed in a deep breath of air.

The woman came over to Rapp and turned him around. Hands on her hips she frowned at him. "Now what are you doing here? Not sneaking in to see the girls are you?"

Rapp blushed profusely. Gross! He didn't want to see any naked women. "No, ma'am."

He didn't know if the woman believed him, but she scolded him, took off the robe he had been using, and shooed him out. By then, the men had gone farther down the street, and Rapp was able to slip off in the other direction.

An hour later, he informed Kelln he had in fact found Berlain and that she was the Guild of Thieves' guildmaster's daughter. Kelln couldn't believe it.

Kelln told Rapp he had a plan to get Alessandra to see her mother, but it would require keeping the guildmaster himself busy at the time so as not to interfere. They also needed to keep the Preacher away from his daughter for a time.

They decided to meet that night with Tali and her father and discuss the plans.

* * * * * * * * * * * * * * *

Christine tried to eat, but she had no appetite. She was bloated and sick every morning now. Her clothes were already becoming tighter on her. Finally, the general had called in a doctor to examine her. He couldn't very well negotiate with a dead or sickly queen.

The doctor was a lady, which was unusual for Christine. In the Realm, all doctors were men. Christine watched her walk into the room. She seemed to be her mother's age, but the eyes said she was older. A thin-boned woman, she was shorter than Christine with graying dark hair and a light brown face. She greeted Christine with a smile.

"Oh my. Aren't you a lovely girl?" the woman said in the language of the Realm but with a slight accent. "The general said I needed to see you. Something about not eating properly and getting sick. Your face is pale. Come and sit down on this chair next to me."

Christine smiled and almost laughed for the first time in a week. This lady liked to talk. Maybe she could get some information out of her. She already knew what the doctor would find. She just hoped she could keep it secret from the general a while longer.

"So nice to have someone else visit me," Christine said. "What is your name? Mine is Christine."

The woman frowned. "Oh, I don't want to know your name, young miss. The general swore me to secrecy, and I don't want to disappoint him. You can guess what happens to people that disappoint the general." The woman didn't stop for an answer. "They disappear. Bad thing, I say. Now let's take a look at you."

The lady ran her hands over Christine's body. A power from the lady tingled over her body. "You're a wizard?"

"Of course I'm a wizard. All doctors in Gildan are wizards. Where are you from, anyway, that you wouldn't know that?" Again, she didn't stop for an answer. "Oh, I can see by your blonde hair that you are not from around here. Where are you from? No, don't tell me. I can't know those things."

The woman smiled, told Christine to stand up, and ran her hands over her belly. "Well my dear, there is nothing wrong with you."

"Oh, I know that."

The doctor seemed surprised by the admission.

"You're pregnant. You're going to have a baby. Can't tell if it's a boy or girl yet. Strange, but I should be able to tell by this point, but I'm getting mixed signals. Do you know who the father is? Well, of course you do. But don't tell me," the lady babbled.

Christine knew who the father was. It could be none other than Darius, the only man she had ever been with. Drops of moisture fell from her eyelids. He would be so happy at the news.

The old wizard doctor came over and patted her head. "Now, dearie, don't cry. You'll be fine. I'll make sure you take some herbs that will help the sickness and keep both of you healthy. You must eat well and exercise and stay positive."

Christine sat up. The doctor had misunderstood her tears for sadness other than her memories of Darius. "How can I exercise? I am locked in this room all day long. How can I stay positive? I am being held prisoner. My husband doesn't know where I am, and the general has threatened to use me to take over the Realm."

"No, no, no," the wizard wailed. "You cannot tell me these things; I told you that." She held her hands over her ears. "Now I am doomed. I know too much."

Christine took the woman's hands in hers, looked her directly in the eyes, her own still full of tears, and whispered, "You could help me escape."

"No, no. I can't do that. Were you not listening to me? I won't live another day if the general finds out."

"My husband can protect you. He is also friends with Prince Mezar." Christine wiped her tears away, feeling hope for the first time since being taken.

The lady put her fingers to her lips. "You must not mention the general's son. He has done something and escaped."

"Please help me?" Christine begged the lady. "Don't you think it would be wrong for my husband to never see his child?"

"And who is your husband?" The doctor paused. "No. Don't tell me," she amended.

"He is Darius DarSan Williams, King of the Realm."

The lady, for being a wizard and all, didn't have much control. "Oh no. No, no. What have you gotten me into?" Her face contorted with anguish.

A knock sounded on the door, and a servant entered. "My lady." He spoke to Christine. "The general would like you to dine with him tonight."

Christine looked afraid and glanced at the doctor for help.

The doctor took a deep breath and tried to compose herself. “Inform the general I will dine with the two of them tonight also. The lady needs to take care of herself. I will work with her to make sure she is eating properly.”

The servant nodded and left.

Christie hugged the doctor. “Thank you.”

The doctor smiled in a resigned fashion. “Pray your husband finds us soon. I don’t know how long I can keep myself alive.”

* * * * * * * * * * * * * * *

Chapter Fifteen
HISTORY OF THE CREMELINOS

Darius paced the library in the governor of Sur's office. It had been commandeered for his headquarters while staying in the most northwestern city of the Realm. A week ago, a sudden early winter storm blew down from the north. Temperatures plummeted, and the snow fell at a rate unheard of this time of year. The entire region was shut down.

The King was frustrated and anxious to find his wife. Between the time traveling to White Island, Sur, and the battle, it had now been almost two months since he had last seen her. He had made amends with Mezar and had apologized for his distraught behavior. While Darius had slept that first day, Mezar rode out and inspected the attack area himself. Instantly obvious to him by hoof prints in the earth, the horses were indeed from Gildan and not from Arc. The horseshoes used in Gildan, especially in the royal stables, showed a very distinct design and a slight altered state to a common shoe.

Upon hearing of this news as well as Mezar's account of what he overheard his father and the other men in Gildan saying, Darius was relieved at least to have a direction to go in. He also felt remorse for the battle that had ensued in the mountains with Prince Bronwyn over the apparent abduction.

The Gildanians under Mezar's father had done a very fine job of trying to lay blame on the Arcs.

Darius had expressed his apology to the High Wizard on this accord. Wizard Olan, however, had told the King that although his reason for battle may have been misled, the intent of the prince was to sow discord and invade. This made Darius feel a little better for his somewhat-reckless behavior. Men had still died on both sides, and as King, he would have to hold at least some responsibility for that.

Once in the last few days, Lightning communicated to Darius she had felt a strong surge of feeling from Christine. Immense joy followed by sorrow. She tried to establish more of the link, but once again the bonding crumbled. The good news was she was still alive.

"Please sit down, Sire," High Wizard Sallir said. "I am an old man, and you are making me tired just watching you wear out the carpets."

Darius gave a short smile and flopped himself in a large chair in front of the roaring fireplace. Looking out the window nearby, all he could see was white. The flakes decreased, giving him some hope, but the ground would need to be cleared or melted before they could travel again.

Olan continued. "That is a fine gift you gave to my apprentice. I am not sure if she is ready for it yet."

"It is not my choice, High Wizard. The Cremelinos have a mind and will of their own in these things." Darius felt amusement float through his bond with Thunder. "What do you know about them anyway?"

"The Cremelinos?" The High Wizard thought for a moment, apparently accessing knowledge learned long ago. "The Cremelinos are originally thought to have come from the eastern kingdoms a thousand years ago. At the time, those in the east were enlightened with magic and lived in peace with the land and each other. Fairies and other magical creatures, like the Cremelinos, flourished in this environment. All the land was ruled by a wizard's council, the wisest among the land. The population grew and spread across lush forests, deserts, highlands, and into the mountains. The unique abilities of the Cremelinos to communicate with each other and with those they bonded with were used by each of these groups of people to stay connected."

"How did a Cremelino choose who to bond to?" Darius asked, enthralled with the history.

"It is said each wizard was chosen by the herd for a specific Cremelino to bond with. This bond could not change except upon death of the wizard or the horse." The High Wizard paused to take a drink.

"That makes sense," Darius agreed. "They told me which Cremelino to take for Christine as well as the others that came with me from the island."

Mezar, who had been dozing off on the far side of the room, joined the two of them. "But how did they get so far from the eastern kingdoms?"

"You are jumping ahead, my friend." Olan winked. "As the groups of people spread across the eastern lands, they began forming kingdoms of their own. The wizards tried to keep a common governing body, but after a while, it became more and more difficult to control everyone. As the population grew, need for land, cities, and food grew. This started small skirmishes and even battles. A few wizards even began to side with these kingdoms in their own exclusive relationships, dragging their Cremelinos into the fray."

Roland came into the room and interrupted the story to tell the group clear skies were seen to the north and west, and the storm should be gone by the end of the day. The governor invited all of them to join him for dinner that evening.

"Finally, we can begin to make plans." Darius let out a sigh. "Now let's hear the rest of this story."

The High Wizard continued, "The Cremelinos were goodhearted creatures. They could not be tempted or turned to evil; however, some of the wizards were. In order to gain favor and wealth from their benefactors, men set themselves up as kings in these new lands and delved into the darker side of sorcery. They created spells and creatures that should have never been. Through the bond, the Cremelinos felt this evil and could barely stand the pain to their pure hearts."

"As you recall, I said a bond was made that could only end at death. Some of the Cremelinos started to find ways to put themselves in danger, to seek death as a means to escape the evil hearts of their masters. However, their masters found out about this and held them more in line. They started using their evil magic on them to control them and force them to communicate their evil plans with others. These wizards even drew energy from their Cremelinos to increase their powers. This was unholy and disgraceful."

Darius felt sadness through his bond that almost overwhelmed him. He swooned to the side, almost collapsing.

Mezar reached out a hand to steady him. "Darius, are you sick?"

"Thunder, my Cremelino, was not aware of all these events." Darius straightened. "He is grieved for his kind."

"The wizard council stood intact, although they lost some prestige and power over the land." Olan seemed to enjoy the storytelling. "They formed a plan with the Cremelinos without their masters knowing. They would lure them to a battle in which the wizard council would take the evil wizards captive, killing them, and destroying the evil bond. The council laid a plan to invite all the wizards in the land to an event at the Wizards' Conclave. It was thought to be an invitation to expand the council and let the other wizards take more power. All of the Cremelinos who were bonded came with their masters. Those that were not bonded were told to gather on the western shores of the land, where some of the most powerful wizards would meet with them."

"At the Wizards' Conclave, something went wrong. A traitor among them thwarted their plans to capture the evil wizards. A battle ensued, one of power and magic. Wizards on both sides died, Cremelinos perished, and the land around the conclave was left utterly desolate. Many of the Cremelinos at this time, seeing their plans to eradicate the evil wizards to be a lost cause, turned against their masters as a last resort. This was thought impossible, but their grief and pain was so deep through the bond. They reached out and, with personal pain to themselves, severed the bonds and destroy many of evil wizards' minds. At this point, the wizards took to killing their own Cremelinos before they could be destroyed themselves."

"What about those that fled?" Darius asked.

The High Wizard smiled. "Almost there, Sire. In the end, the Wizards' Conclave fell. This organization for wizards had been intact for a thousand years, helping to bring stability to these kingdoms; however, greed won out. It was supposed that some good wizards and Cremelinos had escaped but not many. Those that turned evil, though they lost their Cremelinos, became victorious and returned to their separate kingdoms with a loosely agreed upon set of rules. For many years afterward, the eastern kingdoms struggled and battled for lands and kingdoms. There are many stories from that time until now that describe how they grew into the great continent they are now, but those will have to wait for another snowstorm, I am afraid."

"So?" Darius asked again.

"So, Darius, those Cremelinos that escaped to the western shores of the continent were loaded on large ships by a few remaining wizards, men and women. They sailed across the Eastern Sea until arriving at what we know now as White Island. There were no inhabitants of the island at that time, there was fresh water and land for growing grass and grain, and it became a refuge and a place of repair for the horses for many years. Soon the herd grew, and the wizards began venturing out into the western lands. The Cremelinos' abilities were kept in strict confidences from the rulers of these early primitive lands."

Darius sat on the edge of his seat opposite the old wizard.

Olan took a sip of wine before continuing. "Gildan was much smaller then, the Realm had not been formed, and the Kingdom of Arc was basically bands of nomads. Once the original wizards died out, their descendants became the caretakers we have today. Some of them most likely have power flowing in their veins and, though not full wizards, are able to care for the horses."

"My wife is not a wizard, but she communicates with her Cremelino."

Thunder's voice answered Darius's statement before Olan could. *It was done as a favor to you, young wizard, as part of the prophecy. Your wife has enough wizard blood flowing through her veins for us to communicate with her. We needed Lightning close to you to watch over the prophecy. We recognized in you the one from the prophecy, the one that would bring us back to our glory. Now we communicate with all wizards as needed. It is a time of changing for all of us.*

Darius relayed this information to Mezar and Olan.

"Tell me the prophecy," Olan said.

Darius smiled. "I am not sure I know it all. The Cremelinos can be a little secretive. It seems I am only given bits and pieces."

Thunder sent a wave of amusement to his mind and asked Darius to touch both Mezar and Olan so he could communicate to them all.

Darius did so and Thunder spoke to them all.

Forgotten lines of ancient magic
and the power of the throne.
One will make them both his own
if his heart sees the true power.

He will bring light to fight darkness
and love to fight hate
if he reaches into the power of his heart.
He will find new allies, turn enemy to friend, and
find the binding of all power on the path of peace.

Olan sat back and smiled. "Amazing. Amazing. So this is how you speak to them?"

Darius nodded.

"I wonder what it means to 'find the binding of all power?"

Darius shook his head. He didn't understand most of what the prophecy said until after each part was fulfilled.

The High Wizard looked wistful. "You gave a very great gift to Danijela and to our kingdom. King Anwar will be happy and proud to meet with you and enact any treaties you desire. We would be happy to have you visit our esteemed capital."

Darius smiled, then frowned and sighed. "All in good time, my new friend. First, I must rescue my beloved and help Mezar reestablish peace in his empire."

Mezar bowed his head slightly to his neighboring King. "At your coronation, I pledged my support to you until the end of my days, Darius. I do not take that lightly. At first light, I will ride with my men back to Gildan. I will find your queen for you."

Darius's eyes misted over, and he thanked his good friend.

Soon Roland came back in to call them to dinner. They walked over to the large festival hall, where other nobles from the city were gathered. Cray and some of his officers had also been invited. What surprised and somewhat worried Darius was when he saw Danijela enter, hanging on Sean's arm. Sean looked his way and smiled. It was not the scornful smile he usually had for Darius through the years, but a smile of peace. Darius still didn't trust the man who had betrayed him too often and who had caused much pain to him personally. For now, he would keep a close eye on him and especially his interest in the young wizard girl.

The feast was a scrumptious affair with roasted pork and gravy, freshly baked bread, fall vegetables, and plenty of drink to go around. The group on the whole seemed to enjoy themselves, though Darius sat a little somber, thinking of his wife and kingdom.

Mezar excused himself early, saying he was firm on his pledge to leave in the morning. Darius followed him out to inform him that the Cremelinos requested his presence in the stables. With mild curiosity, the two friends did as requested.

Once there, a young male Cremelino strode toward Mezar and nuzzled up against him. Mezar's face registered shock.

"He has chosen me. I never thought . . ." Turning to Darius, he asked, "Did you know?"

Darius shook his head. "I was asked to bring these Cremelinos with me, but they wouldn't tell me why. One went to a young wizard girl in Mar, one to me, one to Danijela, and now one to you. Each has chosen us in turn."

"I wonder who the remaining two are for." Mezar said.

Darius did not know. "What will you name him?'

Mezar thought a moment and then said, "Star. He shines like the brightest star in my homeland."

Darius and Mezar spent a few more minutes with all of the Cremelinos. Thunder had communicated recently with Radiance and informed Darius of Kelln's findings on Alessandra's mother. Kelln still didn't know how to reach the Preacher without getting himself killed. Darius was just happy that, for the time being, the Preacher seemed to not be more of a problem, though he still felt uncomfortable with not having the man in a prison.

"So now we are able to communicate in Mar with Tali and Kelln, here in Sur or Arc with Danijela, wherever you go in Gildan, and with me." Darius mouth went wide in a broad smile. Things were definitely looking up.

"Just like the old days." Mezar moved his hand over the smooth mane of his new Cremelino one more time. "Like the High Wizard said."

"Let's just hope ours ends more peacefully," Darius mused.

While Mezar went to get ready to leave the following day, Darius returned to the feast. Still thinking about Kelln and the Preacher, Darius saw Sean laughing with animated gestures with a group of nobles from Sur, and a plan began to form in his mind, a plan that definitely held an edge of danger and risk, but one that may prove Sean's newfound loyalties once and for all.

* * * * * * * * * * * * * * *

Chapter Sixteen
PLANS

The sturdy horse sloshed through the mud-filled road on its way to Mar. It's sturdy pace and strength let Sean's mind wander. The dirty and uncomfortable surroundings did little to dampen Sean's spirits. He sat atop the black Friesian and whistled a merry little tune he'd picked up at a bar in Sur. Even though the ground was still trying to soak up the record-breaking snow and rain over the past ten days, the skies were clear and bright blue. The storm seemed to have forced the change in seasons from fall to winter, but all in all, it wasn't a bad day for traveling.

The more Sean thought about his situation, the more amazed he became. When Darius asked him to go to Mar and help Kelln find the Preacher, he bristled at first. The Preacher might kill him for his failure in Arc and Sur. Darius still questioned his loyalty to the Realm and looked at this assignment as a test of sorts. Sean still even questioned it himself. Could he be trusted?

Sean wished for Danijela as a traveling companion. He had seen her power, and she would be a strong ally in a fight. He was intrigued by her power and her sharp wit and feisty persona challenged him. She, as a wizard apprentice of Arc, and he, being a noble of the Realm, knew nothing serious would ever happen, but the flirting during the storm had helped to pass the time—though the age difference was slightly scandalous at best.

Alone, he rode the empty miles between Sur and Mar, a week-long trip with the muddy roads. Why did Darius allow him to go alone? Why did he trust him? Should he trust him? What if he was once again blinded by the Preacher's power and charisma? Sean realized he was weak for those things.

With all his personal doubts, the one thing that kept him focused was the moment when Darius could have let him be killed-after all that Sean had said and done to him personally, yet he struck at the prince with his power instead and saved his life. Moments later, as the King held the inconsolable Danijela after her brother fell off the cliff, the power of peace, love, and comfort that emanated from Darius was something that Sean would never forget. Those two memories burned a change to the deep recesses of his mind.

Yes, he still wished for power. He wished people would bow to him. But he now saw Darius as one worthy of what he might never achieve himself. Maybe in the King's good grace, someday he would be fully pardoned for his crimes and given a small spot to rule in the Realm.

Each night he stayed in a clean inn and ate well with money provided by Darius. He had to stay an additional day in a small town that sat on the banks of the Black River. The river had swollen with the recent rains, and the bridge needed to be repaired.

Finally after eight long days riding, he glimpsed the white walls of Mar beginning to rise in his line of sight off in the distance. With his credential papers in his pocket, there wouldn't be any problem entering the city. Darius told Kelln through his and Tali's Cremelinos what was happening. He had told them he was sending someone to help but held back who it was. Sean smiled at the thought of Kelln's surprise when he found out. Another one of Darius's tests of his loyalty, he assumed.

Entering through the city gates, Sean surveyed the market district. It was not as wet here, and people were dressed in loose-fitting, colorful clothing. Vendors reached out to sell him clothes, jewelry, and other trinkets. He was amazed at the colors that swirled around him. Women in their dazzling multi-colored skirts and vendors with colorful tent-tops made it hard to concentrate on where he was going. He dismounted and walked next to his horse through the city.

The smell of spiced food filled the air, making his stomach growl in anticipation of a meal. He made his way through the market district and toward an inn Darius recommended he meet Kelln at.

Before stepping up on the inn's porch, a young man grabbed his arm and pulled him to the side.

"Hey, you urchin." Sean tried to kick the boy. "What is the meaning of this?"

The young boy deftly escaped the kick and glanced around quickly. "You are here to see a special person?"

"What are you talking about? Who are you?" Sean was getting annoyed.

The boy leaned in and whispered, "You are looking for the ambassador?"

Sean stopped in his tracks and took better stock of the situation. "And who are you that I should be telling you my business?" He noticed a few people glancing their way as they walked down the street.

"My name is Rapp. I'm the governor's runner and let's say a friend to the ambassador."

"Rapp, you say? Well, I'm supposed to meet him here by direction of your King."

Rapp's eyes opened wider. "You know the King?"

"Of course I do," Sean snapped. "Now let me go in there." He tried to move around the boy but was stopped again.

"He's not there. I will take you to where he is."

Sean didn't know what to make of the situation but decided there wasn't any choice but to trust the boy. As they passed the edge of the inn, a dark-haired beauty joined the two of them walking down the street. She appeared to be only a few years younger than Sean, not nearly as young as Danijela. But there was something about her that reminded him of Danijela, though not in looks, for they were completely opposite—one smaller with short blonde hair and one tall with long dark hair. The similarities were more in the way they carried themselves. Confident.

She smiled at him, and Sean thought it more of a predator grin than a welcoming smile.

"Tali is going our way, too, " Rapp offered. "So do you know the ambassador?"

Sean smiled. "Let's just say, he and I have had our moments together. This may be quite a reunion for him. A surprise!"

The girl turned to him and glared. "I wonder if you are to be trusted."

"The King sent me, didn't he?" was all Sean said. Tali shrugged.

With apparent surprise, the girl threw herself in front of Sean and pushed him up against the wall of a close-by building. She pushed herself in tight against him, as if to kiss him.

"Pretend we are lovers. Don't look around."

Sean smiled at the fun. "Sounds fun, honey, but don't we have business to get to?"

She leaned in closer, and Sean smelled a slight wave of perfume. He wrapped his arms around her tighter, and she flashed her brown eyes at him. Her face was smooth and porcelain, quite a contrast to the dark brown hair hanging down past her shoulders. Sean moved in for the kiss.

Rapp continued walking around the corner. He whistled a signal. Two men came around a corner and glanced momentarily at the couple kissing at the edge of the building. After walking a few steps away, the girl moved her hand in a slight wave. Two bricks from the walkway moved, and the men tripped on them, sprawling on the ground.

With the distraction, Tali grabbed Sean's hand and proceeded around the corner, joining once again with the young boy.

"Done already?" Sean quipped. Then instantly felt a sting on his behind. Turning around, he tried to figure out what happened.

"Tali, King Darius told you not to do that with your magic," Rapp said.

She glared at the boy. "But young men sometimes deserve it." Then she glared at Sean.

"What did I do? And who are you? How did you do that?" Sean was full of questions. Taken out of his controlled environment, he was not his usual self.

The girl came around in front of him and sarcastically offered him her hand to kiss. "I am Taliana Penrose, daughter of Governor Penrose, and a wizard of some means."

"Great, another wizard," Sean mumbled under his breath. He kissed her hand, and she smiled at him, flipped her hair, and continued walking.

Turning to Rapp, he said, "Is she always like this?"

Rapp rolled his eyes. "Oh, yes. She enjoys the teasing. You should see her with the ambassador."

Sean laughed at that. He couldn't imagine the thin, redheaded Kelln El'Han handling anything so sophisticated as this woman.

Composing himself once again, he became more serious. "Who were those men?"

"Those were high-ranking members of the Guild of Thieves. They are aware of who I am and would wonder what I am doing here in this part of town," Tali said.

"And what are you doing here?" Sean asked.

"Making sure you stay safe on your way to meet with the ambassador and the governor."

"Wizards," Sean sighed. "Can't seem to get away from them anymore."

"So you are here to help Kelln find the Preacher?" Rapp asked.

Sean was surprised that the information had been shared. He nodded, not wanting to say anything more.

"How will you do that?" the boy asked.

"We have a history together," was all Sean said. "Nothing more until we meet Kelln."

Thirty minutes later, they entered a back alley that ran between sets of nice homes nearer to the water. Rapp signaled to stop in front of a door that he entered first. A minute later, he came back out and ushered them in.

The house was pleasant with painted white walls and comfortable furnishings. An open window afforded views of the Blue Sea. Sean breathed deeply, smelling the ocean air in his nostrils, and realized that this was his first time being this close to the ocean. Coming upon a room, two men sat in chairs. The one facing him was obviously the governor, and the other held a mop of red hair sticking up over the top of the chair. As soon as the three entered the room, the two men stood up and faced them.

Kelln about fell over himself. "Sean? What are you doing here?" He pulled his dirk out and headed toward one of his most hated enemies.

Sean stepped back a few feet and put up his hands. "Kelln. Stop. Darius sent me."

"If he did, then you tricked him again." Kelln's face was red.

Tali, her height between the two men, stepped between them. "Kelln, at least listen to him. He says he knows the Preacher."

"Of course he knows him, Tali. He kidnapped Darius, helped the Preacher escape, and has sided with him in creating havoc in the kingdom."

The three others in the room glared at Sean for an explanation.

"Please, put down the weapon, Kelln. Let's just talk."

The governor stepped closer. "Ambassador, my daughter and I can handle this young man if he is not who he claims to be. I agree with your assessment, but our King did send him to help. Let's at least hear him out."

Kelln mumbled a retort but reluctantly put his dirk down.

Sean stepped up to the governor and bowed, reverting to his noble upbringing. "Governor Penrose, I am Sean San Ghant of Anikari. I do indeed hold some history with the Preacher. But let me assure you, King Darius has sent me here in good faith to help the situation." He took out his papers, which he gave to the governor. Darius had written a note to him and the ambassador.

"I still don't believe it," Kelln mumbled.

Sean turned to him. "Just so you understand, Kelln, I was not the one that let the Preacher escape; that was your beautiful raven-haired friend, Alessandra. It was all her doing. I was just offered a way out with them, and I took it."

Kelln jumped toward Sean again and tried to grab him.

Tali swatted him back with a push of air. "Now boys, we can't tolerate this fighting if we are going to get anything done."

"A feisty one, she is." Sean smiled a toothy grin at Kelln. "She likes to tease the boys it seems." That remark got him another pinch on the bottom. "Ouch." He scowled. "Stop that."

"Then stop acting childish," Tali said, hands on her hips.

Her father smiled and regained control of the situation. "Let's all sit, please. We need to plan on how we find the Preacher and stop his influence from growing in the city. Rapp, make sure the place is secure, then ask someone to bring us some food. This might be a long night."

* * * * * * * * * * * * * * * *

In the three weeks since Christine had been under the care of her newfound friend, her nausea had abated, her skin tone was healthier, and her energy level was up. The two developed a schedule of spending time together each day and taking walks. First, it was just inside the large building she was held prisoner in, but in time, they ventured to an outside garden area.

The fresh air and sunlight lifted the queen's spirit. With winter approaching, the days were getting shorter and the nights cooler; however this much further south, the daytime temperatures were still comfortable enough to wear a light coat.

The doctor never shared her own name with Christine and still seemed very skittish and nervous any time that Christine talked about her home or the chance to escape.

Christine discovered through listening to the servants that she was being held in Gildan in a large estate of one of the general's most faithful followers.

"There must be hidden doorways in the garden walls," Christine mentioned one day.

"Dear, you must stop thinking about escape."

"I can't," Christine said. "Darius is out there searching for me. General Alrishitar is planning on invading the Realm. I must warn my husband. There is no one else."

The wizard smiled. "How did such a young girl become so bold in life? I could never be like you."

"But you are a wizard with powers I can never even dream of."

"But I am a weak wizard. I am a wizard of the mind. I do not fight or battle. I use my power for studies and scholarly work. That is how I learned about healing."

"My husband is a wizard of the heart," Christine mentioned proudly.

That got the doctor's attention. There hadn't been many wizards with the power of the heart over time. They were thought to be some of the most powerful but also more volatile and open to sudden mood changes. "The general will not have such an easy time then."

"No, he will not," Christine became more firm and serious. "That is why I need to escape." She stood taller, face flushed. Her golden hair flowed down her back over a light silk coat that was more to hide the pregnancy than to provide warmth. She stood a good hand taller than the woman.

"And you will help me," Christine continued. "I will leave either way, doctor. If you would see me safe, your help would be better for me. If not, I will still try on my own. I must reach my husband or reestablish the bond to my Cremelino."

At mention of the mythical animal, the wizard doctor took immediate interest. She had made a lifetime pursuit in studying ancient creatures, particularly the Cremelinos. Having never seen one herself, she was full of questions. The Gildanian wizard did not know about communicating through the bond. They contemplated together why it was weakened now for Christine. They could come up with no answer.

In the end, with the excited expectation of maybe meeting a Cremelino horse, the wizard decided to help the young queen find a way to escape. The wizard promised to discretely search out those who were not sympathetic to the general and to find out the whereabouts of Prince Mezar. Christine knew if they could find him, he would help.

Later that week on one of their morning walks, the doctor confided in Christine that contact had been made with someone who caught rumors the prince was back in Gildan. Contact would be made if possible.

Christine's hope lifted for the first time. She tried to be strong on the outside for the doctor and others around her, but inside she was only a moment away from weeping each time she thought about her dear husband. He must be frantically searching for her and out of his mind. She hoped that his grief was not distorting his powers. The power of love and compassion were strongest in him, but feelings of anger and frustration could bring havoc and even deadly results.

She missed Darius and found herself reliving more and more their times together as younger teenagers. Times were so simple then. She marveled how the daughter of a poor farmer had become the queen of the Realm.

As much as she missed Darius, the lost bond to her Cremelino was sometimes even more debilitating. For years, the constant comforting presence had sat in the back of her mind, urging her on, giving her strength, and bringing hope.

She sat on her bed, feeling sorry for the missed bond, when the door to her room crashed open. It was General Alrishitar.

The heir to the throne of Gildan was livid. His face was red, and dark veins stood out on his light brown face. His hair, although dark in his younger years, now held tips of gray. His hand came up out of his dark black robes and pointed at Christine.

"You deceived me, girl!" he roared, his voice filled with an expanse of power. The walls shook, and Christine winced.

He took three large strides and grabbed the queen off of the bed. With rough hands, he pulled her to her feet. Christine felt tears sting her eyes. Her lips quivered with his rough handling.

The general grabbed her cloak and ripped it from her body in one fluid motion. Christine stood still in her light blue silk gown, her baby bump obvious.

"You are pregnant and hid this news from me? You and that wretched doctor of yours."

With the mention of the doctor, Christine's fear grew deeper, but her resolve slid into place. "Where is my doctor?"

"She has been taken away. She is a traitor to the crown, and her use to me is over."

The doctor had been right. If the general found out, she would be killed. The realization hit Christine, and she fought hard to stay in control. "You are the traitor, General."

The older but muscled man slapped her hard across the face, sending her falling into the bed. "Your use is not so great that I can't accomplish my purposes without you. I am not a traitor. I am a patriot acting on behalf of those that won't. Our empire has been denied their destiny for greatness for far too long. There are others who believe in me and are guiding us toward becoming one land together.

Christine stood up again and continued to glare at her captor, a far more dangerous man than she at first realized. Her hand went instinctively to her face, rubbing what was sure to be a swollen bruise.

"Tomorrow we ride to the border and attack your precious land. My wizards will demolish anyone who interferes. Within a month, your husband and his army will be backed into Anikari and will be pleading for your life, and now the life of your baby, in trade for his entire kingdom."

"He won't do it."

The general laughed. "Oh, you naïve girl. Kingdoms greater than yours have fallen for the sake of a woman. I hear about the passion and love your King has for you. He will have no choice but to follow his heart."

Christine realized that the general was correct. Darius would give up all he had for her. It was a sad but proud feeling at the same time. Tears came to her eyes and fell unashamed down her reddened face.

"You are now confined to this room, day and night. There will be no visitors. Food will be brought to you three times a day, and the chamber pot will be emptied once. Any disobedience will bring swift action to you and your baby," he roared.

Christine's hand went to her stomach. Her baby! She must stay safe for the baby. She would obey the general and hope for a miracle.

General Alrishitar ran his hand around the inside of her doorframe, and blue light spread across it. "No one without my permission will enter or leave this room". With that, he walked out and closed the door.

Falling back to the bed, the young farmer-girl-turned-queen sobbed until her throat was raw and sleep overtook her.

* * * * * * * * * * * * * * *

Chapter Seventeen
TO THE BORDER

Mezar rode Star, his new Cremelino, in furious strides, racing ahead of Leandra and his other companions to get to Gildan first. Amazed at the bond, he reveled in the peace, power, and direction it brought him. And the speed! They took three days in what would normally be a week-long journey.

Slipping through the Gildanian border just west of Denir, he noticed the march of thousands of troops on the Gildan side heading for the Realm. His father was planning on invading. Mezar had very little time to stop it all.

Riding through Gildan was slower. Not wanting to call any more attention to himself, he laid a brown blanket over the horse to hide his blinding white color. Taking up at an inn on the outskirts of the capital city, he now sat with Star in the stable.

Without warning, Star went up on his hind legs and made a screeching sound. Mezar stood up from a bucket he had been sitting on and tried to soothe the Cremelino.

"Star, what is wrong?" Mezar felt the horse's horror through the bond.

Lightning just felt the horrible pain through her bond.

"From Christine?"

Yes. She could hardly bear it, even at this distance—abrupt and intense physical pain, followed by overwhelming distraught.

"Does she know from where it came?" Mezar asked.

It's close to us here. She transferred the feelings to me as soon as she felt them, and now I can sense Christine close by.

Mezar didn't know they were able to do that, but he was anxious about the possibility of finding Christine. Mezar's men and Leandra were still a few days behind, and Darius would be farther behind than that. With forces building up on the border, he must act fast to stop his father.

The prince of Gildan struggled with thoughts about the general. He had always been a tough man to please, a man used to giving orders rather than following others. Until recent days, he never showed any signs whatsoever of deceit to the empire. Once Mezar's grandfather passed away, his father was already chosen to rule. Why wouldn't he just wait? Something didn't make sense.

Hoping he wouldn't have to directly confront his father, Mezar mounted Star, and they headed out into the city. It was nearing dusk, and although people were still about, the crowds were, for the most part, heading to their warm homes. With the last rays of sun disappearing, Mezar was struck once again by the beauty of his city, especially the multi-colored domes reflecting off of the setting sun. Looking up on a nearby hill, he caught a glimpse of a large building, an estate of a formidable Gildanian noble.

Over there. The thought came charging from Star, who seemed to know where Mezar was looking. *She is there!*

* * * * * * * * * * * * * * * *

Richard sat in council with the other members. His mind was wandering during the ongoing boring rhetoric from some of the younger councilors. A rear door to the room opened, breaking the silence, and one of the aides approached the senior councilor. He leaned down to whisper in Richard's ear.

"Sir, a rider from Sur has just stumbled in. News from the King."

Richard's boredom vanished. He jumped up, dismissed himself, and left the room. "Have him meet me in my study."

The young rider's hair was disheveled, mud splattered his clothes, and his face was gaunt and tired. The councilor told him to sit and handed him a drink. Parched, the man drank in eager gulps before saying anything.

Finally, the young man related to Richard the news from Sur, the battle with Arc, the Preacher in Mar, and the abduction of the queen.

Richard sat back in exhaustion. Worried for weeks with no news from his son's party since the queen had ridden back through Anikari on their way to Sur, he was relieved to at least know something. He was also distraught about news from Mar and the sudden appearance of the Preacher there.

"General Cray asked to send two battalions of men toward the border with Gildan immediately," the messenger continued. "As soon as the snow melts, the King, the general, and the rest of their men are heading south to Denir – to the border with Gildan. The King means to find his wife."

Richard knew what Christine meant to his son. Though he didn't understand the attraction at first. His son and him had not seen eye to eye on many things, but he had learned to accept and respect the young queen, and he had pledged his support and loyalty to his son. He admitted that she held up quite well, she was good for his son, and he had actually begun to grow fond of her. The Realm should be a safer place so that they didn't have to worry about their queen being abducted. The failure was on all of them. The task to find her again would be everyone's top priority.

The senior councilor stood. "You get some rest, soldier. The ride you made may well save our kingdom. I will find the battalion leaders myself." He hoped his son wouldn't let his anger get in the way of things. The power he held, still new to all of them, had a way of getting him in trouble.

On the way to the battalion leaders, he stopped back in the council room and shared the news with the rest of the men and women. Jarad San Newlyn, the religious councilor, offered to pray for the King and their queen. Richard, although not overly religious, consented for the time to be taken to do so before they dismissed. He knew that Darius would think it was important. And maybe it was. The additional peace and clarity he felt after the prayer did much to bolster his spirits.

* * * * * * * * * * * * * * * *

Darius rode beside General Cray and High Wizard Sallir. Troops from Sur, Anikari, and a small presence of Arc soldiers rode behind. Danijela had stayed in sur in preparation to returning back to be with her father in Arc. The prior day, Darius's group met up with the two battalions that his father had sent south to Denir as he had instructed. Given the size of the troops and the wagons to support them, they were still days away from reaching the border of Gildan.

Darius itched to ride forward on his own. Thunder could make the journey in much less time, but this once, he held to the advice of others. He was the King of the Realm, and duty held him to stay with his troops in this situation. He did bristle with impatience as he slowed down for their sakes. All he could think of was getting to Christine.

The communication from Mezar informing him of the whereabouts of his wife had been both a blessing and a curse to his impatience. Lightning, who traveled with Darius, communicated to him, the same as to Mezar and Star, the intense feelings she felt from Christine for a brief moment earlier. He wanted to barrel ahead, crushing everyone between him and Gildan to reach her, but he also knew that he trusted Mezar. The prince would do as well as Darius could in getting her out safely, even more so, being from Gildan and being able to blend in. Darius as King entering into Gildan unannounced could provoke war.

"My Lord" Roland came up beside his master. "Riders coming up the road toward us."

Darius watched Roland's pointing fingers and called a halt to the troops. He'd sent riders up ahead to ascertain the situation on the border.

Three riders skidded to a stop in front of him. All three were handed a waterskin to drink their fill before talking.

"Sire," one of the men began, "there are signs of large battalions of troops gathering a short distance south of the border. The governor of Denir has begun gathering in the farmers and others who live outside of the city."

Denir, being on the border with a foreign kingdom, always maintained a high amount of food stores and extra livestock inside the city for such possibilities as this. It was a double-walled city, with killing fields between the two walls, fifty feet of empty space in which archers from the walls could kill anyone in between. A siege on Denir would be a long one.

One of the other men took over speaking. "However, my Lord, even though we did not see it with our own eyes, it is rumored there are wizards with them."

Darius frowned at that. Wizards might negate much of the strength of the walls. "Of course, we also have wizards with us," he said to firm up the men's hopes, though inside he wondered how much two of them could do against those fully trained in Gildan. The High Wizard was a formidable foe for sure, but Darius was still learning the possibilities of his powers. Being a wizard of the heart, he was not as equipped for battle as other types of wizards, but he was sure that if need be, he could provide some solid resistance to the Gildanian army.

After a short rest, he motioned for the army to begin marching again. Darius was deep in thought as he rode. They would need to reach Denir before the Gildanian army attacked. They must contain the foreign army on their side of the border.

The King thought back to his first assignment as commander of the King's Elite Army. It, too, had been in Denir. They had marched from their training grounds in the Superstition Mountains. Through a lucky plan and opponents that were overly confident with themselves, Darius had been able to capture a group of Gildanians with their commander, Mezar. At the time, he hadn't been aware that Mezar was second in line to the throne of the Empire of Gildan. Of course, he also hadn't known he was in line to be King of the Realm either.

He discussed the situation of the upcoming battle with Cray and Olan. Was there something they could do besides an outright battle? The Realm had already lost many fine soldiers fighting the army from Arc up in the pass. An open battle with Gildan would put many more lives at risk and would put a strain on the relationship between Mezar and himself. He knew that Mezar had a duty to his empire and to help the Emperor reestablish peace there, but it would be difficult with Mezar's father, the general, building up an army to invade the Realm.

The High Wizard, being a wizard of the mind and having had more history of studying wars and battles, told Darius he would think on it. After that, they rode in silence with only the sounds of the horses' hooves, soldiers' feet sloshing in mud, and the supply wagons' wheels creaking along the long road.

Darius's thoughts of course went to his wife.

* * * * * * * * * * * * * * *

Chapter Eighteen
WIZARD POWER

Rapp sat hunkered down behind some crates close to the docks of Mar. Through the slats in the wooden boxes, he watched the sailors and deckhands loading and unloading goods from the ships. Trade between Mar and Gildan, and even farther south, were conducted through this port. It wasn't uncommon to see a few elves from Elvyn or ships from the eastern kingdoms, or Southern Territories.

The early winter sun barely touched Rapp through the wet fog. He pulled a wool coat more protectively around his small body and tugged his black cap down tighter over his ears. His legs were getting stiff, but he was used to these kinds of assignments from the governor, and now from the ambassador, and he learned long ago how to relax and tighten his muscles to keep the circulation going.

Earlier in the day, he had followed Mr. El'Lan—or the Preacher, as the ambassador called him—down to the docks. His orders from the ambassador were to keep the Preacher in sight at all times and occupied as long as possible. The ambassador, on the other hand, was going to try and bring Alessandra's mother to her without the Preacher finding out.

The Preacher had gone silently to one of the larger ships at the dock. By the look of the colors and riggings, Rapp concluded it was from one of the eastern kingdoms. The Preacher had been inside for almost an hour, and Rapp was getting bored. Looking around, he pulled himself out from behind the crates and walked in a haphazard manner around the docks, trying to blend in. He wanted to know what was happening inside the ship.

Three sailors, who he surmised were in actuality guards, stood outside the ship. Their skin was darker, and tattoos adorned their arms. Glancing around for ideas, he spied a few jugs of wine sitting outside another ship, waiting to be loaded. The sailors of that ship seemed to be preoccupied. With a swift move, Rapp grabbed a few jugs and continued walking back toward the ship where the Preacher had gone inside. Coming up to the sailor guards he changed his persona and put on his dumb but happy face.

"Hey, blokes." He grabbed their attentions. "Got some drink here from the harbor master as a thanks for your business."

The men, wet and cold, smiled at the possibility of some wine warming their bellies. They reached out for one of the jugs.

Rapp gave them one, and with smiles, they passed it around between the three of them. "Cold night standing guard out here."

One of the men mumbled in agreement. They continued sharing the wine.

Rapp moved in closer and whispered, "Guarding something important in there?"

Another man laughed. "Wouldn't you like to know, harbor boy?"

Rapp continued to play the simpleton. "You sailors must be important to guard something in such a big ship." He handed them another jug of wine.

The third sailor, loosened up by the wine, began to talk more, though Rapp had to concentrate real hard to understand the accent.

"There are important men in the ship discussing important business. They don't want to be disturbed." The man began slurring his words rather quickly. He was obviously someone who couldn't hold his drink well. Rapp latched on to him for more information.

Rapp looked surprised and envious. "I've never seen a ship this big before. They must be important."

"Magic users," one of the other men whispered, then laughed.

All three sailors put their hands in the air and moved their fingers around as if imitating a wizard. Rapp joined in, laughing.

Two of the men sat down and took the last jug of wine. They began grabbing it from each other and almost came to blows, when the third man took the wine jug from them and put it up to his lips, taking a long drink. The two others jumped up and grabbed the third man back down.

Rapp smiled and skirted around the three drunken sailors onto the large ship. Hearing voices from an inside cabin, he ducked down some stairs and into an empty storage room. He listened to the discussion on the other side of the thin wooden walls.

"You overstepped your boundaries, Preacher," came a deep voice with a strong foreign accent. "You are not in a position to give orders."

"I am preparing the land for your people. I deserve some credit," came the familiar voice of the Preacher.

"You failed in Belor. That was your assignment. You allowed a wizard to become King of the Realm, and from what I can tell, you have done nothing else to secure this land. We have had to turn our attention to Gildan now and see if they can take the Realm since you have not been able to do so."

There was silence for a moment.

"I am sowing discord around the Realm. I have contacts in Sur and Arc that are starting a war there, I am disturbing the hierarchy in Mar, and I will take down the young wizard who thinks of himself as a King. I do not need the Gildanians' help."

A third voice spoke for the first time. Rapp wished he could see who was talking. "The discussion is ended, my old pupil." The voice was old and raspy. "We had high hopes for you in the east. You were to be our eyes and ears in this land. It was time for us to expand, but that time is now passed. Current events have changed things. There are more wizards in the western kingdoms than we were led to believe. We have found another in Gildan to help us in our task. You are no longer in our employ."

Rapp moved around the storage room and tried to find a crack in the wall. Finally, he was successful. He could now glimpse the back of the Preacher. Two other men of brown skin stood opposite him, one very old with white hair.

Necklaces, charms, and earrings adorned their heads and necks, and tattoos seemed to cover their arms and necks. Their eyes were slightly tilted and their bodies much shorter than the Preacher's.

The Preacher abruptly jumped toward the older man. Wizard's fire flew from his fingers, flashing green and blue. The older man swatted it away as an irritant with a calm turn of his hand. The man's eyes glowed, and the Preacher fell backward on his back.

"How dare you attack your master. Have you not learned control yet, you insolent pup?"

The Preacher sat stunned on the floor, gasping for breath. With only a look, the eastern wizard continued squeezing the air out of his old pupil. The man's tattoos seemed to swim around his skin, as if they were alive. Rapp gaped in horror. The old man was going to kill the Preacher right here on the ship.

Somehow the Preacher raised his hand in an effort to stop the attack. The third man in the room motioned for the eastern wizard to stop. It seemed the Preacher had something else to say. The Preacher sat up, still struggling for breath. His eyes were bulged and watery.

In a raspy voice, he croaked. "The Cremelinos. I've found them."

The eastern wizard looked shocked but pleased. His demeanor changed, and he motioned for his former pupil to stand and report. "Why didn't you tell us earlier?"

"There is one in the city now." The Preacher's voice grew stronger. "A gift to a young wizard, the daughter of the governor. And the rest are on an island a short distance from here."

The two eastern men grinned.

The wizard said, "You may redeem yourself after all. The Cremelinos could increase our power at home and here in the west. Your new assignment is to kill the girl and take the Cremelino. Bring it to me, and I will force it to bond to me."

Rapp almost let out an audible sound. He had to warn Tali. Without waiting to hear more, he turned to sneak back out of the room. Upon doing so, his foot knocked over a bucket. The ensuing sound of the bucket rolling around caused the neighboring conversation between the wizards to stop. Without any other stealth, Rapp quickly ran up the stairs and hopped over the railing to another ship close by on the docks. He noticed the three guards, still half-drunken in front of the eastern ship.

* * * * * * * * * * * * * * * *

A short time earlier, Kelln was following and watching Alessandra. When he knew she was alone, he approached. She was in a room above an inn that was known for being used by the Guild of Thieves for some transactions. He entered the inn alone, but Taliana and Radiance stood outside, ready to assist if necessary.

Rapp had earlier informed Kelln and Sean where he had seen Alessandra's mother, Berlain. Since Kelln was too well known in the city in his status as ambassador, Sean took the assignment to confront the woman and convince her to meet with Alessandra. Kelln took upon him the assignment to talk to Alessandra and arrange a meeting with her and her mother.

Walking up the steps to the second floor, Kelln knocked on the door. He heard sounds of movement within, but no one answered.

"Alessandra," he whispered at the door. He thought he heard a gasp. "Open the door. It's Kelln." He hoped she would respond for old time's sake. This would be his last ditch effort to get her away from the Preacher's influence so he could take the man down.

She did. The door opened, and she stood looking at him. Her dark-colored auburn hair still fell in beautiful layers past her shoulders. Her large almond-shaped eyes pulled him in once again. She smiled a melancholy smile.

"Hello, Kelln."

He asked if he could come in, and she opened the door wider. She moved over and sat on the edge of a bed while Kelln closed the door behind him.

"How are you?" He didn't know how to start the conversation.

"Why are you here?" she answered. "My father is looking for you, you know. "

Kelln shrugged. "As are you. I heard you bargained away my life for the chance to visit your mother again."

The statement seemed to catch Alessandra off guard. She looked panicked.

Kelln stood in front of her. "Come with me?' He offered his hand.

Her hand came up as if without thinking, but then she pulled it back in an abrupt move. "My father will be back here soon. You need to leave."

"That is why we need to leave together. I found your mother, Alessandra."

Jumping off the bed, her eyes opened wide in shock. "Is this a trick, Kelln? After all I have done against you, why would you do something nice for me?"

"That's a good question, one I have been asking myself over and over again, Alessandra. I harbor no more notions that we can be together after what you have done. My job is to take in the Preacher, but for the feelings I had once for you, I am willing to help you see your mother before I take both you and your father in to custody."

Tears filled Alessandra's eyes. "Why? Why are you so good to people? I saw the way you never gave up on your friend Darius. You are loyal to a fault, Kelln. I am not worthy of your help."

"Look, Alessandra. I know your father can be manipulating. I know he can be hard to resist, but you can leave him right now and see your mother."

"I don't know."

"Do you want to see her?"

Indecision and pain played across Alessandra's face. After a long silence, she whispered, "Yes."

They left the inn by a back door and met up with Tali outside. Kelln was trusting Sean to bring Alessandra's mother to the rendezvous point but still wasn't fully convinced of Sean's motives.

They had chosen an old courtyard on the eastern outskirts of Mar. It was enclosed on three sides by old dilapidated homes, which over time had been worn down by the harsh salted sea air. The paint had peeled off years ago, and part of the walls and roofs had collapsed. At the center of the courtyard stood a large ruined water fountain and small swimming pool, signifying the wealth the past inhabitants had once enjoyed. Weeds and old scrub bushes sat in cracks of brick, while a thick layer of sand covered it all.

Kelln, Alessandra, Tali, and Radiance stood at one end of the courtyard. Nothing was said as they waited. The sound and smell of the ocean wafted over them in their stillness.

Kelln's hearing picked out the sounds of someone approaching. He felt Alessandra stiffen next two him as two people entered the courtyard opposite them. Sean stood there with Berlain. He nodded his head toward Kelln, and Kelln ushered Alessandra toward her mother.

Berlain whipped her head toward Sean. "You did not tell me she would be here."

Sean just shrugged.

"You told me it was a meeting with my father." Berlain wore brown leather pants with a brown jerkin over a shirt. A blue cloak moved in a slight breeze around her.

Kelln looked at the two women and noticed the similarities. The almond-shaped eyes of both mother and daughter held a firm resolve.

Both ladies stood looking at each other for a moment, then Alessandra rushed into her mother's arms with a cry. Berlain stiffened at first, but then relaxed. She held her daughter and stroked the back of her head.

"You are so beautiful, my dear," her mother said. "I have missed you for so long."

"Why?" Alessandra could hardly speak. "Why did you leave us?"

Berlain backed away from Alessandra an arm's length. Sadness and regret filled her face. "It's complicated. I can't explain it all. Your father, however, was part of it."

The rest of the group backed away to give some privacy to the reunion. Sean stood next to Taliana. "How are you today, sweetheart?" He tried to break the serious tension in the air.

Tali squinted her eyes at him in a mock glare but didn't move away.

Kelln took up the silence. "Sean, thanks for bringing her. I don't know what's going to happen with Alessandra, but it was important for her to see her mother."

Sean nodded his head in acknowledgement and said under his breath, "It actually feels good to do something decent."

Tali looked at him and smiled. "There is hope for the young, arrogant noble."

Sean snorted but smiled anyway.

The quiet moment was shattered by a loud wail coming around the other side of the building. Kelln heard his and Tali's names being called. In an instant, they were all on alert. Kelln pulled his sword, Sean ran to where Alessandra and her mother were visiting, and Taliana moved over closer to her Cremelino.

With shouts and yelling, Rapp came stumbling around the corner, dirty and out of breath. He ran up to the group and tried to talk, but he was breathing too hard.

"Rapp, what's wrong?" Tali tried to get it out of him.

"He's going to kill you," Rapp finally said.

"Who is going to kill who?" Kelln put his hand on the boy's shoulder. Rapp was clearly afraid.

"He's going to kill Tali."

"Who Rapp? Who is trying to kill me?" Taliana looked around the square with nervous glances.

At that instant, another man came around the corner. Tall and broad, calm, overbearing with short red hair. A red cape swirled around him.

"I am," the man said.

"Father?" Alessandra whispered.

"Dominic?" Alessandra's mother said.

"Dominic?" Sean echoed with a slight smile.

Kelln gave Sean a look that said to be quiet and guard the girls. Sean moved between Taliana and Alessandra. Rapp backed up behind the Cremelino.

"Ah," the Preacher continued, "everyone in one place it seems. The little urchin was easy to follow."

Another man came around the corner, flanked by two guards. "Not everyone, Mr. El'Han. What is the meaning of this meeting?" It was the guildmaster.

"Father!" Berlain shouted.

Alessandra's face drained white. "The Guild of Thieves' guildmaster is your father?"

"And your grandfather," Berlain finished. "I told you it was complicated."

The guildmaster walked with intent toward the Preacher. "I told you to stay away from my daughter fifteen years ago." His guards pulled out swords and walked with him.

"I had nothing to do with this meeting." The Preacher's neck pulsed with anger. "I tried to keep my daughter away from this side of the family. It would only bring her pain and suffering. This is the doing of our beloved ambassador, Kelln El'Lan, who has meddled in my affairs for the last time."

"Father," Alessandra said. "You told me you wouldn't hurt him."

"I lied," the Preacher said. "He has interfered too much. You were better off never seeing your mother again. She is the daughter of a thief and will always be living in the underground with them, their guild never sanctioned. I wanted glory for you Alessandra. I told you I would give you a city to rule."

"I don't want a city to rule, Father. I just wanted to see my mother again. You don't understand the bond I had with her as a little girl. I would do anything to see her again."

The Preacher smirked and turned toward Sean. "Nice to see you here, Mr. San Ghant. I trust you have been following my plan?"

Sean nodded noncommittally to the Preacher and smiled. Kelln's face grew red. He shouldn't have trusted Sean.

"Sean, what did you do?' he yelled and ran toward him.

The Preacher lifted his hands in the air. Blue, green, and white fire and lightning circled his hands, crackling in the air. He hurled a hot white fireball toward Kelln as he ran for Sean. "Now you will die once and for all!"

The fire raced from the Preacher's outstretched hand, but Alessandra ran to intervene. As the bolt of flames reached them, Alessandra threw herself in front of Kelln, offering herself in a final moment of redemption. She took the brunt of the magical force and crumbled to the ground as Kelln skidded into Sean.

"What have you done?" Berlain yelled to her former husband. "You would kill your own daughter?"

The Preacher did indeed look shocked as he tried to comprehend what he had done. His eyes glazed over in madness, and he brought another bolt to bear; however, Taliana sent a wave of wind crashing into the Preacher, taking him to the ground before he could launch the fire.

Tali jumped on her Cremelino and, with a few swift strides, rode over to the Preacher to finish the job.

Rapp yelled at her from across the courtyard. "No, Tali. He wants to kill you and take your Cremelino. Stay away!"

Tali paused and looked back at Rapp. It was enough time for the Preacher to stand again. He reached out his hands toward the young wizard and shot blue lightning from his fingers.

"Tali, jump," Sean yelled.

She dove off the horse, the bolt of lightning only hitting her right arm. A scream followed as a burn raced up her forearm.

Kelln sat down next to Alessandra on the ground. The smell of burnt flesh filled the air. A large gap in her clothes showed inflamed and burnt skin across half her middle. Her leg was badly scorched. Hurt eyes pleaded with Kelln to help, and then she passed out.

Kelln looked up, trying to figure out what to do. The two guards with the guildmaster were hanging back and tried to circle around the Preacher. Kelln needed to distract him.

"You are ruined, Preacher. There are more of us here."

"Worthless. All of you!" the Preacher shouted, his voice amplified by his power. Energies of various colors began to circle around him, and Kelln stepped back.

The two guards rushed the Preacher from behind. The first ran a blade toward the Preacher's back, but he, along with the second man, were killed instantly with fire from the Preacher's hand as he turned to face the attack.

When he turned back around, Tali, though untrained, lifted a barrage of pebbles from the ground and threw them at blinding speed toward the evil wizard. They pelted his body, but still the man stood.

Grinning with eyes blazing, the Preacher stomped his foot on the ground, and the ground rose up in bubbles, knocking everyone down. He took an inhuman leap and landed a dozen yards away directly in front of Tali. Reaching out his hand toward her throat, he squeezed in the air, and she began to choke. Her Cremelino made an awful shrieking noise, filling the air around them.

"Stop that, you monster!" Berlain, who had been standing in shock, drew a small knife and threw it at the Preacher's chest. It hit low and stuck in his gut, his power on Tali weakening momentarily.

The Preacher pushed his other hand toward his ex-wife and tossed her like a rag doll into the air, throwing her into the old tile fountain in the courtyard. Her body stayed still. The savage act snapped the guildmaster back to action, and he jumped on the back of the Preacher trying to gouge his eyes from behind.

The distraction enabled Tali to break free from the Preacher's magical hold. She lay on the ground, gasping for breath.

Sean, surprisingly, reached down and pulled Kelln from the ground where he still sat trying to protect Alessandra. "We've got to do something!"

"Haven't you done enough Sean?"

"You mistake me, Kelln. This was not my plan. I have remained loyal since I arrived here." Sean pleaded his case. "I can tell he's a monster. He will kill us all. Now get up and fight."

Kelln stood and grabbed his sword. The Preacher was still busy with the guildmaster, having just thrown him down again. The wizard was relentless. Blood poured from his back and gut; his eyes were bloodshot and crazed. Dirt and pelts of rock covered him, but still he pushed on. Sending a killing burst of fire on the guildmaster, he turned to face his final standing opponents.

Rapp yelled for Sean to come and help Tali, leaving Kelln alone facing the Preacher. His mind raced back in time and covered in mere seconds all the pain and harm this man had caused in his life. His family had been misled by the Preacher's evil dreams, resulting eventually in Kelln's father's death. Kelln himself had been imprisoned and tortured by him on multiple occasions., and Darius had been held under his power for a time. He spared a lingering look at Alessandra lying crumpled on the ground, her chest rising and falling slowly. She was unconscious, which was a blessing in her badly burned state.

Kelln, raised a sword maker's son, now made a stance. He had learned as a toddler how to hold a sword with perfect balance in his hand. He thought of Darius's sword, his relic of power, and wished for that golden sword at this time. Looking around at the carnage, wishes obviously were not being granted that day.

"Fight me!" he yelled at the top of his lungs. "Man to man. Fight me without your powers."

The Preacher stiffened and smiled. He hadn't touched his sword yet, but now with a ring to the air, he drew it from his side and settled into position.

Kelln attacked first, going on the offensive. Back and forth they dueled, clashing swords in the midmorning air. Kelln tasted the salty sea in his mouth. His wild red hair was plastered to his forehead, drenched in sweat. Kelln sliced the Preacher's arm just above the bicep and jumped in to take advantage of the pain; however, the Preacher cut low and caught Kelln across the thigh. Screaming in pain, he limped backward.

Both approached more cautiously this time. Kelln's energy was dwindling; the Preacher was more powerful than him, even without his magic. With the affairs of the ambassador's office, Kelln hadn't trained like he should have recently. He stopped thinking and instinct took over.

Kelln bumped into an old stone bench. He hadn't realized that the Preacher had been pushing him backward a step at a time. Now he was pinned against it, and when the Preacher lunged into a full assault, Kelln's legs couldn't move; all he could do was bend backward at the waist. He would break or fall soon.

Without warning, Kelln felt his legs sweep out from under him by the Preacher's foot, and he fell backward, laying unprotected across the bench. The Preacher smacked the sword out of Kelln's hands and looked down in mad glee at his young opponent.

Kelln looked up at the Preacher, and everything stopped in his mind. This was how it felt to die. He had done his best. He didn't want to die, but he wasn't afraid. The things Alastair, ironically the Preacher's father, had taught him in the cave last year came back to him now. He could leave this world knowing he had done his best. No one could ask for more. May God protect him.

"I will kill you," the Preacher grunted through clenched teeth. With sweat dripping down his face, his eyes shifted momentarily over to Taliana and Rapp. "Then I will destroy you, young girl wizard, and take your bonded Cremelino from you." The mad wizard brought his sword up in the air.

Falling limp to accept his fate, Kelln heard Tali scream at Sean to stop, then a rush of brilliant white blurred the air to his right side. It was accompanied by a loud wailing, deep and painful. Both he and the Preacher turned their heads.

Sean was riding Radiance, and he spurred the speeding horse toward the Preacher. Agony contorted his face in obvious pain from riding a Cremelino he was not invited to ride on or bonded to. In unmeasured speed and in radiant, blinding light, he waylaid into the Preacher.

The man fell on top of Kelln, his weight barely allowing the ambassador to breathe. After a moment of scrambling, the

Preacher slowly pulled himself off. Kelln instinctually rolled to the side and grabbed his sword from the ground once again.

Sean, still on top of the Cremelino, was in apparent physical and mental anguish from not being bonded. The usually docile Cremelino reared up in the air and came down with her front legs toward the Preacher's skull. At the last possible moment, the wizard turned his body and tried to run away, but Kelln stood behind him now, holding his sword out in front of him. As the Cremelino's muscular legs crashed into the Preacher from the back, Kelln's sword impaled him from the front. The man died in one brief moment.

Sean dove off the horse, flying through the air. He hit the ground and lay there for a moment catching his breath.

Rapp sat on the ground next to Taliana, wide-eyed. The young girl wizard was breathing better now and gaped, with newfound affection, at Sean. Kelln stood and stumbled over to the man who surprisingly had saved his life. He helped Sean sit up.

"That was either very brave or very stupid," was all Kelln could find to say.

"Couldn't think of anything else to do." Sean hunched his shoulders up and rubbed his head with his hands. "I thought the pain would kill me, though. Those horses can destroy your mind."

Radiance reared upon her legs again, emitting a loud wailing neigh, permeating the minds of all those present. *"Evil will not take us again! We will prevail!"*

* * * * * * * * * * * * * * *

Chapter Nineteen
ESCAPE

Mezar returned from staking out the building where Christine was being held prisoner. While waiting for the rest of his men and Leandra to join with him, he took up watching the movement of people and detecting patterns. Originally his father was still in the building, so he had to be careful. Now two weeks later, his father had left to ride to the border with his special forces. From informants, he had gathered that the battle on the border would begin in the next few days, so the time to act was dangerously soon. Darius awaited word on the rescue of his wife before taking any further action against the general's army.

In an inn owned by a man loyal to Mezar and the Emperor, Mezar and his companions sat around a dining table, discussing plans to free the queen. Lowell, William, Allon, and Gregor stared expectantly at Leandra. She blushed from the attention, but nodded. Mezar brought forward a plan utilizing Leandra at the center of it. Since the rest were known to some degree in the capital city, it was best for a stranger to infiltrate the building. If something went wrong, it would be easier to get her out without being noticed.

The amulet that Mezar gave to Leandra before leaving Anikari earlier that year had been infused with a new spell.

With a hand touching the amulet and her other hand in contact with another person, she would take on the form of that other person. In fact, they would immediately switch outward appearances with each other. It was only a simple physical transference, the person's personality and thinking remaining intact, and it would only last for a brief time.

"Leandra," Mezar said, "with the small size of the amulet, the spell will only work three different times for Christine after you give it to her. Also the simple illusion seems to work best on someone the same size and sex; otherwise strange shadows and reflections could be seen around both people."

Through Mezar's contact in the building where Christine was being held, they would sneak Leandra inside as part of the kitchen help. It wasn't unheard of for people of other countries to work as servants in Gildan. When the opportunity arose, she would change places with the person bringing food to Christine and then pass the amulet to her with instructions on how to work the spell. The rest of the group would be waiting outside a back gate to take her away.

Leandra stood up. "I'm ready." She wore typical Gildanian servant attire. A serviceable but attractive pale blue dress hung across her slender body, a lacey apron tied around her middle. Her short brown hair hung almost to her shoulders now and included a lace ribbon on top.

"Be careful, Leandra." Mezar worried for her. "If there was another way I could think of to do it, I would."

"You could blast into the mansion with your and Gregor's powers," she said, though he knew she was only joking. They had discussed it already. They didn't know how many other wizards were inside. Most trained wizards could sense the power from another wizard, so they could be detected.

"Just blend in. Don't say a lot. We are certain it is a woman who takes the food each day and removes the chamber pot. A guard will probably be stationed outside the door, but you should have a brief moment to pass on the amulet," Mezar instructed.

Before leaving, Mezar leaned in and gave Leandra a quick brush of his lips on her soft cheek. The others bade her luck, and she left with Lowell and William. The two friends of Mezar's would escort her safely to the back gate of the building where their contact would be later that night to let her in.

Mezar himself had one last place to go. He meant to visit his grandfather, the Emperor.

* * * * * * * * * * * * * * * * *

Christine sat alone in her room. She had not been treated badly but was definitely a prisoner. Her only contacts with others were the three meals a day that were dropped off and the changing of the chamber pot each morning. The servants came in and left without a word. The third day of her confinement, one of the servants left some books for her to read along with her meal. This and gazing out of the window at the city below were her only companions. Two days ago, she watched as a column of soldiers on foot and horse left the city with General Alrishitar in the lead. She spent her time looking for a way to escape, but in all that she did, she had to be protective of the new life growing inside of her.

The architecture and colored lights around the city below gave her some notion of internal calmness, but her mind wandered into a realm of nothingness more often. The beginning of winter lengthened the shadows over the city. Thoughts of missing Darius and what he must be going through brought her to tears, so she tried to push those negative thoughts to the back of her mind.

Every once in a while, Christine felt a faint tugging on her mind. It must have been Lightning trying to reach out to her. The missing one left a gaping hole inside her. It was like a part of her was missing, and she still did not understand why it wasn't working. She went deep inside herself, trying to concentrate on the bond, but to no avail. It always just unraveled like something blocked it.

One of the happier parts of her life was the baby that she carried inside. More often recently, she felt a small kick and beginnings of a slight stirring. Amazed at the size her stomach had grown, Christine would sit with her hand on her belly and talk to her little one. She told the baby about her life growing up, meeting Darius, and the new Diamond Palace that was being built in the Field of Diamonds, where the baby would live part time, growing up surrounded by the beauties of the farmlands. She thought back to the times she had started feeling nauseous and then how long she had traveled and been held prisoner since then. She surmised that she must be around five months pregnant by now; however, she was growing much larger than she would have thought.

Twice today a woman entered her room and brought food to her. Due to a lack of exercise and the baby pushing on her stomach, she hadn't finished either meal yet. She reached over and picked up an apple and absently bit into the fruit. It was a little too ripe, leftover from the fall harvest, but it still tasted good.

The door handle turned. Christine was surprised it was already time for another meal. She didn't even turn around to look at the servant. What use was there? There would be no recognition or talk.

"Christine," the servant whispered.

Christine whipped around, suddenly knocking the food on the floor. Never had they spoken to her.

The guard stuck his head in the room.

"Just an accident, sir," the nervous servant said. "It will just take me a minute to clean up."

Christine gaped hard at the woman as the servant bent down to pick up the food.

"It's me. Leandra."

Christine looked but stayed silent. She had only spoken to Leandra a few times, and although the voice was familiar, the face was someone else's.

"I only have a moment while we clean this up." She handed Christine the amulet. "Take this. Hold one hand on it while you touch another person. The two of you will exchange physical looks. It will not change who you are, just your appearance."

The guard walked in. "What is taking so long? Orders are that no one is allowed in the room."

Leandra picked up the last remaining bowl and stood up. The guard turned around to resume his post at the outside of the door.

"The change doesn't last long. Help will be waiting outside the back of the stables whenever you can leave. It won't last long, but you can use it three different times.." With that, Leandra left the room and closed the door.

Christine heard the guard and Leandra arguing outside of the door, but her heart leapt with joy. She fingered the golden amulet, wondering how it worked but accepting the gift happily. Finally a way out. She planned her escape for the next meal.

She didn't sleep that night, her mind fresh and new again with thoughts of seeing Darius. He still didn't know about the pregnancy. Examining her belly, she laughed for the first time in weeks. Once he saw her, he would surely know. All of a sudden, she felt fat and wondered if she would still be attractive to him. She took a brush from the nightstand and brushed her hair out.

The morning sun woke the queen of the Realm earlier than expected. She used the cloth and pail of water they left for her each night to wash herself. They supplied her with a few changes of clothes, mostly to accommodate her slight change in size due to the pregnancy. None were made to run in. She chose the plainest dress and readied herself for the servant. She had nothing else to take with her.

It seemed like hours, but a short time later, the door clicked and a maid stepped in. She was the usual morning servant, a few years older than Christine, with shorter black hair, a small mouth, and slightly tilted eyes. Her plain attire made her appear younger than she was.

Using the same unplanned distraction that worked the previous evening, Christine knocked into the girl, spilling the contents of the food on the ground. As they both bent to pick it up, Christine held the amulet in one hand and touched the arm of the servant with the other. She didn't know what to expect, but she gasped as she saw a mirror image of herself appear on the form of the servant. They had instantly switched identities.

Not knowing if she had changed or not but assuming so, Christine picked herself up off the floor, grabbed the dishes, and started walking out of the room.

"Wait. You can't go out there," the servant wailed, but as she looked at Christine, she gasped and panicked without saying anything for a moment. That moment was all it took for Christine to swiftly leave the room.

The guard came to the door to find out what was going on. Seeing what looked like Christine still in the room he went to shut the door.

"No, no," the servant yelled. "It's me. It's Sarah. She tricked me somehow." Christine could understand enough Gildan to make out what was going on.

The guard's eyes followed Christine in the hallway, seeing her as the servant. A questioning expression flickered across his face. Not wanting to speak and give herself away, she just shrugged and rolled her eyes like the lady in the room was crazy. The guard laughed, and Christine, being careful, walked back down the hall.

Not really knowing where she was in the large compound or how long the deception would last, Christine found some stairs and ran down with long strides. On her way down, she encountered two other servants coming up and started to panic. One of the servants turned to her and said something that Christine couldn't understand. She assumed it was in the language of Gildan, which she didn't speak. To keep from getting caught she forced herself into a coughing fit. Signaling that she couldn't speak and needed water, the two servants left her on her own.

Finding herself in a large marble hallway, she looked up and down its length. The walls were all a creamy plaster with large displays of weapons, art, and tapestries covering its length. She heard a noisc and saw a younger boy walk around the corner holding a large plate of food. That gave her the directions to the kitchen. Approaching the boy, she saw her reflection in a nearby mirror on the wall and noticed the deceptive spell had begun failing.

The boy almost dropped his food as right in front of his eyes, a short dark-haired Gildanian changed into a taller, blonde Anikarian. He opened his mouth to scream.

Christine, still holding the amulet, touched him on the arm, and her appearance changed once again, now into the form of a young page. On the other hand, the boy started screaming hysterically. Christine actually smiled at his antics but knew she had to leave.

Up on the higher floor, the maid's deception had obviously also worn off, and lots of yelling meant they were searching for Christine. Running into the kitchens, she almost bowled over the cook.

"Look here. What are you doing back?" the lady said to her. "I just gave you food. What have you done with it now? You couldn't have eaten that much."

Christine didn't dare talk to her. She was having a hard time moving around with the illusion of the boy. Her belly still stuck out, even though others couldn't see it. She found herself bumping into a few counters.

"Now what has got into you, boy?" the cook continued. "You haven't gotten into the master's wine have you?"

Christine gave a sick guise as if she was going to throw up. The cook raised her hands in the air and started yelling while pointing the way to the back door. Obviously she didn't want a mess in her kitchen. Finding the door, Christine opened it and ran outside.

The morning air felt cool, but she drank the freedom in and ran as far away from the buildings as she could. Hearing a fervent increase of drama in the household, Christine ran toward where she thought the stables would be. Halfway across the large expanse of yard, she had the feeling that her own form was back once again. She only had one more spell to work with. She skirted behind trees to stay away from any prying eyes but still ran toward her destination.

"Hey, what are you doing here?" A groomsman reached out for her as she walked into the stables. She was about to touch him and put the illusion on again when someone hit the man from behind. The groomsman crinkled to the ground. The attacker then proceeded to grab Christine by the arm.

"Come on. We have to hurry. Mezar is waiting for you." The attacker was young, only a few years older than Christine, though since he had grabbed Christine while she was still holding the amulet, they suddenly switched appearances. It was strange to see herself beside her.

"Oh no!" the young man said. "Why did you do that?"

"You grabbed me," she said as they continued to run.

"How do you run like this?" The man glanced down to his illusioned belly, which was now protruding from him. "You're pregnant." He spoke in the language of the Realm but with a Gildan accent.

Christine just smiled. The man had mentioned Mezar, so she assumed she could trust him. At this point, she would go with anyone that was taking her away from her captivity. She knew from sounds in the estate that she couldn't go back there.

Running for a few minutes, they encountered a back fence. They didn't know who should help who over the fence, so they managed on their own.

Dogs barking and people yelling could be seen and heard gathering throughout the compound. Christine imagined the wrath they feared from General Alrishitar if she escaped. Through some bushes, she saw a flash of white. A Cremelino came riding into view. It wasn't Lightning, but she could feel this Cremelino's presence in the air and as a trickle in her mind.

Mezar sat on top of the horse and seemed confused at first. He reached for the man that looked like her and offered a hand up.

"That's her." He frowned and pointed toward Christine.

Mezar broke in to a loud laughter. "Lowell?"

"That's enough, Mezar. It's not funny." Lowell grinned.

"We have to hurry," Mezar said, reaching out his hand for the real Christine. As he did so, she changed back. "That's better. Welcome back, my lady. My noble steed and I are here to take you away."

Tears blurred Christine's eyes. She had never beheld such a beautiful sight. The young prince pulled her up to sit behind him on the Cremelino. "Star said it's fine for you to ride. You are one of the bonded."

"You have a Cremelino, too?" Christine's voice rose in excitement.

Embracing the full force of the Cremelino's speed, Mezar took off through some backcountry. The trees and bushes blurred by as they rode toward a cover of thicker trees, putting as much distance between them and her captors as possible.

The whisper of the wind against her face made Christine feel alive again. Memories of times when she rode Lightning flashed through her mind. She held her stomach with one hand, trying to cushion the baby.

Suddenly, Star skidded to a stop and went up on his hind legs. Christine grabbed both hands around Mezar, who hung onto his horse's neck.

A loud wail screeched through the bond. *We will prevail!*

It was as if for a moment they both felt the combined weight, power, and intelligence of all the Cremelinos. Many voices ran through her mind at the same time. In that mix, Christine felt Lightning for the first time in almost two months.

"Lightning!" The joy almost overwhelmed her. Tears came unbidden to her eyes and slid down her cheeks.

Christine! It is good to hear you again.

Then before she could figure out why the bond worked again, Mezar's Cremelino came back down on all fours, the voices dissipated, and the bond with her Cremelino was once again gone.

Now she had to find Darius and inform him of the general's plans.

* * * * * * * * * * * * * * *

Chapter Twenty
PREPARING FOR BATTLE

Danijela stood next to her Cremelino, Spring. The horse's quick step and bright personality reminded the young earth wizard of springtime. Thinking of springtime, she shivered and wrapped a dark cloak tighter around her. Snow had fallen up in the mountains the previous day, and now thick clouds rolled in, engulfing the area around Denir. Winter was a horrible time to have a battle. She missed the warm deserts of Arc.

The young girl stared wide-eyed at the troops that had been amassing on both sides over the past few days. At the request that was more of a demand from the High Wizard, she had ridden her Cremelino from Sur to join with Darius and the others. The ride had been exhilarating, and it allowed her some time to get used to the incredible bond without others being around.

The wind gusted, and she brushed her blonde bangs out of her eyes. It was hard to imagine that fifteen months ago she was taken under the tutelage of the High Wizard. They traveled to the Wizard's Conclave in the Kingdom of Arc, where she'd began her studies. Then upon news of problems on the border, she had traveled there to witness those horrifying events in which her brother had died.

Now she stood to the side of not only the High Wizard, but the King of the Realm also. The sixteen-year-old girl felt a little out of place in such esteemed company, however, the gifts of comfort and the Cremelino from Darius would forever hold him in her heart. She pouted momentarily wondering if she would ever grow taller and slender. She felt self-conscious next to these great men.

Danijela looked up at the King standing next to her. He was talking with Roland and giving him instructions. He seemed so confident. His firm jaw, brown hair, and gray eyes made her heart flutter. He wore the red and purple of the Realm well. She envied his wife and the deep love that he had for her. She hoped that someday someone would care for her as much, and not just think of her as their little sister, which seemed to be the relationship she had with most men.

Darius must have sensed her looking. He turned toward her, smiled, and waved her over to join him. She hoped her reddening cheeks were covered by the cold.

"The High Wizard would like to speak to us." Darius motioned toward his tent. "I think he has a plan, now that you are here."

Their two Cremelinos walked beside them on their way to the command tent. She could see Jakob off to one side with Lightning and the other two horses, feeding and caring for them. The young boy took pride in his work and was a very serious young man.

Without warning, a scream sounded in her mind. It was like the screeching and whining of hundreds of horses. She covered her ears, but the sound was internal to her. Spring and

Thunder rose up on their hind legs and made an awful, loud sound. Off to the side, Jakob tried to grab the other Cremelinos he was watching, but they too reared up on their hind legs.

Soldiers and servants stopped and backed away.

Then as if in one solid chorus, she heard, *We will prevail!* echo through her mind. A powerful magical force seemed to rip through her body, giving her clarity of thought, vision, and hearing beyond a normal person. She could hear the sounds of the camp magnified around her.

Then it stopped.

Lightning raced to Darius, almost sliding into Thunder.

"She is free!" Darius yelled. "The queen has escaped!" A large smile engulfed his entire face, and tears filled his eyes.

Followers around the field clapped and yelled in delight. They had mourned with their young King. He had tried to hide the sorrow from them at first, but it was too much for them not to notice how it affected him.

Turning to Danijela, he said. "Now it is time to end this battle here before it even gets started." The two walked into his tent, where High Wizard Sallir was already seated.

"What was all that noise?" the Wizard asked.

"The Cremelinos. It seems to have been brought on by a fight with the Preacher," Darius informed him, "and my wife has escaped with Mezar. They ride his Cremelino to us now." Darius didn't stop smiling as he practically bounced on the balls of his feet.

The High Wizard looked slightly forlorn.

Darius looked concerned. "What is the matter, master wizard?"

"Oh, nothing." Olan tried to brush it off.

"Tell me."

"It actually seems kind of silly. I am, what, three times your age or more, been High Wizard for many kings in Arc, and am one of the most knowledgeable practitioners of magic in the western lands, yet you two have been given this amazing opportunity to communicate with your Cremelinos."

Danijela reached her hand over and patted the High Wizard's knee. "Oppa, you know so much more than we do." She glanced at Darius to make sure she wasn't overstepping her bounds. "We may have the opportunity, but we don't have the knowledge to do what we must do. We need your guidance. We always will."

The High Wizard smiled. "Thank you for your words, young one. And I do believe their sincerity. But alas, I have seen your magic. You won't have need of me for long and will surely surpass all of us soon."

"Danijela is right in one thing, High Wizard. We are untrained in our power." Darius stopped for a moment as if listening. "I am sorry. Thunder has just told me that the situation in Mar has been handled. The Preacher is indeed dead." Darius paused as if to gather his thoughts. "It's just been so long it is hard to imagine the Preacher being dead. Sean San Ghant and Ambassador Kelln, along with another young wizard, defeated him. There does however seem to be some eastern kingdom wizards on a ship in the harbor."

"My Lord. This means of communicating will change warfare, politics, and trade in our kingdoms forever." The High Wizard spoke in awe. "It really is amazing."

A servant brought some meat, cheese, and biscuits in for the three of them. Danijela was too nervous to eat anything, but High Wizard Sallir motioned for her to eat. She would need her energy later.

After the servant left, Darius continued. "It may be amazing, and we may have potential power, but we really do need your guidance, High Wizard. I do not know why you were not chosen to have a Cremelino, but I do know I cannot stop this war myself."

High Wizard Sallir took a deep drink from a glass of wine he was holding and then, with a twinkle in his eye, said, "I do have a plan."

Darius motioned for him to continue.

"There are instructions I have read before about constructing a large magical barrier. It takes great power and energy. But the thing it takes the most is balance and representation from all the wizard power disciples. An earth wizard, a mind wizard, and a heart wizard it seems is needed to make it work."

"Luck would have it, we have those here." Darius smiled. "How do we form this barrier?"

The High Wizard sat deep in thought for a moment. "That is the problem. I think I can remember it, but there seems to be something missing that I can't quite remember."

"We could try it"—Danijela motioned, always anxious to try new things with her earth power—"on a small scale."

"That is a great idea, young apprentice."

The three got up and exited the tent. They walked together to the edge of the camp. Danijela could see soldiers training and getting ready for a battle they were sure would come soon. There had been reports of thousands of foot and cavalry soldiers from Gildan camped within a short distance. Danijela was already sick of war, and she had only seen one battle.

Pointing to some trees not far away, the High Wizard instructed her and Darius to calm their minds, pull on their powers, and think about each other. Danijela closed her eyes so not to be distracted by what was going on around them. She felt the familiar stirrings of her power of the earth. She felt the power from the dirt, the trees, the wind around her, the rocks beneath her and brought it forth.

Soon she felt the light touch of her mentor and his power of the mind. It seemed more firm and thoughtful than hers, then she felt the almost wild and volatile power of the heart come from Darius. The three powers circled each other in her mind, trying to come together. But they wouldn't quite mesh. It was as if there was nothing to bind them together.

You are missing a piece, her Cremelino said. She opened her eyes and saw the King and High Wizard looking at her.

She told them what her Cremelino had said.

Tell the King and wizard to open their minds. It is time for them to know the final piece of what is missing.

Her Cremelino then spoke to all three of them. She watched a broad smile spread across her mentor's face as he was granted the ability to hear the magical horse like she had.

The power of the mind, heart, and earth are only three parts of the powers of a wizard.

"That is all we have been taught," the High Wizard said into all their minds.

There is one more, one that has been hidden since the persecution of our kind, one power that held the wizards of old together and brought them to such great heights, one other discipline of magic.

The three wizards stood in anticipation. Spring continued teaching.

You have been missing the power of the spirit. A wizard of the spirit is one that binds and bonds all others together into one great whole.

"Who?" The High Wizard was the voice of their question. *"Where do we find a wizard of the spirit?"*

Collectively, the Cremelinos in the camp answered. *You have already found us. The Cremelinos are the wizards of the spirit—the power to bond, the power to bind, the power to guide the other powers.*

Danijela laughed in delight. She watched Darius gasp and Olan smile with tears in his eyes.

Now concentrate your powers again, wizards, came the command from Thunder, *and we will guide you.*

Danijela closed her eyes again, felt the power of the earth, mind, and heart circle each other again, but now a fourth power came forth. Magnifying itself in a brilliant white, it engulfed the others, bound them to each other and became not four powers, but one.

The youngest wizard opened her eyes. All three of them looked out at the trees and saw a shimmering barrier of light. It began to grow until it covered their side of the camp. Darius ordered Roland to walk toward it and tell him about it. It was semi-transparent to look at, but when touched, it was as solid as a wall. Sight and sound permeated its barrier, though muffled, but nothing physical could push through.

"Looks like we have a way to stop that army now." Darius smiled. "I do not want to fight or kill our southern neighbors. I don't want any more innocent people to die because of someone's thirst for power. We will stop them with the barrier and then try to negotiate with their general when he arrives."

The King called his commanders to his tent to plan the final defensive strike to diffuse the war with Gildan.

* * * * * * * * * * * * * * *

Mezar stood with Christine, Leandra, and his friends in a copse of trees just behind and to the east of the main Gildanian army. He estimated that General Alrishitar had amassed over three thousand troops. He could see the flag of his father's house along with that of Gildan flying high over the command tent in the middle of the camp. A mist still hung in the air, and the ground was wet from a soggy night.

By sending William and Allon into the camp disguised as soldiers, Mezar had learned most of what he needed. It seemed that today would be the day to march over the border and attack the Realm armies. The general had not yet received word of Christine's escape. His plan to invade the Realm and then hold the land hostage over Darius for the exchange of the queen was still in play.

One disturbing piece of news that was rumored around the camp was of a stranger in their midst. A shorter, darker man with large tattoos accompanied the general everywhere and seemed to have great influence with the Mezar's father.

Commanders began forming ranks of the soldiers, a company of sharp bowmen accompanying them. They would march first, with horsemen in the rear and the side. The army was disciplined and formed straight lines. Soldiers began marching to the cadence of the drummers, blindly obeying their senior officers.

Through his Cremelino, Mezar learned that Darius had a plan and hoped it would stop any bloodshed, for the force of the Gildan army was fierce and strong. These were career soldiers who trained each day. Their strength, agility, and skills were the best in the empire. The general had spared nothing in his mad plans to annex the Realm.

The troops began their march north as the winter sun burned away some of the night's fog. Visibility returned, and Mezar could see a few miles further. A mass of dark signaled the armies of the Realm at the border. There was a strange silence with only foot and horse steps marching in unison, occasionally being squawked at by large crows. Anticipation filled the air. The two nations had had a few skirmishes but no full-scale battles in over two hundred years.

As the soldiers moved out, they left behind their camp servants and followers. This would make it easier for Mezar and his group. They were still intending on getting Christine across the border. They had hoped to do so before the battle began but had been slowed down trying to stay hidden from the main army and it's outriders.

Mezar tried to keep his Cremelino hidden by once again putting on a large brown blanket on him. The brilliant white coat of the horse would be too easy to spot. They made their way down a small hill. Each of them had a horse they kept quiet. Skirting to the east of the main army, they would try to reach the border with the Realm in the next hour or so. They rode east of Denir, where the ground was mostly grass plains—unlike the west, which rose in quick, rocky heights to become the Superstition Mountains—and with the full attention of the army facing north, they hoped to remain unspotted.

Suddenly, a white light rose in the air between the two armies. The party stopped and looked toward the border. A milky translucent sheen filled the air. Mezar could hear shouts of confusion as the apparent barrier seemed to spread and grow larger.

A warm feeling of accomplishment from Star came through Mezar's bond with his Cremelino. His tilted eyes opened wide as Star informed him of the barrier and the fourth wizard power.

"How long can they hold?" Christine asked after Mezar had relayed the information to the group.

"A long time apparently, especially with the powers of the Cremelinos now helping," Mezar informed her. "Let's get closer.

The group rode up to the rear of the army. The ranks of the Gildanians held, just barely. Their disciplined training kept soldiers from running away from the barrier.

Mezar felt power crackle in the air and saw a bolt of fire hit the wall. That would be his father or one of his wizards. They must have marched forth with the army. Multiple barrages of power tried to crack the barrier, but to no avail. It stood firm.

Soon, however, he noticed smaller groups of men going off to the sides, trying to circumvent the barrier to the west and east. As they did, the barrier just expanded further. Mezar stood in awe at such power.

"How will we get back?" Christine asked. "The barrier is growing."

"You are right. We can't have you trapped on this side. We need to get you back to Darius." Mezar motioned for the group to follow. "Ride quickly to the eastern side. Let's try to get around the barrier!"

They rode to the edge of the barrier, but as they neared it, it expanded once again and they bumped into the invisible barricade. Mezar got down from his horse and walked next to Star, examining the wall.

"Star. Do something," Mezar cried. "We have to get the Queen back to Darius."

Suddenly a group of soldiers approached them. Leandra and Christine hung back, while the men walked out to meet the commander of the small group.

"I am Prince Mezar Alrishitar," Mezar shouted while they still approached.

The leader of the soldiers hesitated. "My Prince. We have ongoing orders to bring you in should we find you."

Gregor, the other wizard in Mezar's group, brought forth his hands. Mezar felt power building.

"No, Gregor." Mezar put his hand on his friend's arm. "We will not fight our own people."

Gregor stopped but glared at the soldiers.

Mezar stepped forward. "I will allow you to take me, but the others will be free to go."

The head soldier inclined his head. "The orders are only for you, Prince Mezar." He said it almost apologetically. A soldier only doing his duty. "I am fine with the Gildanians leaving. However, the two Realm ladies I will have to take in for questioning."

Christine looked at Mezar and shook her head to the side. He could not let her be taken again. Two of the soldiers raised bows.

Star touched his nose to the barrier, and an irregularly shaped door appeared. Without thought, Christine grabbed Leandra's hand and dove through.

Arrows whizzed through the air and into the opening. One hit Christine in the side. She screamed, and Leandra caught her. The barrier closed and sealed itself again. Mezar could see the wound bleeding in Christine's side as Leandra lowered her to the ground.

Gregor wheeled on the group of soldiers and shot out a blast of air, knocking two of them to the ground but not killing them.

The commander motioned for his men to grab Mezar.

"I told you I would come. Shooting them was not necessary." Mezar gritted his teeth.

"Just doing my duty, my Lord."

Duty. That is what Mezar had to do now. Duty to his country above supporting his father. He looked back through the shimmer again at Christine and whispered under his breath, "Darius, it's up to you now. I returned her to your land as promised."

He nodded to his friends, and they took off on their horses. The two Gildanian soldiers picked themselves up off the ground.

Mezar grimaced in determination as he allowed the soldiers to tie his hands and march him to the middle of his father's army camp. Now he would meet his father head on and stop this battle from destroying two kingdoms.

* * * * * * * * * * * * * * *

Chapter Twenty-One
THE POWER TO BIND

Wizard, Christine is through the barrier, but she is injured. Lightning spoke to Darius. *I felt a spike of pain through the bond southeast of here.*

"Christine!" Darius's heart leapt with joy at the thought of seeing her again, but pain filled his soul to think of her hurt. How long had it been now since they bade farewell on the road south of Mar? Seven weeks? Eight? So much had happened.

"I have to go and find her," Darius said out loud.

Roland stood by him. "My Lord, the barrier?"

"Don't you think I know that, Captain?" Darius snapped at him. Thousands of people were being protected by the barrier that the High Wizard, Danijela, the Cremelinos, and himself held up. If it came down, there would be war, and thousands would die on both sides.

He took a deep breath and turned back to Roland. His shoulders sagged. "You are right Roland. I cannot leave. But you can."

"Sire?"

One more time, he thought about running to find Christine and leaving the others to hold the barrier. All he wanted right now was to hold her again, to feel her in his arms. His mouth tightened in frustration. Darius looked at the other wizards holding up the barrier with him. He could see a tightening around the High Wizard's eyes. It wasn't fair for him to choose between his wife and his people. But wasn't that the choice a King faced all the time? It was his duty to use his powers to protect his people.

"Captain Commander, as much as I want to find my wife myself and hold her again," Darius spoke with thick emotion, "my main duty is to all of my people. I now entrust you to find and rescue my wife and return her to me. It is the greatest trust I can give you."

Roland gave a formal bow. "I will not fail you, my Lord. I will find her and return her to you as soon as possible."

"Take Jakob and Lightning with you. Maybe the bond with her Cremelino will help you find her," Darius instructed.

"I want to go also," Jain said, walking up to the group. He had accompanied Cray and had been helping the battalion as they traveled. "After all, she is my sister. If anything happened to her . . ."

Darius smiled at his brother-in-law. "Very well. I understand. Please hurry and bring her back safely."

Roland obeyed, gathering the two young men in quick fashion, and headed southeast out of the camp. Once they cleared the camp, they began to run.

Darius closed his eyes and pleaded with God for his wife's safety. He could feel the power soaring through his veins. He tried to reach out through the Cremelinos to find his wife but was met with nothing. Tears leaked from his eyes and ran down his face. He was not ashamed. It was his wife!

Scanning the two armies, he wondered how they would disarm the conflict. He noticed flashes of light hit the barrier from the other side and surmised that the general had wizards with him also. Could they hold on? Was it only a matter of time until they broke through?

For now, the three wizards and the Cremelino wizards held the barrier, but it would not hold forever.

* * * * * * * * * * * * * * * *

Prince Mezar was brought before his father. They stood facing one another in the command tent. Mezar held his father's gaze with fierce determination to see this through according to the Emperor's wishes. Guards circled the perimeter inside and outside of the large tent. Other commanders joined them inside.

"Mezar, I could guess you were involved in this," he said to his son.

"Involved?" Mezar let his anger show. "You are the cause of this." He spread his arms around, pointing at the camp. "I have done nothing against you. This is your doing, and it needs to stop. What has possessed you in this ridiculous endeavor, Father?"

"Stop?" The general took a step forward. "You are telling me to stop? I am your commanding officer. You obey me, both as your general, heir to the throne, and as your father, Mezar."

A man standing with a hooded cloak back in the shadows walked up, put his hand on the general's arm, leaned in, and whispered something in his ear. He was short with skin color slightly darker than Mezar's own. His skin was covered with intricate tattoos. Mezar felt power radiating from the man, and realization dawned on him that this was one of the eastern kingdom wizards he had read about in his studies.

"What is he doing here? What have you done, Father?"

"He is helping me to understand what needs to be done to bring peace to our western lands," Mezar's father said almost mechanically.

Mezar recoiled and took a step back. His father was mad, but this eastern wizard was dangerous. He breathed in deeply and proceeded with his plan. Pulling a scroll out of the inside of his shirt he handed it to his father.

His father's face contorted with rage as he read the document. "How dare he."

"You brought this on yourself, Father. As the scroll says, you are now relieved as general of the army, effective immediately."

The guards and commanders in the room gasped. A scowl covered the face of the eastern man.

"I will not obey this," his father stated. Pointing to two of the guards, he said, "Take my son out of my sight. He is a traitor to his kingdom."

The guards hesitated. One of the general's commanders stepped forward in front of Mezar. "Is this true, my Prince? Does this come from the Emperor himself?"

"It does, Commander. The Emperor, in light of the general making his own decision in direct disregard to the Emperor's wishes, has formally removed him from command. A hearing will be held back in Gildan to determine if any further action is needed and who else might be responsible." Mezar glanced at the eastern man, but the man seemed to be slipping away further behind the crowd. Mezar would have to deal with him later.

"Take him," his father yelled again, his veins bulging out from his neck.

"I am sorry, General Alrishitar," the commander said. "The Emperor has ordered this. We had assumed that you were acting under his authority. Guards, please escort the former general out of the command tent. He is no longer in command."

Mezar's father looked around frantically for his eastern supporter, but the man had totally disappeared. Turning back to the room, he struck out physically at first, then magically. He punched two guards and drew his sword on a third. The tent was small, and chaos reigned. Blue fire grew around his hands, and he twisted it out at the others, burning a hole in the side of the tent.

"I will have that barrier down and we will attack," he screamed.

Other wizards, beholden to the general, ran to the tent and escorted him away among flinging fire. They raced together toward the barrier. Mezar and the others gave chase. Star came running up beside the prince, and he jumped gracefully up in the air. In one fluid motion, he landed on top of the Cremelino. Reaching the barrier, he noticed his father and four other wizards joining hands.

"No Father. You cannot form a circle with that many wizards!" Mezar yelled at the wizards. "It's too dangerous! You will burn yourself out."

But his father gave no heed. Power built up around the five wizards. The air churned with a howling wind. Soldiers had a hard time standing in place. Lightning crackled in the air, and dark clouds formed on their side of the barrier.

"We need more!" his father yelled. "Beltzar, where are you?"

At the sound of his name, the eastern wizard came forward. He pulled his hood back and tattoos seemed to slither across his face and down his neck. He grabbed the general's hand with his left and another wizard with his right. The circle of six wizards joined their power together in an awesome force.

Looking through the barrier, Mezar watched as King Darius, High Wizard Sallir, the young wizard Danijela, and their remaining Cremelinos drew closer. Their faces showed the strain of power to hold the barrier in place.

"Darius," he voiced through his Cremelino, hoping he could get a message to him through the barrier. *"The general and his wizards are drawing a circle of power."*

"I don't understand," came the reply.

"It's too dangerous with that many wizards together. The power will burst the barrier and destroy thousands on both sides. You must retreat." Mezar couldn't bear to see the army of his friend destroyed for his father's vengeance and greed.

"Get your people back also, Mezar," Darius said through the Cremelinos. *"We will try and hold it. If we do, the backlash will hit your armies instead."*

Mezar motioned for the troops to get back from the barrier. It was now raining, lightning and deafening thunder filling the air. A large display of power began to encircle the six wizards. The eastern lord held his head upward, and fire seemed to dance across his tattoos. Evil saturated the air.

"You will burn yourself out!" Mezar yelled at his father's wizards through the storm, but once again there was no response. On the other side, he could see Darius's army retreating, leaving only the wizards on either side of the barrier.

A force pulsed out from the circle of Gildanian wizards against the barrier. A loud rumble filled the air, causing people to cover their ears. A high pitched sound was heard over the battlefield. Once again the wizards attacked the barrier, this time causing it to shake. Mezar saw the strain on Darius's face.

To the east of Darius, a white horse rode in to view. Christine was slumped over the front of Lightning, a bright red crimson stain spreading across her clothes.

Darius looked toward her. Through the bond of the Cremelinos, Mezar felt Darius groan and saw his lips move in a wailing sound of despair.

Darius moved toward his wife, his concentration on the barrier waning.

The wizard circle struck again, timing the strike with Darius's change of focus. The barrier began to crack and open, wind and power pulling through like a siphon to the other side.

Darius turned back to the barrier in shock. He wrestled with his attention alternating between his bleeding wife and the barrier.

Mezar needed to do something. He closed his eyes and dug deep inside of himself. He called upon the reserves of Star, who in turn called upon the Cremelino family back on White Island. Unlike Darius, Mezar had been taught and trained to wield magic. This was not a circle of wizards bound together, but the drawing of power from others. He brought power into him from the Cremelinos, as much as he dared. He had never known such power. The power of the spirit—the power to bind. The sudden knowledge was staggering. He briefly swayed, then set his resolve and opened his eyes. With the increased power came clarity of thought and a heightened awareness to his senses.

"Father!" he screamed one more time, his voice booming and echoing across the battlefield of two armies.

This time his father did look at him, but Mezar hardly recognized the horrible visage looking back at him. Rage, anger, and greed had corrupted the general's face. His eyes were bloodshot and his eyelids receded. His face was drawn and wrinkled, a snarl forming on his lips. He had taken too much power into himself from the circle of his wizards. The general was burning out but seemed intent to try and take the army of the Realm with him when he did.

"Hold, Darius," he yelled to his friend. He couldn't imagine the turmoil Darius was feeling, being torn between his wife and the barrier. It must be eating him up inside.

Darius had begun to sag to the ground but stood straight again with new resolve at Mezar's command. Flanked on one side by the High Wizard and his apprentice and on the other side by Thunder and Spring, all their faces showed exhaustion and strain beyond what a normal creature could bare, yet still they held on to hope.

The circle of the general's wizards began one last gathering of power, and just at the apex, right before they let it loose into the barrier, Mezar grabbed the hands of his father and the eastern wizard, and forced all the power he held into the circle itself. A seventh wizard.

Mezar felt the evil, corrupt power and hatred of these wizards course through him, almost overwhelming him. Pulling upon the purity and power of the Cremelinos, he pushed out into the circle with all he had, then let go and fell to the ground.

The six wizards turned into shimmering firelight. Beings of elemental light, pulsing with power and energy, their physical bodies burned out. A bright burst of light filled the air between them as one by one the six wizards burned out in total, their elemental energy following their physical bodies into oblivion. Mezar's father was the last to disappear.

The wind and rain stopped. The clouds disappeared immediately. An eerie silence permeated the air.

Mezar pulled himself up to his knees and leaned his head against his Cremelino, Star, who sagged to the ground himself. The prince of Gildan watched as Darius, Danijela, and Olan released the barrier. The shimmering light winked out. The three wizards collapsed to the ground.

Panic struck the two armies, many of which had not been privy to the general's fate. Soldiers surged forward on both sides. Darius stumbled to his wife's side, barely able to hold himself up. Her eyes remained closed. With the help of Roland, he lifted her from the horse to the ground. Mezar tried to regain control of the Gildanian army, but he was too weak to yell or to use his wizard powers for anything more.

Unexpectedly, the young wizard girl Danijela slowly brought herself up off the ground. She looked so small and fragile in the middle of the chaos swirling around her, her short blonde hair hanging straight on the sides, dirt smudges covering her soft and innocent face.

Gradually but deliberately, she raised her hands to the sky and then in one swift motion, brought them down hard against the ground. The earth cracked below her and spread dramatically outward through where the barrier had been and into the armies of Gildan. Men scrambled to keep from falling into the growing crevice. Again she brought her hands up and back down, swifter this time, and the earth quaked, rocking back and forth, bringing up rocks from its depths. Rocks that suddenly melted and flowed together and began to form new solid walls. Small rocks came up out of the fissure and flew through the air, knocking down soldiers on both sides of the battle.

Soldiers and commanders both ran and screamed at each other, backing off from the battle. The earth shook again as the ground rolled through the remaining men, knocking many of them to the ground.

"Enough!" screamed the young wizard, her high voice amplified to be heard over the entire battlefield. "Enough fighting. Go back to your homes. This battle is over!" One last quake shook the area, then the ground stopped moving.

Mezar summoned a reserve of energy and jumped on Star. He was amazed that after the power of the barrier, the young earth wizard was still able to command the elements around her. He rode toward her, against the tide of Gildanian soldiers leaving the battlefield. She must be in danger of taking too much power into herself and burning out like his father and the other wizards had. He had to warn her.

The strength of her power and words, however, had the intended effect. Men on both sides backed away from each other and returned to their camps.

Mezar reached Danijela at the same time High Wizard Sallir did. Together they approached the young wizard in trepidation.

The High Wizard put his hand tenderly on the young girl's arm. "Danijela, stop. You will burn yourself out."

The young girl turned and looked up at the two wizards at her side. Flecks of orange power floated in her eyes, a sign of the immense power she held. Eyes sparkling, she smiled.

"I am fine," she said softly.

"That was a lot of power," Mezar exclaimed in amazement.

"That was not near my limit," Danijela said, a devious smile adorning her lips..

"Protect us all." The High Wizard sighed. "You are an extremely dangerous wizard. For now, however, you are still my apprentice, young lady."

"Am I?' she said with a challenging but friendly smile.

"We will discuss that later," her mentor said.

* * * * * * * * * * * * * * * *

Darius sat kneeling on the ground next to Christine, ignoring the shaking and rumbling of the ground. He hardly noticed when it ended. All he cared about was his wife. Her eyes were still closed, but her chest rose and fell in a stable pattern. She was still alive. Leandra, Roland, and Jakob sat on the other side of her, Jain standing next to him.

"Darius!" Mezar came running up to him.

"Oh, Mezar," Darius sobbed. "You brought her back."

Mezar only nodded.

"She is back, and pregnant with our child." Darius could barely speak. "How did I not know? How could I let her leave me? This is all my fault. My fault."

That is why the bond was acting irregular, Lightning said. *The pregnancy was interfering with the bond somehow. It must be a very powerful child.*

"She has lost a lot of blood, my friend. You must do something quick or you will lose her." Mezar leaned down next to Darius.

Darius's bloodshot eyes held pain for his wife's condition. "I don't know if I have the strength." He sagged down against his wife.

Remember where your power comes from, wizard of the heart, Thunder and Lightning both said in his head. *Remember the prophecy!*

Darius closed his eyes and did remember. He remembered the first time he had met Christine, picking her up off the ground outside of the city gates. He remembered her smile, the time of their first kiss, the hours and days talking to her in the Field of Diamonds. He remembered his longing for her as he left her to go off to training. He remembered with some embarrassment pushing thoughts of her to the side as he sought for power in the army. He remembered being captured and almost losing everything to despair when he couldn't access his power. It was then that he thought about Christine and his mother. It was then he felt love once again. And with that love, his power had returned. As his heart had turned from anger to love, he had felt peace. That is where his power came from. Deep inside his heart. He had put duty to his people first, now he must heal with his heart.

He leaned over Christine and put his hands over her wound. Her body flinched out of instinct. Delving deeper into his soul, he remembered returning to Anikari and seeing her again. At that moment, his life had clicked into place. At that moment, he had found true meaning to everything. His path had been set right once again.

The kingship, the engagement, the announcement, and wedding—it all flooded back through his mind, bringing up feelings and thoughts of love and concern and compassion. He felt his hands grow warm; he felt the healing powers of a wizard of the heart seep deep into his wife's wound. The arrow had missed the baby, going less than an inch to the side. He gasped at what he felt inside of his wife. Two powers growing inside of her. He opened his mouth to declare what he found, but the powers hushed him and bade him to remain silent for now.

Delving deeper, Darius pushed his powers to the limit. Blood vessels began to heal, torn muscles fused back together, and new skin began to grow back around the wound. He poured all he could into his wife, his queen, his beloved, his reason for living. He pulled strength from Thunder and the other Cremelinos. He used the power of their binding and bond to seal the wound and to heal.

Opening his eyes, Darius realized silence prevailed around him. Friends, wizards, and soldiers alike stood with tears streaming in abundance down their dirty faces. Love filled the air. In open wonder and admiration, they began to kneel one by one.

"My King," voiced one of thousands of soldiers who knelt in honor.

"My Lord" Roland, Leandra, and Jakob knelt.

"Darius, my friend forever." Mezar went to one knee with head bowed.

"Wizard of the heart." Danijela Anwar, High Wizard Sallir, and the remaining Cremelinos bowed their heads in respect and esteem.

Christine stirred, and her eyes fluttered open. A large smile crept across her face.

"Darius!" she whispered.

Darius hugged and kissed her, picking her up in his arms. His heart was so full of love and tenderness, it poured out to all those standing and kneeling beside him.

"Rise," he said to those still kneeling. "My wife, your queen has returned to us." Cheers erupted all around the field of soldiers as the news spread rapidly.

Mezar turned to leave, and Darius caught him by the sleeve. The King's other arm was around Christine. He would not let her go a foot away from him now that he had her back.

"Thank you, my friend. I am forever in your debt. What can I do to repay your friendship and loyalty?"

"I didn't do it for repayment."

"I know," Darius replied. "But what will happen now?"

"The general is dead." Mezar smiled sadly. "Hopefully the Emperor will recover from his treatment. I will ensure that the right wizards are helping him."

Darius got the meaning. "I understand. You are now first heir to the throne of the Gildanian Empire, Mezar."

Mezar nodded his head. "But I have a lot of damage to undo. It seems my father was blinded by the eastern wizard."

"It was the same in Belor." Darius remembered what he had heard through Tali's Cremelino. "The Preacher was being directed by another eastern lord. Seems they are intent on trying to spread their influence to the west."

"Hopefully they have been stopped for now." Mezar said.

"Go in peace, Prince Mezar," Darius bowed his head. "We will stay in contact through the Cremelinos. I still have a formal visit to make to your empire. I would like to meet your grandfather. But . . ."

"But . . ." Mezar looked at Christine's stomach. "You have other things that will occupy your time for a while. Congratulations. An heir to the throne."

The two clasped arms and bid farewell. Mezar stopped for a moment with Leandra before he remounted his Cremelino and rode back to his side of the border.

Darius turned back to Christine. After a short meal, they walked over to their Cremelinos. Darius kissed her hard on the mouth and hugged her tight. Lifting her up gently on her Cremelino, he jumped on his. Exhaustion filled his core, but he pushed it away. There would be time to sleep later once they were safely back in Anikari.

"We ride in victory to Anikari!" he shouted for all to hear. A deafening roar met his words.

Word of the queen being healed by the King ran with the wind, northeast to Anikari, around to Sur, Mar, and Belor, then overland to the Kingdom of Arc, and south to the Gildanian Empire. In the coming weeks, all knew a powerful wizard of the heart ruled the Realm. News spread of the battle, the barrier, the young earth wizard Danijela standing by her mentor and defying an army, and the Gildanian prince's selfless act of power to stop his father and the other evil wizards. Word spread, growing greater with each telling. Bards and musicians already began writing tales and songs of mythical proportions. With the help of the powerful and magical Cremelinos, the path to peace had been found.

* * * * * * * * * * * * * * *

Chapter Twenty-Two
REWARDS

Kelln helped Alessandra into a carriage, half carrying her. She could talk, but she was weak. Her burns were not healing well, and Kelln didn't know how much longer she had to live. He'd tried to wash and wrap the blackened skin, but his touch was very painful for her.

It had been a week since the attack with the Preacher, and for the first three days, Alessandra had laid unconscious. Governor Penrose and his daughter tried healing her, but neither one were practiced in that part of the power. Either way, it didn't seem as if her body wanted to heal. She had said very little, and seemed to be giving up on her life.

After the attack, Sean went with Rapp, Taliana, and her father to the shipyard with a group of soldiers. They found an empty slot in the dock where the eastern ship had been anchored. Witnesses said the ship left in an obvious hurry less than an hour before, not even bothering to gather a full crew.

Taliana had healed, and Sean was never found far from her side, a development that she didn't seem to mind. Through her Cremelino, they had been asked by Darius to accompany Kelln and Alessandra to the capital. Each of them sat on horses on either side of the carriage. Rapp had stayed behind to help the governor. With the Guild of Thieves having lost their guildmaster and his daughter to the Preacher's attack, things were in an uproar around town. Guilds that the Preacher had been courting felt betrayed. The governor needed Rapp to run errands and take care of things that he couldn't do himself. Both of them now stood beside the carriage, bidding the ambassador's party farewell.

"I will have the King send additional troops to help keep the peace until affairs are back in order," Kelln said to the governor.

"There will be a new order now. Mar shouldn't be so much trouble for the King. You will return my daughter to me though, won't you?"

"That is up to the King" Kelln smiled. "But I will put in a good word for it. I can see you are lost without her."

The governor wizard laughed. Looking at his daughter, he surmised, "Well, she seems to at least be smitten by the young noble Mr. San Ghant. They have hardly left each other's side since the fight with Mr. El'Han—the Preacher."

Kelln turned to Rappatorian. "And you, my new friend. The King and I are definitely in your debt. None of this could have happened here without your help. I will see you are rewarded also." He punched the young man on the shoulder.

Rapp smiled a big smile. "Things really got exciting once you came to town, Mr. Ambassador. That's for sure."

Climbing in to the carriage with Alessandra, Kelln motioned for the driver to proceed. At a slow pace, the drive to Anikari would take quite a few days. As Mar shrunk behind them, Kelln breathed out a deep sigh. It was still hard for him to believe that the Preacher was dead. He hoped all assignments from the King would not be so harrowing. He looked over at Alessandra bundled within warm blankets. She sat with her eyes closed. Kelln's heart was deeply troubled over what would happen to her. In the end, she had jumped out and saved him from her father's wrath. That should count for something, shouldn't it?

* * * * * * * * * * * * * * *

Darius walked by himself through the Cremelino stable. It had been three weeks since they'd returned from the battle. He had just given Jakob Widing leave to go and get ready for the banquet that evening to honor all those who helped in the recent events in establishing peace once again in the Realm.

He brushed Thunder's gleaming white coat. It was still hard to comprehend that the Cremelinos were wizards in their own right. The fourth wizard power – the power of spirit; the power to bind. Lightning was in the next stall over. Looking at her turned the King's thoughts to his wife. After his healing of her and some rest, she was back to normal. Well, at least as normal as could be while being pregnant.

Christine's moods had been stable, but her appetite was horrendous and she never seemed to be full. Darius smiled at the thought of the servant's faces each time Christine asked for more food. He wondered if any of it had to do with the healing. Her body had been through a lot and needed to recharge itself. Of course, none of them knew the secret that he held inside. He smiled again. She was eating for more than one additional life.

In the stall over from Lightning were the two remaining Cremelinos who had not bonded with anyone yet. If Taliana and her father were any measurement, there must be other wizards throughout the Realm. He had been thinking about what to do about that for some time now.

Through the Cremelinos, word had come to him that Danijela had been named a full wizard, was ordained to follow in the High Wizard's footsteps as advisor to Kings, and eventually would be High Wizard herself. He grinned and almost laughed out loud at the High Wizard's decision. After the young girl's showing at the battlefront, how could the High Wizard do anything else? She would definitely be a handful, but hopefully she would always be a powerful ally.

The Emperor of Gildan had recovered from his slow poisoning but was not as strong as he once was. He named Mezar as his heir to the throne, which Mezar accepted - but he declined to be the general of the armies. Being both the heir to the Gildanian throne and leader of the army had been too much for his father. The greed and influence that the eastern kingdom wizard had on the general seemed to have been too much for him to pass up. Darius wished to be able to spend more time with his southern friend under different circumstances. He had looked forward to visiting the wizard library in Gildan. That trip would have to wait.

Footsteps came around the corner, and Darius turned. It was his father, Richard.

"Where are the guards?" his father asked.

Darius smiled. "You know I have no need of guards to protect me."

"I know. But you must keep up appearances." His father smiled genuinely at his only son. "You are the King."

Darius sighed and walked closer to his father. “I never wanted all of this, Father. Sometimes the burden is too great.”

“That is why it is yours, Darius. A better king is one who doesn’t want to be, but who learns his duty and serves the people.”

“Are you a philosopher now, too, besides my councilor?” Darius laughed. “I will name you first philosopher of the Realm.”

Richard laughed heartily. “You are a good King, my boy.” He slapped his son on the back. “Better than I would have been under the circumstances.”

Darius hid the moisture in his eyes. They turned and walked out of the stables together.

After Darius donned the rest of his attire, they entered the banquet room. All eyes turned to their King. The gathered crowd rose as one and bowed.

“Long live the King. Hail Darius DarSan Williams, King of the Realm,” his father voiced.

“Long live the King,” a monstrous voice of people answered.

Darius walked in long strides down the red carpet toward the throne. His purple cape swirled around his broad shoulders, and his black boots were muffled against the carpet in the large hall. Windows in the high ceiling let the late afternoon sun filter through the room. The golden light danced across the King’s crown. Long banquet tables adorned the grand hall, set up between the marble columns. Along with the filtered sunlight, candles adorned the sides of the walls and the tables, filling the room with light.

The King waved and bowed his head slightly at those he knew in the crowd. A King he was in decree, in look, and now by deed. His actions had saved their realm from certain war on three sides.

The Throne of Power had been brought in from the throne room. Darius sat and motioned for the others to do the same. He ran his hands over the golden armrests and felt a power course through his veins. He looked to his side, where Christine already sat on a smaller throne, then back out over his people and smiled. His heart was full.

"Before we feast, I would like to make some formal announcements and declarations. There are many to thank for the success of the most recent events in Mar, Sur, and Denir. I cannot name them all, but their deeds have made the Realm a safer place and one once again looked at as a leader of the western lands. However, there are a few specific individuals."

Picking up a scroll, the King began to read. "Be it known throughout the Realm that Ambassador Kelln El'Lan is now known as Kelln San El'Lan, and title to lands will be transferred, affording him the noble title of baron." He smiled at his oldest friend. They had talked extensively earlier about Alessandra. Darius had privately forgiven her treason in light of her condition. Kelln would take her to Belor to be with her grandfather, Alastair, for the remainder of her days. With the burns being from wizard fire and her lack of desire to live, she had not been able to be healed and would not live more than a few months.

"Be it known that Rappatorian Wells of Mar has earned the title of squire to the King and will be rewarded as such and given responsibilities in the Realm." He had heard of Rapp's abilities and thought it may come in handy to have some eyes and ears throughout the Realm to help keep track of things.

"Be it known that General Cray and all those that fought under his command be given additional pay and a special commendation from the crown.

"Be it known that a new university will be built on White Island dedicated to the study and schooling of wizards. This school will work in tandem with the Conclave of Wizards in Arc and the School of Wizards in Gildan to further the research and training of wizards dedicated to good. Jakob Widing is named as head caretaker of the Cremelinos at that university. Be it known that Governor Penrose of Mar is named head of that university once it is built and open. In the meantime, he will be transitioning his role as governor of Mar to another." Many of the nobles perked up. To be named as a governor of one of the major cities of the Realm was a high honor and afforded them privilege only just below the King and his three senior councilors in Anikari.

"Be it known that due to extraordinary service to the Realm under extremely personal and dangerous circumstances, Sean San Ghant is hereby now named governor of Mar upon the transition of Governor Penrose. He, along with his newly betrothed, Taliana Penrose, will be my representative in ruling Mar."

Darius gave a broad smile to Sean, who looked almost sick with shock. He could see tears fill Sean's eyes with the announcement. Richard had not been excited about this announcement, but Darius had informed him that he had seen into Sean's heart and that he was loyal to Darius and to the Realm now. Taliana, standing in a beautiful multi-colored gown cinched tight at the waist, hugged Sean closely.

"Our success in Arc and Gildan could not have been made possible without the help of High Wizard Olan Sallir of Arc, Wizard Danijela Anwar of Arc, and prince and heir to the Gildanian Empire, Mezar Alrishitar. Since they are not of the Realm, I have no authority to add rank or privilege to them, but they are hereby honored and always welcomed in this land. Once recent affairs have been settled, we will meet together, and new formal treaties will be reestablished."

Enthusiastic claps echoed through the crowd at the announcements. He glanced over at Christine. She looked radiant in her golden dress, made that week to fit her changing shape. A small golden diadem was fixed in her curled and flowing golden hair. He nodded to her brother, sister, and mother, who sat as special guests at the head table. Christine beamed back a smile of love at Darius, and his heart fluttered with joy. He vowed to never lose her again.

"Let the feast begin!" he bellowed, voice echoing around the hall.

* * * * * * * * * * * * * * *

EPILOGUE

Darius paced the floor of the Diamond Palace. One wing had been completed the prior week, and Christine had chosen to deliver her baby there. As he paced, he looked out of the twenty-foot-tall glass windows at the Lake of Reflection. Dark storm clouds hung over the Superstition Mountains to the west. A large storm had blown through the previous day, bringing a barrage of spring rain. It had almost been a year since he returned to Anikari and found out he would be the next King.

Christine had started contractions two days before, about a month earlier than normal. For the last month, the doctors had been concerned about her condition and put her on bed rest. A doctor and two midwives were now in the room with her. They were convinced the baby was coming soon. Darius smiled at the thought.

A father! It would certainly be a new experience. Strange, exciting, and fearful all at the same time. He had held in the secret since healing Christine. He had been tempted to tell it many times over the last few months since returning back to Anikari. Now, soon, all would know.

He stood in front of the window and marveled in the beauty. His thoughts drifted to the first time they ran into this field after a rainstorm. Christine named it the Field of

Diamonds. That was three years ago. He had been captivated by her the first time and now loved her far more than he thought could have been possible. Almost losing her to the greed of General Alrishitar the past winter made him appreciate her even more.

He heard his wife cry out, and he continued his pacing. He was not allowed in the room until the baby was born. Too many men seemed to pass out when they saw their wife in labor and bleeding. He worried about her, though. What if she was in danger? He couldn't lose her. He wouldn't lose her.

Servants came and went into the room. He could hear the noises of construction going on in a far wing of the new palace. He'd excused himself from all duties that day. His father and other councilors would be able to handle anything that came up.

Since returning from the battle with Gildan, things had returned to normal. The prior problems with the farmers and the city people started improving. Groups met together more often and talked and planned the next year's crops together.

A loud wail broke the King's concentration. He rushed to the door and opened it rashly. The doctor glared at him and told him to leave.

"We are going to have to operate, my Lord. The baby hasn't turned." The doctor looked worried. "You must leave."

"But I can help." Darius wasn't going to leave her in this condition. "I can calm her down." He sat down on the bed next to her. Christine gave him a weak and tired smile. Her hair was plastered to her head in sweat, and her eyes drooped due to the valerian root they had given to sedate her. Darius took

Christine's hand in his and caressed it. Her fingers moved slightly in response. He reached deep inside his heart and brought out his feelings for her. Along with Lightning and Thunder, he sent a ray of calmness into her soul. She breathed deeply and smiled.

The doctor didn't look at all happy with him there, but he was the King, and so he continued with his procedure. They would have to cut into her and lift the baby out. It was not a common procedure but had been done enough in the last few years to make the doctor comfortable with the operation's outcome.

The midwife brought some additional numbing herbs to Christine's lips, and she drank. Darius continued to hold her hand softly, helping her stay calm.

The doctor began the incision, cutting through her belly with careful precision. The two midwives stood to either side, helping to guide his hands. There was a lot of blood, and Darius noticed his wife's face growing paler. He sent his healing power into her, and she looked better.

Abruptly, the doctor lifted out a new baby. "It's a beautiful girl, Sire."

"Let me see her," Christine cried, and the doctor handed her to one of the midwives to bring to Christine.

The doctor gasped and reached in again and held up another baby. "And a boy, Sire."

"Twins?" Christine cried out again. "No wonder I felt so big and bloated. I had wondered but didn't dare say anything."

Darius looked down at his wife and their two babies. He couldn't contain his smile and was glad the secret was out. Christine looked up at him.

"You knew," she accused him with a smile.

Darius nodded. "I knew. When I healed you, I felt the two babies stirring inside of you, but I did not know if they were boys or girls."

The nurses cleaned off the babies, sewed Christine back up, and handed the twins to the happy and joyous mother and father. Tears streamed down their faces as they beheld their two babies. The boy was smaller, and one of his feet twisted at a slight angle, but Darius felt power from both of them.

"Christine, both are wizards. I can feel it." It was a wonder. "The boy will be Liam, and he is a wizard of the mind."

Christine smiled then added, "And the girl we will call Breanna."

"She is a wizard of the earth," Darius said.

The two remaining Cremelinos in the King's stables were ready and anxious to touch the two new wizards. They communicated their choice to Darius of which twin each of them would bond to. Christine and Darius felt all the Cremelinos in the land rejoice. Two more wizards added to their ranks.

The prophecy is now truly and finally fulfilled, Lightning said to both of them from outside in the stables.

The time that had long been foretold for wizards and Cremelinos to join together once again was now here. In

Darius DarSan Williams, King of the Realm and wizard of the heart, the prophecy was fulfilled.

Forgotten lines of ancient magic
and the power of the throne.
One will make them both his own
if his heart sees the true power.
He will bring light to fight darkness
and love to fight hate
if he reaches into the power of his heart.
He will find new allies, turn enemy to friend, and
find the binding of all power on the path of peace.
His inheritance is the heart, but his twin legacy
will be split between the earth and the mind.

Thus ends The Cremelino Prophecy

* * * * * * * * * * * * * * * *

If you liked this book and the series, please feel free to leave a short review on Amazon. Also sign up at www.MichaelSheltonBooks.com to get information on forthcoming books by Mike Shelton.

About the Author

Mike was born in California and has lived in multiple states from the west coast to the east coast. He cannot remember a time when he wasn't reading a book. At school, home, on vacation, at work at lunch time, and yes even a few pages in the car (at times when he just couldn't put that great book down). Though he has read all sorts of genres he has always been drawn to fantasy. It is his way of escaping to a simpler time filled with magic, wonders and heroics of young men and women.

Other than reading, Mike has always enjoyed the outdoors. From the beaches in Southern California to the warm waters of North Carolina. From the waterfalls in the Northwest to the Rocky Mountains in Utah. Mike has appreciated the beauty that God provides for us. He also enjoys hiking, discovering nature, playing a little basketball or volleyball, and most recently disc golf. He has a lovely wife who has always supported him, and three beautiful children who have been the center of his life.

Mike began writing stories in elementary school and moved on to larger novels in his early adult years. He has worked in corporate finance for most of his career. That, along with spending time with his wonderful family and obligations at church has made it difficult to find the time to truly dedicate to writing. In the last few years as his children have become older he has returned to doing what he truly enjoys – writing!

www.MichaelSheltonBooks.com

Made in the USA
San Bernardino, CA
13 December 2016